SONG OF THE NILE

I dedicate this book with love
to my daughter Tracey Lynne

Song Of
The Nile

by
Irene Roberts

Dales Large Print Books
Long Preston, North Yorkshire,
England.

British Library Cataloguing in Publication Data.

Roberts, Irene
    Song of the Nile.

    A catalogue record for this book is
    available from the British Library

    ISBN 1-85389-880-5 pbk

First published in Great Britain by Mills & Boon
Ltd., 1987

Published in Large Print 1998 by arrangement with Judith
Murdoch Literary Agency

Dales Large Print is an imprint of
Library Magna Books Ltd.
Printed and bound in Great Britain by
T.J. International Ltd., Cornwall, PL28 8RW.

PROLOGUE

Thutmose the Third 1490–1436 BC

When he became Pharaoh, Thutmose the Third liked to recall an incident in his childhood. A procession which had formed behind the statue of the god Amun left the road it should have taken, and came towards the place where the young Prince Thutmose was standing. It stopped directly in front of him. It seemed as if god meant to designate his son.

Thutmose's claim was not incontestable. He was certainly the son of Thutmose the Second, but his mother, Isis, a secondary wife, was not of royal blood. However, because of the incident during the procession, the young prince was designated to the throne. He gave himself titles and people began to count the years of his reign. This would have been authenticated had the widow Queen, Hatshepsut, married him. She refused and swiftly seized power, holding on to it jealously until her death in the year 22.

At the outset of his kingship, Thutmose

7

the Third made it clear that he would no longer tolerate the near presence of his enemies. They had been gathering en masse at the frontiers during Hatshepsut's long and peaceful reign. He declared war, and such was his might and valour that Pharaoh Thutmose, whose Horus name was Valiant Bull, became the greatest of all the warrior kings of the Eighteenth Dynasty.

Nefer's story begins in July. This, the time of the Inundation, was Egypt's New Year.

CHAPTER ONE

Zarah, wife of the great lord Per Ibsen, stood thoughtfully on the river bank. Small and lovely for all she was in her middle years, she was staring at the golden nimbus the sun made over the Nile. Egypt, she thought, is above all a land of mystery and magic. A great and wondrous world and I am part of it. But oh, the vagary of the gods. How perverse they are!

They do not seem to be listening to me, yet I continue to call them all—to Bast, Hapi and Hathor and even the Unseen One, Amun. Yet, in spite of everything, they remain deaf. Now I have no faith and I am afraid.

There came the sound of familiar, well loved footsteps and her expression of doubt and distress was banished as she turned and smiled. Her Lord Husband, a large, steady, very powerful man, smiled back and there was adoration in his eyes.

'Princess,' he said as he joined her, 'you are well.'

'Very well, my lord.'

'You seem to be too quiet and too thoughtful lately. Are you certain that there is nothing wrong?'

'No, but—I have been thinking about the kind of problems that might arise—should, should something occur to anger the deities.'

He frowned, worry lines crinkling at the corners of his eyes.

'I do not understand, my Morning Light.'

'I meant if—if something bad should happen.'

'Bad?' His concern grew. 'What is this? Nothing out of the way can arise, surely? There is no cloud on our horizon. If that was not so, Thickneck would have realised it long before now. He senses these things. He knows!' He looked round, frowning. 'Where is he, by the way?'

'I sent him on a message. It was just an excuse. His care and concern for me was getting unbearable. I—he made me want to scream.'

Seriously perturbed now, Per Ibsen said quickly: 'But beloved, Thickneck is the friend you have adored all of your life. You never cease to boast about how black and beautiful he is. He is your shadow, your twin soul and he—'

'Was watching me!' Her voice trembled as she fought back nervous tears. 'Yes, *watching* for all he cannot see. He was going to lecture me, to order me to rest,

10

and I—I felt that I needed to be alone, to be quiet. The man fusses and frets too much and I just could not face it today.'

Per Ibsen pointed out the truth of things.

'Thickneck, above everyone, would have understood. He has always read your moods right.'

'Nevertheless,' she replied obstinately, 'I found it necessary to send him away.'

Per Ibsen put his arm round Zarah's thickening waist and led her to where the bank was grassy and shadowed by a group of palms. There were wild flowers growing and the air was marbled with delicate veins of their perfume.

'Let us sit together,' he persuaded. 'Tell me what it is that makes your face look so worried.'

'It is nothing, my lord,' she said, evasively and turned her head away.

He would have none of it.

'Princess,' he said firmly, 'this simply will not do.'

She gave in then and allowed him to help her to sit comfortably on the ground. Her back was rested against a palm and cornflowers, wild celery and tiny star-lilies rustled gently against her feet. Per Ibsen's concern grew, for he saw the brightness of unshed tears gleaming in her large khol-outlined eyes.

'My Lord Husband,' she whispered, 'I am afraid.'

'Of what, my love?'

'The Black Jackal of Death.'

'Don't!' His voice was sharp now. 'I beg of you, don't even think such a thing. Nothing bad can happen. No, it cannot!'

'But if it did,' she whispered desperately, 'my soul would have no peace in the Everlasting, for there is something I have, as yet, left undone. Ramose wished—'

'You are fit and well,' he cut in firmly. 'Nothing can go wrong.'

'My lord,' she pleaded. 'My insides do not feel as they should. When I had Nefer growing under my heart, and then our own darling little Twosre, all went correctly and well. This time it is quite different.'

'But this was explained to you!'

'Yet I do not feel that things are right.'

'My love,' he said firmly. 'The belly doctor told us that the manner of bearing is quite different for a boy child.'

'Yes, yes, my lord, I heard!' she insisted. 'But I am still afraid for my unborn. I cannot forget that I am neither as young nor as strong as I was when I had the girls. I have moments of black despair. I—I feel—I don't know how I feel. All I know is that my fear grows for our unborn and for myself.'

'Don't!' he said urgently and cupped

her face between his hands. The light had gone from his eyes and his face was bleak. 'I swear by the gods that I'll never let you go.'

'You must not let me leave this earth,' she sobbed and clung to him. 'I could not hold the Feather of Truth, let alone step into the joy of the other world if I had failed in my duty to Ramose. You see, my love, there is a certain thing I must do, if only for my own peace of mind.'

'What thing?'

'I must put Ramose's estates in Nefer's name—now!'

Per Ibsen's frown deepened. He could not make sense of either his wife's words or her distress.

'No matter what happens,' he tried to comfort her, 'Nefer will automatically inherit her natural father's estates and wealth should the worst happen. My dear heart, I cannot understand what has got into you. You are not going to die, but living or dead, Nefer's future is assured. The papyrus stating Ramose's wishes was signed and sealed long ago.'

'You don't understand!'

'I know that you are unwell, and confused, and thinking of things that have no significance in the here and now. Come, let me take you home. Thickneck was right to be concerned after all. How

13

well the old man knows you.'

Zarah could stand no more. She had to break a promise she had made to Pharaoh's first wife. It was not in her nature to act without Per Ibsen's approval; she needed his strength to help her to carry out the duty that must be done in all haste.

'Pharaoh has made a new decree,' she said softly. 'And no one must learn of it until the moon is past. The people will therefore have no time—to do what I mean to do now. My lord, we must go to the Temple of Law and I must sign over Ramose's property to Nefer. Then—and this is the terrible part—Nefer must leave us and take up residence in Ramose House.'

'What nonsense is this?'

'I must and will continue to live at your side, my lord. I will never leave your house. But Nefer's property is at risk. It has been decreed that all estates left untenanted by their owners will be taken over and kept or sold as the Throne wishes. My love, remember, Thutmose needs all the gold and grain he can lay his royal hands on—to help him pay for the wars.'

'This rule will not apply to us. We are Pharaoh's friends.'

'It will apply to everyone and that is why Great Wife whispered in my ear. She risked death in doing so—as so shall we if

14

My Majesty ever finds out that we were actually warned. Beloved, Nefer must not lose her heritage.'

'Her future is assured. I will see to it.'

'Only for as long as Thutmose does not ask for your all. Oh, Per Ibsen, be honest with me. If Pharaoh asked you to strip yourself bare in his cause, you would do it gladly—and so would I. But Nefer must inherit her father's might. His soul would never rest else!'

'I will take you to the Temple,' Per Ibsen said slowly, 'and you shall do what you believe is right. I will lay down my life to achieve that which you have set your heart on. But I beg of you, no more talk of dying.'

Her hand fluttered out to rest on his arm.

'I have no intention of leaving you, my Lord Husband. Not now or ever. We will sail the waters of the Styx together for we are one in our mutual love, but that will not be yet. We will live and watch our son grow to manhood, that I promise you.'

'Our—son!'

'It is a feeling I have,' she told him serenely. 'A dream, nothing more.'

'We will give him gold,' Per Ibsen exploded joyously. 'Piles of gold that will reach pyramid high. He will vie with all of Pharaoh's sons in wealth.'

'Which he, and they, will give to him to help pay for the battles he fights. Oh, my lord, Egypt will be on the road of aggression for many years to come, I feel it in my bones. I feared and hated Queen Hatshepsut, but at least while she was on the throne we had peace. Thutmose loves war.'

'Then it must be as he wishes, since Pharaoh is god.'

'Oh dear! Speaking of deities, my lord, we have an avenging god bearing down on us right now. Just look at the expression on poor Thickneck's face!'

'He seems to be very cross with you, my love,' Per Ibsen agreed. 'But admit it, you can be a great trial at times.'

'So he tells me—often. He glowers at me and stares with his sightless eyes. Then he growls in his most furious voice saying that I must listen to him, and stay off my feet.'

Per Ibsen's eyes twinkled as he watched the old eunuch marching towards them.

'Here he comes,' he said, 'the only person I know who is as clever as you at getting his own way. By Set, I swear that he is more sure-footed than me and he is certainly more majestic. Look how proudly he wears his headband with its feathers, and his full-tailed leopard skin. How tall he is, how firmly he walks. No

16

one could tell he is blind.'

'He sees with his heart,' she replied and her fingers curled trustingly round her Lord Husband's hand. 'And I love him almost as much as I love you.'

'You adore everyone,' he said with mock severity. 'Our friends, our servants, and you openly spoil the slaves.'

'And our children,' she reminded him. 'You are always accusing me of being very silly where they are concerned.'

He nodded and threw back his head and laughed aloud.

Thickneck had his way, as they knew he would. For the rest of the sun-laden day Zarah lay, pampered and spoiled on her magnificent bed. That evening when the air was cool, Per Ibsen called for litters and they were taken to the Temple of Law.

Zarah's wishes were written down on papyrus and were authenticated with the official seal. Even the Head Man of the House of Law exacted one promise.

'The owner of Ramose House and Estates will reside on the premises from now on?'

'Hand on Heart,' Zarah replied devoutly and placed her opened palm across her chest.

'Hand on Heart,' Per Ibsen swore.

'So it is written,' the Head Man of Law pronounced. 'So it is done!'

17

He clapped his hands together three times and the interview was at an end.

Nefer, Nefer, Nefer, the beloved Thrice Beautiful, eldest daughter of the great and noble Per Ibsen House was now the undisputed owner of her natural father's estates.

At the big house there was much joy and celebration. It seemed that the gods smiled and Zarah's eyes were bright, her cheeks flushed. She had at last, ensured a golden future for her first born. This, no matter what either Pharaoh or Fate decreed. She turned to Per Ibsen, her eyes wide with love, with joy and with sadness.

'I will visit her often. She will always be sure of our love. And this I know. When Nefer is a young woman and Twosre is also past puberty, my lord, I promise you that we shall have the most beautiful daughters in the world. They will be admired by everyone and we will be proud even to everlasting!'

He smiled down at her, knowing that she spoke no more than the truth.

During the years that followed, Thutmose the Third, greatest of warrior kings, continued to raise the military glory of Eygpt to its highest point. In campaign after campaign he subdued the Asiatics of the north and east, the Nubians of the south and the Libyans of the western desert. Even the islands of the eastern Mediterranean were subjugated. Again and again he returned to his imperial capital of Thebes, bearing the spoils of the world to lay before the ram-headed Theban god, Amun.

It was Pharaoh's greatest delight and duty to return to his homeland at the New Year, to praise and bless the river, to welcome the floods, to raise high his crook and flail and declare aloud to the nation that he ruled in the name of Amun, that he, and he alone was the living Horus, God of the World.

This is all too spiritual, Nefer thought, and I am afraid! She stood with many others, on one of the highest steps that led from the river. There was a sense of quiet expectancy.

Heaven was a mere promise of the fuschia, saffron, pink and blue glory that was to come. The fertile valley below was shadowed and seemed to be all but quivering with anticipation. Palms stood, dark and still, like guards with headdresses of spiky fronds. Beneath them, all along the banks of the mighty Egyptian river, multitudes waited. They were eager to witness the most striking sight on earth. The arrival of the sun.

There was a feeling of awe in the air and reverence for the Unseen One, Amun. Amun who was all about them, who was the sweet breath of life. A god so mighty, that he could and did caress the face of the Divine Living Horus, Thutmose the King. Pharaoh of the Two Lands.

Thutmose sat on his gold chair, on a dais raised high above his people. He was a determined-looking man. His nose was his dominant feature, giving strength and character to his face. Round his neck he wore a wide collar studded thickly with precious stones. Beneath this a pectoral hung against his broad chest. It was a scarab of lapis lazuli mounted on gold. This was in turn decorated with little cornelian pendants in the shapes of ankhs, Symbol of Life. Over the red and white crown of two hands, Pharaoh wore a gold headband, at its centre the rearing cobra. The uraeus, Symbol of Supremacy, cold, gold, glinting, it was ready at all times to spit fire in the eyes of the enemies of My Majesty. Thutmose's arms were crossed across his breasts, in his hands he held the ceremonial crook and flail. He looked and was omnipotent.

His black-outlined eyes glittered momentarily as he lowered his sights to rest on the slim and beautiful Nefer.

Per Ibsen, tall, proud, dignified, favourite

at court, stirred uneasily. He stood with other trusted officials and guards in the group surrounding Pharaoh. At Per Ibsen's side there stood Amenemhab, old warrior, the King's most beloved Companion-in-Arms. It was well known that Thutmose would lay down his life for both these men. They, in their turn, had risked flesh and blood on Pharaoh's behalf, many times. With them, second in rank only to the King, there stood the proud, silent figure of the Vizier, Rekhmire.

Loving her father, watching him with great sad eyes, Nefer wondered why her parents were so determined to send her away. Once again she was being forced to take up her inheritance, the House of Ramose and all the estates. She found it all bitterly grievous, and killingly unfair. She felt Pharaoh's sudden whip-lash of a glance. She shivered and turned away.

Gradually the special occasion, and her surroundings, got to the lovely young girl. She stood there, her eyes reaching for the far distances now, silently drinking it all in.

The air was full of hushed, whispering sounds. Awed voices, the movement of restless feet, the faint tinkling of ornamental bells. There was the muted cough of a disgruntled camel tethered somewhere out of sight and the far away barking of a dog.

Suddenly a vermilion dagger cut clear across the sky. Luminous colours were flung outwards like vast banners. Then great and glorious, the shining golden ball pounced joyously into the day. A prodigious roar from a thousand throats reached upwards. It was flood time, renewal time, the good-to-be-alive time. It was the time of New Year!

Pharaoh stood tall and the multitude fell silent. He opened his arms and raised his voice to praise and bless the waters and the river god Hapi for obeying his commands. For the signs were there, that they had heard his call. From this moment on, the holy river would climb high. It would overthrow the banks, bringing with it alluvial mud. And the land would be replenished and refreshed. All living things would rejoice and multiply.

'Amun!' the people called. 'Amun!'

When Pharaoh acknowledged their homage, he waited until the High Priest of the Temple stepped forward.

The High Priest also called upon Amun, thanking him for sending Egypt a great and wondrous king who was such an effective living god. Who was Ruler of Two Lands; Ruler of the River; Ruler even of the far away salty Great Green.

Then, as Thutmose made his way majestically down the steps to finally walk into the sweet waters, a million voices raised in the stingingly beautiful national theme. The Song of the Nile.

And Nefer's lovely face was tear-streaked as she too, sang emotionally and felt her heart encompassing the whole of this beloved land. It was New Year, the time for celebrations, the giving and receiving of presents, for drinking wine, eating food and for placing offerings at the shrines. It was family time!

Suddenly Nefer felt apart from her family. This even though her father, Per Ibsen, said that he loved her. Zarah, her most precious mother of the world, had even used the word 'adore'! They had reiterated that she was their sweet breath of life. Then why, oh why were they sending her away? Isolating her yet again?

A laughing girlish voice rang out.

'Nefer! Wait for me!'

Nefer smiled a little, then her expression changed to one of fear for her younger sister.

'Twosre, take care!'

Twosre, pretty, happy, and with golden lilies in her hair, paid no heed to the warning. She leapt along the outside steps, at the very edge, unmindful of the danger. Joyously ignoring the jostling crowds and the swirling water below, she made her way upwards as sure in her movements as a mountain gazelle. She reached Nefer, bright-eyed and smiling.

'O Sister,' she teased, 'what a sad-face you are. Aren't you even curious about the gifts we are to receive? Do you not feel the least bit excited about the celebrations at Court tonight? What a solemn bird you are.'

'And you are a naughty kitten, too daring by far,' Nefer chided, her eyes warm with love and concern. 'You could have fallen and—'

'But I did not fall, Nefer! I am here, as always, to tease the life out of you. Tell me, why are you looking so down? Has Sebni been trying to persuade you to be kind to Longnose again?'

'Twosre!'

The younger girl was delighted at Nefer's look of outrage and her chuckle was rich and mellow, like warm cream. Twosre went on:

'With Longnose in the family, Sebni will be certain to pass all the examinations set in the House of Medicine. Had you thought of that?'

In spite of herself, Nefer laughed and, at that moment, she was beautiful. Like Twosre, she adored Sebni. There was a stillness about him, and a shy, remote air. Even when he smiled, there was a kind of anxious caution glowing at the back of his sickle-shaped eyes. Sebni had been apprenticed to their father when a mere child.

'O Sister, how wicked you are!' Nefer sighed with mock severity. 'And as for Sebni, he will never be a man of medicine, nor law, nor any other of your fanciful ideas. He will be as great a man as our father, in architecture and design. As for Longnose, you keep on about him so much that I believe you must have plans of your own in that direction.'

The thought was outrageous. Longnose, a particularly pompous Doctor-of-the-Stomach, was a very unlikeable man. The two sisters gave little cries of derision and delight. Twosre pulled the flowers out of her hair and pelted Nefer with them.

'By Set,' she laughed, 'the very idea makes my toes curl. Nefer, what a wicked person you are.'

They were unaware of the picture they made and of the fact that Thutmose's glance had turned their way. There was a look that was far from god-like in Pharaoh's eyes as he looked Nefer up and down. Then with great dignity he returned to his chair.

Per Ibsen sent up a silent prayer to the gods and felt relief when Pharaoh turned and signalled to his Carriers. They came forward twelve in number. Six stood to

25

his left. The second six, to his right. At the command they lifted the side poles and the chair was raised shoulder high. Palace guards took up positions. Per Ibsen and Amenemhab flanked the chair. The High Priest of Amun, abreast with the Grand Vizier, Rekhmire, stood a few paces ahead of the procession. Such was the magic and power of these two men that their mere presence was sufficient to send evil spirits scuttling out of My Majesty's way.

Now the trumpets blared and bells and flutes played. Drums beat and tambourines were flourished. People cheered and shouted and laughed aloud. Flower petals were spilled on the ground. The air was thick with perfume and warm with cries of praise for the noble ones that passed. Pharaoh smiled his tight, painted smile and his eyes gleamed behind the thick lines of black khol. And such was his pleasure that he threw gold rings to his people, coloured baubles that glittered, little stone scarabs, and miniature figures of gods. The shrieks of delight grew even more mighty. It seemed the whole world rang with the sound of Thutmose's name.

Nefer and Twosre pushed their way through the crowds to where Zarah, their mother, waited. With her, Thickneck as always and the fat merry little man named

Ay. He was Thickneck's friend and who acted as his eyes!

'It is going to be a wonderful day,' Zarah said. 'Your father will be home quite early and then we shall see what fine gifts he has had hidden away. We will eat, drink and be merry and see that every member of our house enjoys the New Year.' She hesitated, then went on, 'After that, the evening, point of our day. The royal celebration at Court!'

Nefer felt that her mother's tone had not sounded so sure during the last part of her speech. Again the treacherous tears were burning against her eyelids, her merriment gone.

'Mother,' she said wistfully, 'I do not wish to spend my last precious hours here, dangling like a wilting flower against the pillars of Pharaoh's great hall.'

'There you go again!' Twosre chanted impatiently and went off to tease a particularly handsome guard. Zarah watched her younger daughter for a moment, then she turned back to Nefer, her expression sad.

'O Nefer, Nefer, Nefer,' she said unsteadily. 'My sweet and precious Thrice Beautiful, won't you accept, even now, that none of this is our choice.'

'Then—then father—'

'Must bend his knee to the mighty

27

Thutmose who he loves. But even though he must never admit it, Nefer, your father does not love Pharaoh above all of us. For you and you only, he is going to attempt to side-step the will of My Majesty. Oh beloved, don't you understand even now? It is not the first time your father has risked his life for you. Think Nefer—think!'

Suddenly Nefer felt a thrill of fear rushing through her veins. As she looked into her mother's compassionate eyes, she knew! For the first time her mind was opened to the truth and she was filled with the desire to run, to get away now, before it was too late, and she became trapped.

'Mother,' she whispered. 'I will go now at once!'

'This cannot be. You must attend the celebrations as expected. This because My Majesty will look for you and be suspicious if you are not there. Your father has timed things perfectly. At dawn tomorrow, Pharaoh is to hold a council of war. His mind will not be on sweeter, more gentle things. Your father hopes that, in time, and with you out of sight, Thutmose our King will forget.' She tried to laugh, but the sound was a sad little whisper on the air. 'I find it in my heart to wish that Pharaoh had taken a liking to our little one. Twosre has always been more forward in the matters of life than you. It is strange that parents never know how their children are to turn out.'

'You—you admire Twosre more than me, Mother?'

'How can I, my blossom? You are so very like me when I was young. Yet, there was once a time when you were such a very happy, confident little girl.'

'Mother,' Nefer's voice shook as she asked, 'what if—if I am recalled to the Palace?'

'It is the will of Amun and there will be nothing that we can do,' Zarah said sadly. 'O, my darling, would you mind so much?'

'To be a lesser wife of Pharaoh would be a great honour,' Nefer said quietly. 'And First Mistress of the Great House is like a dear aunt to me, the others, sisters and friends. Prince Amenhotep is like an elder brother. Prince Khaleb, well, he—'

'Is like a brother too? O Nefer!' Zarah said quietly. 'Do you honestly think that your father and I are as blind as Napata?'

'Ha!' Thickneck said hoarsely. 'Who is taking my name in vain?'

'Would I ever?' Zarah chided and lovingly reached out to stroke the old man's hand. 'You are very dear to my heart and very precious to us all.'

'I know, Morning Light,' he told her

29

and his face split in a wide, white toothed smile. 'But I like to hear you say it just the same. I cannot see, so I can only imagine the look of your face. I do not need to imagine when you speak. I was always the one to choose reality, remember?'

'You choose things that are good for you, Thickneck,' Zarah laughed softly. 'And you get your own way all the time and so, old friend, it shall be as you wish. We shall change the subject here and now.'

'I can smell the goose cooking from here,' Thickneck said and smacked his lips. 'And I must confess that I am sinfully obsessed with the idea of good food.'

Zarah laughed at that, as did Nefer, trying to hide her fear for Thickneck's sake. He was a very special person in all their lives, for he had looked after and guarded Zarah when, as a tiny lovely child, she had been sold as a slave.

They began to walk home. Nefer and Zarah on either side of their old Kushite friend. He did not really need to be led, since he moved about with sure instinctive steps knowing the area well. But he liked to be pampered and petted, and to do so was their joy. Twosre held on to Ay's hand and whatever it was that she was saying was making the little plump man throw back his head and laugh.

30

They made their way to the large beautiful home set near the Palace, and parted to wash and refresh. They would meet later, in the main hall where it would be shady and cool, to eat and drink. This when Per Ibsen returned. Had they not been invited to the King's House, their evening celebrations would have been held on the large square roof, under the moon and stars. Nefer wished that was where her own New Year celebrations could be. Under the large plaited reed canopy held up by poles, that shaded one from the sun during the day and shielded one from the river bank breezes at night.

She sighed deeply and allowed her maid servants to fuss and fret, as they washed her, and anointed her with sweet smelling oil. Then they combed her hair and decorated it with little lotus-shaped flowers cut from turquoise that hung from a circlet of gold. Her brows and eyes were outlined in black, her lips shadowed green. Lips and cheeks were rouged red as were the nails on her hands and feet. She wore a white sheath dress held up by shoulder straps and a wide collar of turquoise and gold. Her bracelets were of blue faience beads and her anklet too. Long blue and gold loops hung from her ears.

Nefer sat very still, having sent her servants away, enthroned like a little princess in her carved wooden chair. She was staring at her image that glowed from the polished bronze mirror she held in her hand, and wishing that she looked like Longnose's twin. For in her slim loveliness her downfall lay—should the House of Ramose not be escape enough.

She sighed, realising that she loved being here and she would choose to live in no other place. She knew, because her mother had told her, that Per Ibsen had once lived much further away. At Pharaoh's command he had taken up residence near the Palace at Thebes. Nefer also knew that she herself had been born in a tent set in the desert. That only Per Ibsen and an old woman had been in attendance at the time. Her own natural father, the Great Lord Ramose, had been murdered before she had been born on orders of the old Queen.

It was a miracle, that Zarah, Beloved Mother, had not perished too. Now the House of Ramose was once again to be her haven of security and content. But first she had to get through the night of rejoicing at the Palace, where the wine would flow. Where Pharaoh might well have roving eyes. Where life as she had always known it, might come to a quick and dramatic end.

Twosre, a picture in saffron and gold came running in.

'Father is arriving. Come, let us hurry out to meet him. We will make the servants rush his anointing by saying that the meal is getting stale. Much better, we will say that Thickneck has fallen asleep since he became bored with waiting.' She laughed merrily. 'I really think that Thickneck in his rough and rascally way all but rules everyone in this house.'

'Even *you* listen to Thickneck,' Nefer said lightly, dismissing her own fears for Twosre's sake. 'And frankly, that is a marvel in itself.'

With the arrival of their father and Sebni, who Per Ibsen looked upon as a son, the whole house came alive. The geese were cooked to perfection, the meal-cakes were hot and nutty to the taste, the grapes and other fruits were warm and juicy, the honey wine potent and sweet—and the gifts Per Ibsen brought were out of this world. Jewels and combs, make-up plates, mirrors and woven flax materials in every conceivable shade. For Thickneck, vain as ever even though he could not see, there were ostrich plumes and a new shoulder pouch in which to hold the carving tools he now used to such advantage on wood. Thickneck gave away his own carving which Ay had painted for him. Thickneck also wove baskets and mats, but carving beautiful shapes had always been his greatest love. Each member of the family received a tiny replica of something special. Nefer stared down at Thickneck's present to her. A beautiful cat, perfect in shape and form, for all Thickneck could not see. Ay had painted it black with green eyes.

'In memory of your first cat, Great Mother,' Thickneck said gruffly. 'And her family of kittens who you called One, Two, Three, Four and Five. Remember?'

'Yes and thank you,' Nefer replied quietly. 'It shall be as precious to me as the scarab you gave Mother, your first gift to her. You bought it for her many years ago, do you remember?'

'I still have it,' Zarah cried overhearing. 'O beloved, Napata, I treasure it still!'

The whole family had worked together to bring pleasure to the large, quiet Lord of the House they adored. The gifts were replicas of things he enjoyed and loved in this life. There were fashioned from wood, ivory, ebony and red stone. They would all be placed with much pomp and ceremony, in Per Ibsen's tomb.

He was much pleased and he smiled at them all. But his eyes rested longest on the small, nervous figure of his beloved Nefer. He thought for the thousandth time how like her mother she was. How like that helpless long ago little girl his wife had then been. They had called her Zarah, Princess of Anshan. She was a princess to him still.

'We will do all that we can for Nefer,' he said quietly and smiled down to his wife's upturned face. 'Sebni has offered to help, for he loves his sister with all his heart and soul.'

'As I adore him,' Zarah replied gently. 'And look on him as my son. It would please me—'

'I know very well what would please you, my Morning Light,' he teased. 'This is our present to the boy.'

He clapped his hands to get everyone's attention and then beckoned to Sebni who was tall and slow and quiet. And Sebni innocently smiled his rare amiable smile and drew near.

'It is our pleasure to call you Son,' Per Ibsen told him. 'I have been to the Temple and told this to the Scribe. So it was written. So it was done. You are now, and always will be the First Son of Per Ibsen's House.'

Sebni took in a sharp gulp of air and was momentarily incapable of speech. Nefer's large brown eyes seemed to dominate her face. She pushed her long fringe of hair away from her forehead with quick nervousness. But her voice was honey-gold with delight as she ran to the startled Sebni and took hold of his hand.

'You have always been my brother,' she told him, 'whether your name was on the papyrus or not. Welcome to my heart, Sebni. You are dear to me.'

'As I love you,' he told her carefully, his expression showing that he could barely believe what he had heard. 'And I always will, my sister. I shall go with you to the House of Ramose. There I shall stay.' His eyes grew wet with tears as he turned to embrace Per Ibsen. 'My lord!'

'You are my strong right arm,' Per Ibsen told him. 'And it makes me easier in my mind to know that you will do as I requested. You will go to the House of Ramose and stay there to look after Nefer for a while.'

'And I shall go, too,' Twosre laughed up at him. 'Because I relish the idea of having a big brother. I intend to plague the life out of you, Sebni. So stop those tears, else Father will change his mind.'

'You have always plagued me,' he replied in his quiet, diffident way and they all laughed.

After that there was much animated conversation and teasing. Nefer was able to forget her fears for a little while. But they came rushing back when she returned to her room. Whereas before she had feared and dreaded Ramose House, now she would have given anything to be safe there.

Nefer's mind slipped back, to that other time when she had been so young and she and the tiny Twosre had been in Natalia's care at Ramose House. Zarah, her mother had been ailing and had been sent to the great Healing Temple at Thebes. Per Ibsen had taken her and stayed at her side. Nefer had missed her and yet all was bright and beautiful in her little-girl world. There was darling dark, very fat Natalia to love and care for her—and fend off the tall, skinny black-eyed Ese. Yes, Natalia could even do that! Her mother's old nurse was so revered that she stood over and above the Lady Ese, who was there to teach correct manners and social courtesies.

Happy and secure, for she was much adored and surrounded by indulgent servants and slaves—as well as her many beautiful cats—Nefer had been sure of the goodness and richness of things.

One evening, when Natalia was singing Nefer's most favourite song, stopping every so often to wheeze and gurgle, and roll her eyes teasingly and humorously to make her laugh, something awful had happened.

The old lady began to gasp and her eyes distended in an awesome and horrendous way. Wheezing more harshly than she ever had before, and fighting for breath, Natalia had fallen from her chair and on to the floor, her body racked by convulsions. Nefer screamed and the servants came running, also the tall, stone-faced Ese. Ese took a close look at the writhing woman and paid special attention to her eyes. She tried to lift Natalia's head and called for help. The servants drew back. Not even the major domo had the courage to step forward since he and everyone else believed that Natalia's body had been taken over by evil spirits.

'Hurry to the Temple of Physicians,' Ese commanded a trembling youth. 'And mention most particularly this woman's eyes. Tell them all that you see here—and hurry!'

Because the message came from the great Ramose House it was the eminent Wah-Dwa himself who arrived.

'O Chief Occulist,' Ese said in a cool matter-of-fact way, 'it seems that we have much trouble here.'

The physician, a quiet small man with wise eyes, stroked his chin many times as he stood looking down at Natalia, who, apart from the agonising heaving of her chest, lay still. Then he went on his knees and with great care began to examine her head, feeling it all over, then the back of her neck, pressing most particularly behind her ears. Everyone waited with bated breath for

38

the important man's conclusions. Would he diagnose: 'An ailment which I will treat', 'An ailment with which I will contend', or 'An ailment not to be treated'. In other words favourable, uncertain or unfavourable.

After a very long time he rose to his feet and said to Ese:

'I am very sorry. This is an ailment not to be treated. The lady is too old. She should be allowed to step aboard the Boat in Amun's own good time. She should be left in peace. Therefore, I tell you, take her to a comfortable place. Take no notice of her ramblings, she knows nothing of what she says. Do not fret because her eyes remain open, she knows nothing of what she sees. Give her water if you can, but I feel that from now on, it is up to Amun.'

'Amun,' Ese replied. 'Amun!'

Nefer could remember as clearly as though it were yesterday, how her mouth had gone dry at the physician's words. How the grief had throbbed through her, raw-edged and agonising. She was looking at Natalia who was no longer Natalia, and then at Ese, whose eyes were so glittering and hard. There was a sinking sensation in her stomach as she had looked at Ese's face and she had been fiercely glad that the woman could not see her, would not even look. Who cared a fig for a frightened, desolate little girl whose soul, at that moment felt as if it had sunk to the very bottom of the black river Styx?

The physician had gone away, shaking his head. A message was sent to the lord and lady of the house. At the very first opportunity Nefer had slipped away. She hung about near the room where they had taken Natalia. It was a small place, oblong and plain. Ese's face had screwed up in a terrible way when Nefer had begged that the old nurse should stay in her usual place, the room she shared with Twosre and herself.

'Go away and cease to be tiresome and stupid. Play with Twosre. She is in the garden, and, unlike you, behaving herself.'

There had been one time when all the servants and slaves tried to be anywhere but in the sick room and that was just before the sun went down. It had been the time when Nefer crept in to stay with her beloved Natalia, to hold her hand, and all but try to breathe for the old lady who was making such a pain-racked wheezing noise.

The only other furniture in the room, apart from the low bed on which Natalia lay, was a long narrow chest for clothes. There was space for Nefer to creep behind, just, and so her vigil had begun.

Two days later her mother and father returned, her mother looking very weak and ill. Even so they had hurried to the old nurse's bed and Zarah in great agitation had cried:

'We will try other doctors! Let it be known that I will give gold to the person who brings a cure.'

So the new treatments began. And Nefer would wait her chance, when the dreaded Ese believed her to be asleep, to sneak into the room and hide behind the chest and with all her little girl heart and soul, try and will Natalia to get well.

Sickness was caused by evil spirits, so the drum-beating and incantations began. As did the burning of strange things that caused evil smelling vapours to hang heavy in the room.

Unable to stand the fumes, her mother had been led away weeping. Concocted drugs, mixed with the blood of animals and composed of powdered insects as well as magic plants were moulded into plugs. These were pushed into Natalia's nostrils and ears. The doctor's assistant continued to beat the drum in a rhythmic, hypnotic way, all the time, chanting secret healing words. Still Natalia wheezed and had spates of gabbling that had a dull nasal resonance now. It grew later and shadows were black, menacing things waiting to pounce. Oil lamps made the shadows dance horribly on the walls. More evil smelling elements were piled on to the burning altar and obscene smoke belched out, making Nefer's eyes stream and sending a terrible taste in her mouth.

'We must keep the evil night spirits out,' the doctor had intoned. 'Hear how the devils inside this woman cry out to their brethren in the Lower World. They speak in strange, evil tongues. Let them cease!'

Terrified, Nefer had listened. She heard no devils, only poor darling Natalia saying things that no one could understand. But Ese had seemed to go along with it and her cold upright figure had begun to move slightly to left and right in time to the beating of the drum.

Outside, darkness lay over Egypt, but one scarlet gash of sunset had shone through a pass on the opposite bank. It cut between the rocks like a red hot blade and turned into one of the hells that were the lot of fallen *kas*. She knew that she would remember and loathe the stench of that place for all the days of her life. And all the time Natalia's awful sounds continued to emit from her mouth, sounds that gradually faded until the harsh wheezing breathing was the only sound she made.

Nefer knew the exact moment Natalia's soul departed from life. The harsh beating had stopped. The incantations and drum beats died. There was a moment of awful, unearthly hush in the room. Nefer, rigid, shocked, had been unable to understand. Where was Natalia now? It was only her *ka* (double) that had gone to face the Jackal holding the Feather of Truth. But where, oh where was the real, living, loving, laughing Natalia?

She had heard her mother come, weeping and distressed. She remembered the deep concern in her father's voice—but he was not her true father! They had told her that. Ramose House was her true estate. Her real father had been a high and powerful lord. But she did not want to be showered with cubits of land and coffers of gold. She did not need animals and bins of grain. She wanted to live forever in the shadow of Per Ibsen's house. She wanted to belong!

Incredibly, soon after that, Per Ibsen and Beloved Mother had left, taking Twosre with them. Nefer was bereft and alone. But over all else there was the horror of losing Natalia. It had been her first knowledge of death and she could not forget that last look on Natalia's face.

Sick with grief, filled with terror of the unknown, Nefer changed from the happy, confident child she had been. Now she

43

was panic-filled, unsure. Phantoms raged through her dreams. Awful apparitions danced in her mind. Animal headed, human-bodied gods, all with death in their hands. All belonged to that land on the bank of the Styx. The Netherworld! She needed her mother, but her mother had gone.

During those sad times, Nefer came to associate the House of Ramose, her inheritance, with thoughts of loss and evilness—and past tragedies. She learned from Ese of her natural father's fall from grace, of the treachery meted out to him. Of his murder here in the garden of the home of his name. She heard of the terrible pain and subsequent ill-treatment of her mother by a vicious Persian prince. Above all she accepted, and had at last bitterly understood, that she was not a true blood-child of the Per Ibsen line, but a Ramose instead.

At the height of all this emotional upheaval, Amosis, nephew of Pharaoh's Chief Guard had arrived.

Amosis was a rough ram of a youth. Tall, slim, he was good-looking with steady brown eyes. To Nefer, he seemed rock-like in strength. They had become friends, Amosis not minding her nervousness. She looked up at him with great trusting eyes.

'Amosis,' she whispered once, 'I—I do

not know what to do.'

'You allow that awful Ese to overrule you,' he told her. 'Whereas you, as daughter of the house, should tell her what to do. Your mother is too far away to properly understand what is going on.'

'But Ese says that she herself is right, Amosis. And that I must do as she says. I am to stay here with her. I am not truly of Per Ibsen's house! Ese says I must devote all of my life only to god. Just as she has done.'

'You should weigh things up for yourself. You should be strong and determined like me.'

Yes, Amosis had been strong, but Ese had been the strongest. She took a great dislike to the young man who was edging her charge on to have a will of her own. She found them holding hands one day and went into a terrible rage. Nefer, trembling under a deluge of degrading insinuations that she could not understand, did as she was told after that. She stayed like a prisoner in Ramose House. She heard that Amosis had gone away, into Pharaoh's army. He did not come to wish her goodbye, nor did he write ...

It was strange, Nefer thought, how clearly she was remembering the past, how alone she had been. How greatly she had loved Amosis, nephew of Pharaoh's

Chief Guard. She loved the memory of him still.

She looked up, startled, as her mother came in.

'O my Thrice Beautiful,' Zarah said quietly, 'I know how it is. You are sitting here alone, thinking of the time before—when we left you at Ramose House.'

'It is nothing, Mother. I was remembering that's all.'

'I should have been stronger and stayed with you, Nefer, but I was not. And you of all people, must know how very convincing Ese was. I believed that I was acting for the best. Ese came to us from no less a House than the King's!'

As her mother was speaking Nefer remembered the terrifying picture of Ese again. How tall and thin she had been in her body-dress, which had been as pure as the woman believed her own soul to be. Ese had small eyes that glittered blackly under heavy brows. Her lips, thin for all they were thickly painted with red, and her mouth had hardly seemed to move when she had spoken in her metallic, painfully determined voice. She was a religious fanatic with a streak of cruelty running through her veins.

'I still—still do not understand why you left me with her,' Nefer said quietly. 'I still

46

do not know why it was that you could not see how greatly I feared and hated Ese.'

'I will tell you now—even though it makes no difference,' Zarah whispered and her eyes were dark with distress. 'I was out of my mind with shock and with sickness, Nefer! I was taken to the Healing House. But in spite of all the Magic and the Rituals, in spite of all the herbs and potions, there was nothing the alchemists could do. I—I—Your father and I—we lost our son.'

Tears were streaming down Zarah's face and her voice was choked with grief. Shocked out of her own despair, Nefer gazed at her mother, hardly able to believe what she had heard.

'Beloved,' she whispered brokenly, 'you had a child?'

'He was so tiny, Nefer, so perfect, but he did not take in that sweet breath of life. He lies embalmed in your father's tomb even now, in the casket of sandlewood covered by another of silver, then a third casket of gold. How could we let you know? You who wept at the death of a butterfly? Who broke your heart at a fledgling's fall? How could you witness the burial rites of a baby brother and so soon after the shock of losing Natalia, too? I tell you Thrice Beautiful, we acted as we did out of love for you. There was no other reason at all! When we learned about Ese we went to Pharaoh. He allowed us to bring you home and made no claims on your house and estates.'

'O Mother,' Nefer sobbed and cradled Zarah in her arms, 'I did not know!'

'Then we are forgiven for leaving you with Ese?'

'There is nothing to forgive!' Nefer cried. 'And you must take me to visit my little brother that I might offer him my love. I will make him gifts of honey and lotuses. I will—'

'No, beloved,' Zarah sobbed. 'There is no time. We must get to the Palace and pray to the gods to help us through the night. Keep your eyes on your father—for he *is* your father in his heart and soul, Nefer! He will give you the signal the very moment he sees the chance to escape. You will then go at once, with Sebni and perhaps Twosre will follow you. Do not look back, Nefer. The past is over and done with. Now too, is the finish of this part of our lives.'

'Mother?' Nefer felt horror. 'You and Father?'

'Pharaoh will find out in time, Nefer. It will be in the hands of the gods, how he reacts. But it is usually the punishment of death for trying to evade Pharaoh's will, as you well know.'

'Then I will stay!' Nefer said quietly. 'The bed of Pharaoh will not be so bad.'

'For such as you, it will be hell,' Zarah replied. 'Let us do this, Nefer, for you are dear to our hearts. Have faith and pray to Amun that Thutmose remembers all the good things your father has done—should he find out the truth.'

'Amun!' Nefer whispered. 'Amun!'

CHAPTER TWO

Thebes, capital city, was a place of fascination and splendour. The land was rich and verdant on the side of the river. Here, with large gardens, fruit trees and palms, stood the homes of nobility. Great edifices rich with ornate statues, columns and courtyards, and bins full of grain. There were royal palaces, the Houses of State and the great Temple of Amun Re.

It was an every day sight for the family of Per Ibsen, being taken to Pharaoh's Palace in their carrying chairs. They were, and always had been, regular visitors; and the children had often played in the King's garden or his massive home known to the people simply as the Big House.

On the opposite bank of the Nile, where

the cliffs gleamed yellow and rose, was the haunting sadness and mystery of the Western Hills. Here had been built great tombs for those that had left this life. It was called Valley of Kings, or City of the Dead. But, for Per Ibsen's family, the land of the living was now terrifying enough.

At last they came to the high walls and the great golden gates. These were flanked by guards wearing blue and white striped nemset headdresses, short pleated white kilts, and gold collars of valour glinted round their tanned throats. They had daggers with jewelled hilts tucked in their belts. Spearheads gleamed above their heads, the shafts they held rested firmly on the ground.

Once through the gates the chairs were in the open courtyard with its garden, its pool, its separate side buildings that housed animals, slaves and staff. Ahead, the main entrance. Here the carriers stopped and set the chairs down. One by one, helped by obsequious servants, the family prepared to alight.

Nefer found herself silently and frantically praying again, for safety through the night.

Palace porters led, past giant Nubian guards, who stood at short intervals along the way. They wore rich leopard skin loin cloths, thick gold wristbands and anklets;

and chain necklaces that gleamed almost as menacingly as their black dangerous eyes. The family, headed by Per Ibsen, filed through the tremendous square doorway and into the vast Audience Hall. It was gold and scarlet, columned, and luxurious, with vast colourful frescoes on the walls. There were many people milling about. Everyone recognised Per Ibsen and the members of his family and raised their golden cups, calling out:

'Welcome, O Per Ibsen, it is good to see you. Hello, Lady Zarah, are you well? Nefer and Twosre, how lovely you both look. Happy times!'

'Happiness to you,' Nefer heard herself replying. 'I wish you joy and peace.'

'And to you, the sweet breath of life for ever.'

'Amun!' Nefer whispered. 'Amun to that!'

Musicians massed together and were playing the most popular themes of the day. They were encouraged with merry cries and clapping of hands. Inspired, they played joyous lilting airs. This was the time of the New Beginning. The time for fun.

Women, with painted faces and sheath dresses of many bright colours, vied with each other in the showing of jewels. The air was heavy with perfume that came from the hair cones they wore. At the far end of the hall, on a dais, was set Pharaoh's gold chair. With his arrival the giving and receiving would begin, the eating and drinking and celebrations. The revelry would continue till dawn.

'Nefer,' Per Ibsen said quietly, 'very soon now Pharaoh will arrive. Be careful, watch and wait your chance. The very moment that you can, slip away. Go outside into the gardens and stay there. It might be a good idea to wish your mother farewell now.'

'No!' Zarah's eyes were bright with tears as she took hold of Nefer's hand. 'I will always be with you in spirit my beloved Thrice Beautiful. My dearest dear, I love you, we all love you. Now let us drink a dish of wine. Smile, they are watching us.'

Too choked to speak, Nefer accepted a blue glazed faience dish filled with warm red wine and sipped at it, hoping the liquid would give her courage, then almost choked at the sudden rousing fanfare the heralds played.

Through the door set between pillars, the Great One came. Thutmose the Third, Most Powerful Monarch of the World. Behind him walked Chief Wife, Meretre, mother of Amenhotep heir to the throne, and Khaleb her second and younger son. At her side, the wide-eyed elderly, quiet woman, Isis, who had mothered Pharaoh himself. Behind her, two other favourite wives, Nebutu and Satya. Lesser wives followed, all richly clad, all glittering with jewels. Court officials, cousins, and lesser kings were in the group. But it was to Pharaoh the guests cried:

'Thutmose, Hail! Beloved of Ra, Hail! Valiant Bull, Hail! Life, Health, Strength to Thutmose, Pharaoh Divine.'

Thutmose walked with dignity to his throne. He sat down and looked about him. There was a benevolent smile on his face. He clapped his hands together and the time for New Year tributes began.

The fanfares rang out and Pharaoh's guests moved to the sides of the Great Hall leaving the way to the throne clear.

The first row of men appeared at the entrance, behind them, many more. There were Negroes from Nubia, bearded Asiatics from Syria, Cushites, Israelites, Sea Peoples from the Agean. Row after row of men appeared before the King, some carrying necklaces of gold and silver. Some carried wheat. There were ostrich feathers laid down before My Majesty, sandlewood caskets full of precious stones. Great Minoan jars filled with clear oil, and wine made from the juicy red grapes from the south. There were beads, cloth and furs and skins.

And all the time these gifts were being spread before Pharaoh, the guests sat applauding and smiling. The ladies, in their clinging gowns, taking time off to accept sweetmeats from young female slaves. The gentlemen were wondering how long it would all take—for after receiving, Pharaoh would give, and all hoped for elevation at Court. The scribes were, as always, busily counting and writing everything down.

Nefer felt Pharaoh's rapier glance just once, then he became absorbed in all the wealth and abundance being strewn at his feet. Per Ibsen nodded briefly and she knew that for the moment at least, she was safe. The first chance she had to slip away from all the excitement, the laughter and great roars of approval, Nefer made her escape.

She moved like a wraith, back along the passageway with its Nubian guards, and into the gardens that were cool and still, silvered under the light of the moon, almost humming with the far away music of stars. She lifted her face to look up at the sky and breathed in the air that was cool and sweet with the scent of flowers. All around her she felt peacefulness and restfulness and, like a spirit of the evening, she began to walk.

Nefer came upon Prince Khaleb quite

unexpectedly and started back. She had forgotten that like his brother he was bored at such functions and was never impressed with the showers of gifts. He spent his days doing physical things. Hunting, rowing, riding his beloved horses, engaging in all kinds of sports.

As she hesitated, he swung round. He was devastatingly handsome with fringed, shining black shoulder length hair. His eyes were light and twinkling. He was tall and slim and lithe. There was something god-like about him, Nefer thought with confusion, and knew that he had always affected her so, even as a child. She turned round, intending to make a hasty retreat. He smiled at her rakishly, his eyes black and silver in the light of the moon.

'So, my heart, you are as bored with it all as I?'

She nodded not quite certain what to say.

'Would you care to come with me—and see the new horse I have? He is magnificent enough, even for me!'

She hesitated, but his expression was disarming. It would seem churlish to refuse. She had known and adored him all the days of her life. To refuse him now would raise suspicion, and that would never do.

Nefer walked with the Prince, through the moon-lit night that was heavy with the scent of spices and flowers, and felt drugged. It had always been the same. Even as children she had obediently followed where the young Prince led. Not because it was the law—he was next to the heir apparent after all—but because she wanted to. He was the lamp, she as ever, the moth, incapable of flying away.

They came to the stables that were as clean as the Palace, and as fine. A legion of slaves must care for the horses and stay with them night and day. Nefer walked towards the latest mount acquired by the Prince. He was a wonderful creature, long and lean, his coat sleek and fine. It was a good horse, very good indeed and with genuine warmth Nefer told him so. Then she stopped speaking, disconcerted by the laughter that blazed fresh silver sparks in his eyes.

'Forgive me,' he said, 'but Nefer, you still remind me of my pet gazelle. I loved her in those happy long ago days. And I find that I grieve for her still.'

It was a charming, casual flattery and Nefer smiled a little, recognising it for exactly what it was.

'You did love that gazelle,' she whispered. 'But you never fully tamed her, did you, Khaleb?'

'She remained fragile, and innocent-looking to the last,' he agreed. 'She had a thin, bony little face just like yours and eyes with an expression that said, "Any moment now, I am going to run away, O Prince. Run away out of your life." '

'Oh? I do not think—' she began, conscious that her heart was pounding with fear and shock. 'Forgive me, but—'

His next words made her numb with despair.

'It is a great pity, Nefer. You are far too beautiful a prize to choose all that escaping will entail. He will hunt you down, you know.'

'I—I do not know what you mean,' she stammered and felt hot shame speed through her. So, even Khaleb, Second Prince, who was usually concerned only with hunting, and fishing and riding fast as the wind, had heard her sorry little tale. In all probability the whole of Thebes was laughing at her, and at her beloved parents too! Poor Nefer, they would all say, how silly she is. She couldn't see what was happening right under her nose. How could she be so stupid and dim?

Unaccountably she felt tears scalding her cheeks. Not because of fear, nor because the whole world seemed to know of the pathetic plan of escape, but tears because this beloved prince had been the person to point out how obvious everything had been, and too, he had been able to laugh!

Above all, tears because Khaleb had never loved her, not even as much as he had his little pet gazelle.

'You cannot spend your life running,' he told her. 'And it will be so much wasted effort, since my father is used to having his own way. Are you forgetting that he is god?'

'I do love him as god,' she gasped. 'But I cannot love him as a man!'

'My Majesty would give you protection and care all the days of your life. You would be rich beyond your wildest dreams. You would be honoured and revered.'

'I would be a captive for ever,' she cried. 'And unable to roam the land at will. As Pharaoh's wife I would be guarded, protected and loved, but I would have no existence of my own.'

'You would live for Pharaoh.'

'No,' she replied sadly. 'I would die.'

He stroked his chin at that, his eyes thoughtful. At last he said:

'Then I will help you all that I can, little Nefer. I will let it be known that you are with me. So—if Pharaoh, my father, asks for you, that is the knowledge he will receive. He will wait for your return, and perhaps, in that waiting he will forget.'

'Thank you,' she whispered and wanted to fall at his feet.

58

'Tell me,' he asked her, 'what is the news of Amosis?'

'I know nothing of Amosis,' she answered surprised. 'He was dear to me once, long ago, but he left me without a word. I have heard nothing of him to this day.'

'He was sent away. He is a great man now, and rich. He became a mighty warrior and served as Companion-in-Arms, throughout many campaigns. He is at the Border even now. My father trusts him almost as greatly as he trusts your own father and also dear old Amenemhab. I have an idea!'

'Oh?' Nefer wondered why Khaleb could be so excited and happily easy-going about the entanglements of her life, when she was herself feeling so helpless and sad. 'And may I ask you, Khaleb, what is the idea?'

'I will let it be known to Pharaoh that Amosis the Warrior, cannot wait to be recalled. That all his life he has needed and desired a certain Lady Nefer, daughter of Per Ibsen's House. There! That will be enough to gain your freedom from Father's gaze. It is the time of giving—and he always favours his fighting men above all others at this time of year.'

'But—but Amosis will learn of this lie,' Nefer objected, even though hope was flaring in her heart.

59

'He is at the Border, Nefer! By the time he returns, Pharaoh will have set his sights elsewhere. The danger will be passed. But, to be on the safe side, go ahead with your plan. Go to the House of Ramose and stay. Per Ibsen, your father, will stay here with Zarah, your mother, for they are, as ever, dear to Pharaoh's heart. Cheer up! I, Khaleb, Second Son of My Majesty, am, as ever, wholly on your side.'

At that moment the tall figure of Per Ibsen moved out of the shadows.

'It is time,' he said simply. 'With your permission, Prince Khaleb, my daughter will be gone.'

'So shall it be written, so it shall be done,' Khaleb replied in his lazy good-humoured way. 'And, Per Ibsen, later, you and I will speak? For I have conceived of an even stronger plan.'

So! Khaleb had been in on it from the beginning. Nefer thought. Then he was not so casual after all!

There was no time for further talk. Swiftly, she was hurried to the carry chair and helped in. She crouched there, heart beating, conscious of the clamminess of her palms and the dryness of her mouth. She was dimly aware that other chairs were following. They reached the steps that led down to the bank and the wharf where a ship rode at ease on the waves. A small boat floated like a moth in the darkness, carrying Nefer, Twosre and Sebni to the deep water, and to the ship. Gnarled brown hands reached out to help them embark.

Then, as the ship began to move away, Nefer began to breathe again. The waves were painted with silver and held a pathway that seemed to lead direct to the moon. The far banks were the shadowland and the only reality now was the wide, sweeping waters of the holy river Nile.

The journey along the night river seemed to go on forever, Nefer thought. Sick and afraid she looked over the side. She saw other boats, slipping by like phantoms, no human sound coming from them. Only the rhythmic splash of great oars as they hit the water, and the spasmodic flapping sound of the breeze-laden sails.

Nefer strained her ears, afraid even now that Pharaoh's great ship might be following. Even the ebullient Twosre seemed subdued. As well she might be, since defying Pharaoh was as good as courting death.

Standing at the ship's side, watching the dark outline of the bank slowly slipping by, made Nefer experience again the sense of unreality. Would it be too bad, she wondered, to become a lady of Pharaoh's house? She would be elevated to a position above and beyond her wildest dreams, of course, and her every wish would be fulfilled. Pharaoh was renowned for his generosity. She would be given fine linen, gold and jewels and everything of the best. But she did not love Pharaoh, who was her father's dearest friend. He was the living god, high above her—and he was far too old!

It was whispered that Pharaoh was a great lover. That his women would die for the honour of sharing his bed. She should be flattered to have received even a second glance, she knew it, but there was a problem. She had long ago given her heart to someone else. Not Amosis, her first recipient of her love. She had known nothing then, and been merely a child. But the Prince was another matter entirely and she had known him all the days of her life.

'Khaleb. O Khaleb,' she whispered wistfully. 'My dearest dear!'

Twosre came to join her and gently took hold of her hand.

'Do not look so pensive, Nefer. What is done is done. Though—it would have been so much easier, if you allowed Pharaoh his way.' She chuckled softly, adding, 'What a great pity it is that the Divine One did not choose me.'

'You—you would not have been afraid?'

'How could I be? I would love to give pleasure to god. Why are you such a frightened little cat, Sister dear? Do men really terrify you so much?'

'I—I love someone, Twosre.'

'You do?' Twosre was all attention now. 'What a one for keeping secrets you are, who do you love? Tell me!'

'Khaleb.'

'Never! He made our lives miserable when we were small. His teasing was cruel and he always managed to make you cry.'

'I know, but—'

'He only really upset me once and I kicked him—hard.'

'Then he had you whipped, Twosre!'

'And I, in turn, made him pay for that, believe me.'

'How?'

'Never you mind.' Twosre's pretty face was looking rather devilish in the moonlight. 'But for a while at least I had our young lord looking over his shoulder. No, don't look at me like that, Nefer! I swear that I'm telling you nothing but the truth.'

In spite of everything, Nefer found herself smiling at Twosre, who she truly adored.

'Then, if that's the case,' she said, 'Khaleb is sweeter than I thought. For in spite of your terrible revenge, he has put himself out sufficiently to help our father keep Pharaoh's attention on matters other than ourselves.'

Sebni, whose shadowed face was long and solemn under the light of the moon, squinted his sickle-shaped eyes in his usual wary manner.

'Prince Khaleb has a way of exacting full payment for any favours he might give,' he told the girls in his tight, tension-filled way. 'It is too soon to feel relief yet.'

'Sebni!' Twosre said crossly. 'Do you always have to put a damper on things? What a dull sort of person you are. The only time I have seen you really come to life is when you are working alongside Father. As far as I can see, life and living is much more important than fashioning monuments out of stone.'

'It is divine work,' Sebni said in his careful way. 'You should not decry the Great House we are building for the glory of Hathor, the holy cow.'

'There you go again!' Twosre began peevishly. 'How pompous you are at times! And I never—'

'Please,' Nefer said and held up her hand to silence Twosre. 'Don't wrangle, it is not worth the effort. Sebni has a right to his views, just as we all have, and—and I do feel just a little ill.'

Twosre subsided in a mutinous silence. Sebni walked away towards the captain who stood so still in the prow of the ship, seeming almost like a wooden effigy in the light of the swinging lamp. Nefer turned away to look once more upon the quietly moving, infinitely ethereal black and silver world.

It was during the waiting moment, in the strange half light that hovers just before dawn, when the ship reached the landing stage that led direct on to the grounds belonging to the House of Ramose. Nefer clasped hold of Sebni's outstretched hand and he helped her on land. Twosre jumped lightly overboard, spurning all help, and waded ashore. The captain was a quiet, energetic man and anxious to get away. He was aware, as they were, that leaving Pharaoh's Court without permission did not augur well, should the Living Horus be in a bad mood. But he was a friend of Per Ibsen, and the captain found himself praying to the gods that Per Ibsen and also Prince Khaleb were blessed with beguiling tongues, at least for as long as it took for him to get his ship away.

Nefer led the way to the great walled house, to the gates the keeper swung open at their approach. She walked up the path that led to the small family chapel, and stretched her arms before her, palms downwards, her head bent low, in supplication to the figure of Amun who stood in his shrine.

'Thank you,' she breathed, 'for bringing us here unharmed.'

'Amun,' Twosre and Sebni echoed. 'Amun.'

Suddenly, deep down inside, Nefer began to shake. She was remembering how, when a child, she had been forced to pray for hours in this place. She saw Ese again, heard her hard, metallic voice:

'Death is the preparation, Nefer. Learn to be obedient, afraid and prepared. We, none of us can escape. So hear this, we must live our lives in preparation for the final, inevitable event. Then it begins!'

'Yes, Ese.'

'The journey along the Black River.'

'Yes.'

'And at the end we must, in deep humility, have our wicked souls weighed against the Feather of Truth.'

'Yes, yes, yes!'

'The Jackal will be watching, on guard, he will guard the gates. Hail to Anubis!'

'And—and to Amun.'

Black eyes had snapped. Then fingers closed on her arm.

'You are not fooling me, Nefer! You are trying to placate me with your obedience. You are a wicked child, wicked, and Amun

66

knows. He can see you, hear you, know you. To placate him you will one day go to the temple and devote to him every moment of your life ...'

In a vague, but nevertheless certain kind of way, Nefer knew that she could never escape. One day Ese would come for her. The horror of the thought put her fear of Pharaoh in the shade. She turned to Twosre and said quickly:

'I hate this place. It holds bad memories for me.'

'Then we will go,' Twosre replied, 'to where our welcome will be far more down to earth.'

They left the chapel and entered the house through an inner courtyard and a porch where the doorway emblazoned the Ramose seal. Servants, joyful to receive them, ran forward bearing gifts of Lotus flowers and fronds cut from palms.

All was a bustle of welcome now and smiling servants cried out greetings and seemed almost as if they had been expecting their return. Nefer walked along a pillared loggia and into the central hall and from there to the main living room, that had massive red painted pillars supporting the ceiling. She went to the wide limestone slab in the floor and stepped on it, waiting while near-naked servant girls poured cooling water over her hands and feet. And Paihuti, the major domo was bowing most humbly and begging My Lady to prepare herself for the good and nourishing meal that was being brought from the kitchens even now.

'With lots of fresh fruit, my lady,' added Bebu, Paihuti's plump jolly wife.

And such was the joy and pleasure of the house to have members of the family home for a while that Nefer relaxed, and forgot to be afraid, and even enjoyed honey-bread and sweet grapes and warm creamy milk. Then, tired after the journey and needing to be alone for a while, Nefer retired to her own private room that held gilt covered furniture and a lion-pawed bed.

Her memories were wistful as she thought of the Prince. The handsome young man who was as high above her as the stars.

'Oh Khaleb,' she whispered longingly, 'Khaleb, my dear, I love you as deeply as I once loved Amosis. I am bereft.'

Her mind went back to her childhood, to that other time, when she had been filled with the awe and wonder of an innocent first love.

How she had adored Amosis, how she drunk in his every word. He was so handsome, so tall and strong—and so wise.

'He is a rough and ready boy and too

worldly,' tall, thin, hard-faced Ese had said. 'You must forget earthly things and set your thoughts upon the love of god.'

'Which god?' she had dared to ask in her quiet enquiring way. 'There are so many, Ese.'

'Why the highest of all! Amun!'

'But I prefer the Cat Goddess, Bast.'

'I said Amun!'

'Prince Khaleb loves the Goddess of Love, Hathor, above the rest.'

'He would! There is a great deal wrong with that young man.'

'Ese! One day the Prince may become King and rule alongside Amenhotep.'

'Then he will have to bow to Amun above all others. Make no mistake about that. Just as Pharaoh Thutmose, his father, calls upon the Great Unseen.'

'I like Khaleb, Ese, but I love Amosis,' Nefer said obstinately. 'I do not care for gods. I love Amosis best!'

'You are being obscene!' Ese's tone had been coldly vicious. 'Do you know what will happen to you when you die like Natalia? When you leave this life?' The woman had towered over her and looked so demented that Nefer had become afraid. Ese began to rant. The way she had gone on, about god, Punishments of Hell, and the obscenities that were committed in the name of earthly love, had shocked Nefer and made her cringe away, too frightened to cry.

Love, Nefer thought, remembering, is a painful emotion when it is not returned. I so adored Amosis, I would have died for him, had he asked. But he went away without a word, and I have never got over my sense of loss, not even to this day.

She thought of the frightened, nervous little girl she had been. And how out of all the horror Amosis arrived. Tall, strong, down to earth. He had been patient with her, taking her thoughts away from the mystical otherworld things that Ese was for ever pushing into her head. He had allowed her to hold his hand and he had taken her for walks along the river bank. He told her merry, boyish stories of adventures of heroes, men who had been of human blood, flesh and bones. How natural Amosis had been, how warm and real.

Nefer continued to sit alone in the room that had been hers as a child. In spite of the passing of time, the ghost of Ese still seemed to be there, hovering among the people pictured on the walls. Nefer shivered, remembering again the filthy insinuations emitting from the thin-lipped mouth of Ese. The woman's face had worked in a vicious, evil way. She had called Amosis an animal, a disgusting bullock of a boy who needed to be sent to slaughter. That she, Nefer, should know better. That she was not a cow making eyes at a bull, but a high-up young lady belonging to a great and distinguished house. That, by rights, she should be sent to the Temple as a neophyte.

'I want my mother!' Nefer had cried.

'She has no time for you,' Ese had spat out. 'And it's a good thing she is away. She would be heartbroken to learn of the things you have got up to with that boy.'

'He allowed me to hold his hand, Ese. That is not wrong! Please send for my mother. I want her!'

Such had been the demented anger of Ese that she had called on the servant to gather up the pet cats that Nefer so loved. They were placed in rush baskets and taken with great care to the Temple of Bast. There they were loved and cherished by the priestesses of the Cat Goddess. Nefer's punishment could not have been worse. Without her beloved cats she was heartbroken. She cried for her mother again and again. Once she tried to run away and was caught, and taken back, screaming, to the house.

She had been shut up and alone for many days and nights. The servants were afraid of Ese for she was the Authority and High Born. Amosis, the strong, the quiet, the incredibly wonderful had gone away.

Ese had taken to telling the trembling, captive little girl all kinds of stories about the terrible hells. Of wicked demons, of burning fires of torment, and the eerie black, malevolent River of Death. She went on about the punishments meted out to the *kas*—the shadowy doubles of the people who had died. Woe betide any *kas* that did not weigh properly on the scales of the Feather of Truth.

'Don't tell me!' Nefer had cried. 'Please don't tell me such things, Ese. I want Mother. Why doesn't Mother come for me?'

'Because you are a wicked little girl and all the fish-jawed demons with red gleaming eyes will leave their places in the bowels of the tombs one of these dark nights. It is their duty to gobble up wilful, naughty little girls.'

Gradually, the once merry, confident young Nefer, became a pale shadow of herself. She was sure that all of the demons of hell were waiting to chew her up alive. She began to have nightmares and would wake up shrieking. Finally, she took a fever and almost died.

An old servant, who had been in the Ramose household for many years, took his life in his hands, and actually left the estate of his own accord. It was unheard of, to leave a nobleman's cubits without permission, but it had to be done. So, Intef, Grandfather of Paihuti, found Per Ibsen at last and told him the truth about what was going on.

By that time Nefer had been in Ese's sole care for almost nine months of one year.

Ese was sent away in disgrace. No one knew for sure, where she had gone. It was believed that she had returned to her family home on the frontier somewhere. Nefer could still remember the terrible look of hate in Ese's viper-black eyes on that last morning, and hear that high, uncontrolled voice screaming that she would come back one day—to claim Nefer's fallen soul.

Because her memories were almost too painful to bear, Nefer left her room and went in search of Twosre, but came upon Sebni instead. He was sitting by himself in the main hall. He looked uncomfortable, out of place and seemed as though he did not know what to do. He looked up and was clearly relieved to see Nefer.

'Twosre has gone for a walk,' he said. 'She told me that she has gone in search of old friends.'

'Ah!' Nefer said. 'I expect she has gone to look for the relations of Pepi the fisherman. He has many fine, strapping young sons.'

73

'I do not know where she gets all her energy,' Sebni said, despondently. 'Are you rested now?'

'I—I must confess to still feeling shaken and—rather down,' Nefer admitted. She took hold of Sebni's hand then added in her shy, quiet way, 'It is good to know that you are here, Sebni. There's something about you that makes me feel safe.'

He looked at her out of his serious half-moon shaped eyes. He was usually quiet, a young man dedicated to his master, Per Ibsen, and therefore to every member of the family of his lord. He was a slow thinking person, and steady. He had painstakingly learned his craft. Apart from his job and listening to the wisdoms of his master, he seemed to care for little else.

'My lady,' he said carefully.

'Sister,' she told him. 'We are brother and sister now,' she added softly, 'isn't that nice?'

His lips curved and he smiled his self-conscious smile.

'I still cannot believe that it is Per Ibsen's wish to call me Son.'

This was quite true. Sebni was still barely able to grasp that he was now officially one of the family. He had been vaguely aware that his master would not be displeased should he look kindly on his eldest daughter, who seemed so shy and reserved. A son-in-law was most desirable, and especially one so truly able to follow in Per Ibsen's footsteps, for Sebni knew that Pharaoh desired to outdo all past kings in the number of temples he had built in honour of the gods. The work Sebni and his master were set to do would take many years. All of Per Ibsen's lifetime in fact, and probably beyond. Sebni, when first learning of his master's wishes, had looked at Nefer, intrigued. Then he had got on with his work, pushing the idea of taking a wife firmly away.

Now, even he could see that the my lady Nefer was painfully unsure of herself. She looked shaken and ill. Not for the first time, Sebni found Nefer's quiet good manners, her air of timidity, pathetic somehow.

Sebni began to feel a man. He inched nearer to Nefer and saw the colour heighten on her cheeks. He believed that this high born lady, his sister, was somehow affected by him. He felt a sinking sensation in his stomach and drew back.

Her new brother's unease communicated itself to Nefer. It made her forget her own distress at the situation they were in. She looked, truly looked at Sebni for the first time. Before, he had always been there, a shadow at her beloved father's side. He was—well, he was just Sebni. As familiar

75

a figure as were the stone rams that stared imperturbably away from the portals of Per Ibsen House. Now, things were different. In a strange kind of way she was warming towards him.

His wide forehead and scrupulously neat appearance surely showed a scrupulously neat and tidy frame of mind. Nefer found that she was comfortable with him.

During the days that followed, secure in the knowledge that there was still no sign of Pharaoh's barge, Nefer relaxed. She came to look for and enjoy Sebni's company even more. She enjoyed showing him her magnificent house. Gracious and luxurious, it contained rich artefacts from all over the world.

The gardens were a joy, as was the long tiled pool. Palms grew and exotic climbing flowers clambered over the walls. Everywhere there was the feel of luxury, the scent of wealth, the atmosphere of elegance.

Numerous servants and slaves, under the calm but determined eye of the major domo—whose name Paihuti meant peasant—ran the house like a dream. It had been Paihuti's grandfather who had warned Per Ibsen of Ese. It had been his loyalty that had so elevated his family's position. So it was that Paihuti was greatly favoured and taught to run the establishment from the time he'd been old enough to learn.

Paihuti was a nice, decent little man who took his role in life very seriously indeed. Not so Bebu, his plump jolly wife. She took to Sebni at once and would have over fed him with her famous honey cakes given half the chance.

One morning, as Bebu watched Nefer and Sebni walking sedately side by side in the gardens, she turned to her husband, saying:

'My lord Paihuti, I have great hopes for the happiness of Lady Nefer after all. She seems to have taken to Sebni and now looks on him with rather more than sisterly eyes.'

Paihuti frowned.

'I do not care much for such a match. Lady Nefer deserves a real man and one born of high standing.'

'I did not think you would hold Sebni's lack of standing against him! I know that his parents were Wanderers, but there is an uncle who is very worthy indeed.' Bebu became more outraged with every word she uttered. 'O Paihuti, my lord, I did not believe you to be that unkind!'

'Sebni's standing is now elevated to that of the seal of Per Ibsen,' Paihuti pointed out reasonably enough. 'And I am well aware that, next to our master, Sebni is now lord and son of this house. I was not thinking of position, but of character, Wife.'

'The young man has a very good character,' Bebu flared. 'He is slow and quiet and tender. He is—'

'Ineffectual!' Paihuti snapped.

'Merely the insecurity of youth!'

'I prefer to wait and see,' Paihuti doggedly replied.

As the days slipped by and the moons waxed and waned on the orders of Moon God, Chons, the friendship between Nefer and Sebni grew more strong. Twosre was rarely home these days. With wise, wicked, merrily dancing eyes, she went about business of her own. Servants and slaves adored her, but she cheerfully ordered them away.

'I am like the wayward spirit of the wind,' she laughed. 'I go here and there as I please. Go away you old pussy cats, you hamper me!'

Then she would throw presents at them. Sweetmeats, baubles, bangles or beads. They would grin, adore her with their eyes, then scramble at her pretty dainty feet. Yet, for all her determination to be alone, she would allow Sebni to walk with her along the river bank.

A messenger arrived with a letter written on papyrus, for Nefer. It was from the lord their father. Taught by her mother Nefer could read, and Twosre and Sebni waited for news, almost holding their breath. Then Nefer looked up, smiling in a happy, misty way.

'O praise be to Amun,' she whispered. 'We are safe! Prince Khaleb has been successful in persuading Pharaoh that I should be Amosis's prize. Our parents have agreed to this. They are well and happy and continue to shine in the warmth of Thutmose's love.'

'Then we are to return to the city?' Twosre eagerly asked. 'I have many friends at Court and—'

'You may return as quickly as it suits you,' Nefer replied. 'And Sebni also. Indeed our father looks forward to your return very much, my Brother. But at this moment our parents believe it would be best if I stayed here for a little while longer.'

'I would like to leave, then return, and in short, keep up visits to my old uncle,' Sebni said carefully. 'It is important to let him see that I continue in good health.'

'Of course you must see him,' Nefer replied quickly, knowing that she would miss him, and also feeling a little sad for him too. Sebni's uncle was a rough prickly old man who had never forgiven his quiet little sister for running away with a Wanderer. She had returned, alone, to die at Sebni's birth. The boy had been nursed by a slave, and then apprenticed to Per Ibsen when very young.

It was said that the uncle of Sebni boasted that he'd be damned by Set if he didn't outlive his primsie, wish-washy heir. That the gods had been unkind for giving him no wife nor son of his own, so that it would be his sister's son left to continue the family name.

All that talk, Nefer thought, comforting herself, had just been the old man's way. In the nature of things, Sebni would one day come into his own. He would have a house, quite a few cubits of land, animals, servants and slaves.

'We will both stay here with you,' Twosre said. 'And don't you dare to argue about my decision, Sebni.'

'I would not, could not—' Sebni began.

Twosre laughed and tossed back her luxuriant, black hair.

'You are too diffident in look, word and deed, Sebni. I can see that I shall have to take over the handling of you. I will have to if only for Nefer's sake. She spends too much time dreaming while embroidering collars and threading beads. She needs to be looked after, Brother dear, and it will be my delight to show you how.'

'What a lovely idea,' Nefer teased lightly. 'How indulgent you are, Sister, and always thinking of others, never yourself.'

'You are too trusting, Nefer, and you think too kindly of me. For all your teasing you believe me to be sweet and adorable. I am not. With me it is myself that comes first and last. And since you have all but commandeered Sebni since we've been here, I shall take my turn!'

'Twosre!' Nefer was embarrassed for their brother and it showed on her face. Twosre, uncaring, went on.

'I am determined to change him from the old stick-in-the-mud he appears to be.'

Nefer smiled gently into Sebni's discomfited face.

'Go with her,' she said sweetly. 'And let her do her worst.'

And it became the pattern after that, for Twosre to tease Sebni and sometimes to lead him away. He went obediently, but he still seemed to be happier in the company of the quiet and gentle Nefer.

Twosre watched Nefer and Sebni walking sedately by the river bank and her eyes gleamed with amusement. She pursed her lips and began to whistle in a sweet lilting way. One associated whistling with Twosre, and laughter too. Hearing the whistle Sebni's cheeks became pinched and a thin line of sweat beaded his upper lip.

'Do you feel ill?' Nefer asked, seeing the

81

expression on his face, and felt inordinately relieved when he smiled and squeezed her hand.

'Too many of Bebu's honey cakes, I should think,' he said in his slow earnest way. 'Shall we return to the house, Nefer?'

As he walked away from the river, Sebni was unable to get Twosre out of his mind. She frightened him somehow, and yet fear was an absurd word. He frowned, remembering her as he had seen her only that morning, when he had been walking alone by the river. She had moved towards him with ineffable grace. She seemed to be as wild and free as the breezes that tugged at her long, gold ornamented hair. Her eyes had been mocking him, telling him gleefully that he could never be her match.

Sebni turned impulsively to Nefer and smiled into her great melting eyes. How beautiful she was, gentle and fine. She was a dream person who he never seemed to truly reach. Nefer was his beloved, but there was a part of her that she always kept to herself. She was high above him as the Goddess of Dawn, and as ethereal and pure. Her lips were as light as the touch of butterfly wings when she kissed him goodnight.

His mind darted back to Twosre whose lips were as firm and red as passion fruit. He could imagine those lips—his mind flinched away and returned to Nefer. He was grateful to her. He loved her. His relationship with her was a rare and beautiful thing. He had as good as told her that, when Pharaoh had forgotten his promise where Amosis was concerned, he Sebni, would be honoured to have and to hold sweet Nefer as his wife.

Twosre swam in the river, naked as the day she was born. She loved the warmth of the water, the feel of its liquid caress against her skin. She half closed her lids and squinted through wavelets alive with the sun. Then she saw the tough looking fisherman pulling his boat on to the bank. His face was new and he had probably come from a village further along. She saw that the back of his neck was thick, like a bull's. His body seemed firm and strong.

Twosre lifted her body and arched out of the water in a singularly silver-streaked curve. She knew that the fisherman had seen her and her lips curved in a smile. She had recognised her power over men when a very young girl. Aware of the man's eyes on her, thinking how small they were, and hard, like little beads. Twosre began to cavort in the water, teasing him, daring him. Then she swam lazily to the bank, a small way away and waded through the warm mud. She sensuously enjoyed the feeling of a squelching through her toes. She was glad that her fine clothes and jewels were hidden. It would not do for the fisherman to know who she was—it would frighten him away.

She reached a patch of gold grasses and threw herself down, burying her face in a clump of wild scented blue flowers that were growing there. She heard the clumsy footsteps and whistled wickedly in the wind, her eyes mysterious as she thrilled anew with the knowledge of her power. It delighted her, made a goddess of her and because she needed to test its strength again, here and now, she whistled again and waited. Waited with glowing ripples rushing up and down her spine.

He stood over her, legs astride, his beady black eyes hot in his face.

'Yes?' he asked.

'Yes!' she replied.

He lowered himself down and she invited him with the lazy expression in her eyes. He was a good, strong, vigorous man. He used her with a basic ferocity that was her delight. When it was over he rolled away, laid on his back and snored. Laughing softly, well pleased with herself, Twosre slipped away. She found her clothes, and jewels, and put them on. Then returned to Ramose House.

Sebni was alone in the garden and he was aware of the world of knowledge in her eyes. Knowledge that made her bold and defiant and absolutely sure. And the very wantonness dancing in her black eyes, her sheer disregard of what he either said or thought, made her suddenly very desirable—and to Sebni at least, infinitely more dangerous.

'O Brother dear,' she teased, 'what a sour-face you are. You seem to be almost accusing me.'

He stared at her out of his sickle-moon eyes and there was a frown on his face.

'I do not know why I should accuse you, Twosre,' he said.

'No?' She took a step nearer. 'Not any accusations at all? O Brother, you are disappointing me!'

'I—I do not know what you want me to say,' he muttered helplessly and tried to look away, but she would have none of it.

'I want you to *do*, Sebni. There is something I dare you to *do!*'

He stood there, his mouth dry, his heart afraid, but he did not move away as she sidled up against him and put his hand on her pert little breast.

'Tease me, Sebni,' she laughed. 'Play

with me and tease me like a man!'

She began to move against him, coaxing him, half serious and half in play. He was hypnotised and with a sharp cry he clasped her tight against him in a frantically amateurish way.

Nefer, coming on them and hastily hiding behind a large shrub, felt her heart lurch and begin to throb in a deeply painful way. Life without Sebni was unthinkable, yet it seemed it had come to that. Then she gasped and cried out for she felt hands on her shoulders. Hands that effortlessly swung her round.

'Khaleb!'

'I told you,' he said, 'that you cannot spend your days running away—and don't look so surprised. You must have known that I would come, my heart. That I would follow you.'

Before she could help herself, Nefer was nervously smiling up at this incorrigible, absolutely outrageous man.

'You owe me a favour, my heart,' he said, 'but I doubt if, being you, it will ever be paid.'

'I do not know what you mean, Khaleb,' she whispered uncertainly. 'And you're disturbing my peace.'

He threw back his head and laughed.

'Peace? Here? In this great house that stands all but knee deep in the river? So you only half see as well as only half live! The river peaceful? Never! It's vibrantly alive and full of movement. The light of Amun dances on the waves, the might of Hapi lifts it higher up the banks. The water fowl dart in and out of the rushes, birds fly, fish swim. The whole world is alive and surging, kicking and fighting to be alive. Just like our soldiers—at the frontier.'

'Khaleb?' she asked and felt fear. 'What are soldiers to do with me?'

'Pharaoh has promised you to Amosis, had you forgotten? Soon now, very soon I think, you will be leaving this place. I saved you from Pharaoh, my heart, but seemingly, our plan has misfired.'

'You mean—I am to go to Amosis?' She felt the blood drain from her face. 'My parents, surely they—'

'Could do nothing, though they tried. I believe you will be left in peace here for as long as they can get away with it—but my lord father is no fool. Make no mistake about it, Nefer, you will be sent off to the Garrison town or else Amosis will be brought to you here. Either way it has been accomplished. Pharaoh has sent your names together and decreed "So let it be written. So let it be done". Like it or not, My Heart, you belong to Amosis now.'

'I—I do not wish to belong to anyone,' she said quietly. 'I think I'd almost prefer to serve in the Temple of Bast.'

'Really?' His eyes were teasing. 'How strange! Cats are notorious for their delight in producing large numbers of offspring at least twice a year. Tell me, would you like to scream and scratch and yowl up at the moon—with me?' He laughed at her expression. 'Of course you would not!'

'How—how very dull and cowardly you make me sound, Khaleb,' she whispered painfully. 'And I cannot remember a time in my life where you have not seen me in some cause for merriment.'

'But I love you just the same, Nefer. Now how much longer do you intend to sleep? You have never been awakened, and you have certainly never known love.'

'I think you have taken too much for granted, Khaleb, and—'

His eyes reflected the sunlight as he stared intently into her face. His sheer animal attraction almost frightened her. She stood before him, her eyes averted, but all she could hear was his rich confident voice.

'There are two loves,' he told her. 'One like the steady glow that Isis bears for Thutmose her son; and the same as he bears for her. The love my mother bears for my father stays serene and unchangeable for all of life's span. The other love has great, joyous flames leaping up to the gods.

Flames with golden-crested tongues! Such a love is all consuming, Nefer.'

'And—and I?'

'You are capable of the first, made for the second, and as yet you have never experienced even one small genuine spark.'

'That is not true!' she whispered. 'I have loved. I have!'

'Who have you loved?' he teased.

'You are hateful,' she gasped and ran from him, a picture of the young Amosis dancing before her tear-filled eyes.

Late that evening, Nefer once again walked by the river. Khaleb was there, his eyes intent only on the purple shadows at the base of palms, the glow of the sunset that had turned the waters to molten bronze. Of wavelets becoming silver-tipped in the light as they leaped and tumbled and spread in ever widening ripples in the wind. Feeling absurdly like a small child, she stood there, waiting patiently until he turned to her. She blushed before the directness of his gaze.

'Well, My Heart?' he asked her. 'What did you say to that precious pair?'

'Nothing. It was only—a kiss.'

'Where Twosre is concerned,' he said, 'there is always more. Believe me, I know!'

She spun round, as if intending to run away from him again, but his next words stopped her.

'Why not be a little more like Twosre? She is relaxed and happy about life. She takes what she wants and bites into existence with the same relish as she chews at bunches of grapes. Take a man, Nefer, not a pale imitation of one. Take me!'

All her humiliation and hurt rose up in a single tempestuous wave. She thought of Sebni, quiet, comfortable Sebni who had let her down—and now Prince Khaleb, who she adored, was laughing at her again.

She forgot the punishments meted out to a person to even look askance at royalty. Her hand shot out and in that one wild moment, she slapped Khaleb hard across the cheek. Then his face blocked out the sun. She was drowning in his eyes, drowning. And there was the stinging whip-lash of his mouth against hers followed by a sinking feeling as her heart lurched and began to thud against her sides.

He let her go and laughed softly, wickedly, his leonine eyes alight with the dawning joy of the hunt. He seemed savagely sure of himself—and of her.

Terrified she ran from him, her heart beating, her mouth dry. Amid the fear, she felt there was an excitement she had never known before. Deep in her mind, there was the knowledge that she was merely a subject, he a prince. Thus, no matter what happened, the outcome, by law, could only be right.

He caught her, and held her as close as the rushes that now rustled and whispered and held them bound in a solitary secretive world. The setting sun threw out its crimson cloak, tipping the clouds with gold and green. A few birds called sleepily, then the resonant, distant temple bells started to call god's name—Ra! Ra! Ra! Amun—Ra! A slightly scented breeze from the river fanned Nefer's face as she turned blindly to the waiting man.

'This—this is all wrong,' she faltered helplessly. 'I belong to Amosis now.'

'How can you set yourself to judge what is right and what is wrong?' Khaleb asked softly and his lips curved into a smile. A smile that reflected like gold dust in his eyes and lit the whole of his lean, handsome face. 'Only Pharaoh is the supreme judge. Only he who made the royal oath, "With this crook I will shepherd my people and with this Flail protect them from their enemies", can truly assess what is right and wrong.'

'You do not understand—' she whispered. 'How can you?'

'I understand, Nefer, that one must endeavour to accept and to take what is offered.'

91

'I—I do not offer, Khaleb.'

'But I take!'

She stared up at him, her soul reaching out, melting against him, adoring him. Let me always feel as I do now, she thought and felt tears of emotion stinging against her eyes. She was filled with desire and longing and with a sigh gave herself up to his fiery caresses. His lips were moving away from her lips, to cover her neck, her breasts, her thighs. She gasped, then as he looked up and stared ruthlessly into her face, she clung to him, needing him, wanting never to let him go.

Then there was nothing else in the world but the stinging, tumbling, rising ecstasy of passion. With a suddenness that was unexpected, he took her. She cried out, called out his name. And fight it though she had, fear it as she did, she loved Prince Khaleb, Second Son of the Most High Majesty of the World.

Khaleb, hot and sexy, a man among men, knew how to love her. She became alive, reached up to the sky in a rhythm beating in her heart and soul and every fibre of her being. Then the emotion ended in an explosion of stars. She wept, then relaxed where she was in the shelter of Khaleb's arms. They stayed there, in the rushes, and the deep purple night enfolded them in its richness.

When the flamingo-pink clouds trailed across the turquoise sky of dawn, they walked back to the House of Ramose hand in hand. The surroundings, when they reached the large lovely gardens of her home, were as beautiful as love.

'I love you,' Khaleb said. 'I love your wide innocent eyes, your shyness and newness, and everything about you.'

And because Nefer believed the Prince implicitly, because this must surely be the most wonderful day of her life, her eyes became like stars with unshed tears.

Unmindful of Sebni's blank stare, and of Twosre's near black, angrily accusing eyes, Nefer began almost to float through the days.

'Aren't you forgetting that you belong to Amosis now?' Twosre asked tartly. 'What will everyone think? What will they say?'

'Khaleb will sort everything out,' Nefer replied with quiet certainty. 'He has Pharaoh's ear. Khaleb will know exactly what to do.'

'Be careful, O Sister,' Twosre warned. 'You do not know men as I do. You have been given your place by King Thutmose himself. It will do you no good should he learn of what has gone on. And, had it occurred to you that it can bring our parents nothing but harm?'

Nefer experienced fear and decided to

try to send Khaleb away, but it took only one meaningful glance from his dark handsome eyes and she would tingle with pride of submission. Gradually Khaleb won completely and she became wax in his hands.

'We—we should not play at love, O lord,' she whispered again and again. 'It is wrong and always will be, in Pharaoh's eyes.'

'Really?' His smile reflected sunbeams and she could think of nothing else. 'Forget this tiresome talk. Think only of my needs and of my commands.'

And her cheeks glowed as she lowered her head. Her eyes were shy, and full of dreams. She stayed at his side, not daring to remind him that all would be lost if he stayed—if Pharaoh found out!

His eyes would glitter with impatience and words would come. Harsh, dreadful words that made her flinch and that seared against her soul. Then she would freeze and sit like a small desolate shadow until he relented and smiled lazily into her wide shocked eyes once again.

Then he'd begin charming her, wooing her, making her his willing slave once more. His smile would become triumphant and he'd walk towards her savagely sure. She would bow like a reed before the strength of his wanton erotic kisses. He would be delighted with her, tower over her, tangling his long brown fingers in her hair. And when the passion was over, she would lie in his arms listening to her heart singing to the wild tune of her adoration.

Nefer knew that tease her though he had, use her though he did, she was alive as she had never been before. She felt that she would walk in the Elysian Fields for always and ever. She was safe in the warmth of Khaleb's everlasting love.

She pushed away the memory of the greed that had been in his eyes, the lust that seemed as ferocious as Ese's desire for her soul had been. And too, there were times when she had the distinct impression that Khaleb was trying to punish her—or was he needing to punish someone else?

Perhaps she was being fanciful, she thought, and concentrated on the memory of his laughing face.

CHAPTER THREE

Nefer was in love with the world. The happiness that curved the little corners of her mouth upwards in a smile, overspilt to make little diamonds dance in her eyes. The light of her life was Khaleb, the joy of her world was Khaleb, the music in her soul—Khaleb.

She walked with him and talked with him, played board games during the later hours of the day. And the tall pillars of the hall seemed to be holding up the roof of paradise, just as did the arched body of the Sky Goddess, Nut.

Khaleb laughed a lot, teased a lot, made love and cheated at games. She loved him so greatly that just seeing him made her go weak at the knees.

One morning a cry went up. A ship bearing Pharaoh's banner was heading their way.

'By Set!' Khaleb swore. 'He has found out. Let us go back to the house.'

'Then—then we are to die?' she asked him tragically. 'Oh, Khaleb, I cannot bear the thought of you leaving this life.'

'I will not be put to death,' he told her smoothly, giving the lie to all that he had said before. 'My father sets great store by his sons. He has still not got over the death of my older brother Ahmoses who should have been second prince after Amenhotep. No, Nefer, I will not die.'

Nefer prayed that he was right. She found herself wishing that Twosre was near, that Sebni had not gone away yet again to keep sweet that crotchety old uncle of his. She wished that she did not feel suddenly, so very, very cold and alone.

'We will act as though nothing has happened between us,' Khaleb said. 'I will say that I came as a friend of Per Ibsen and that I have been studying, most carefully, plans for the new temple that your father has drawn up.'

'But—what if they should ask to see—'

'Do not worry,' he told her. 'I have many facts and figures on papyrus with me.' He grinned at her. 'You do not think that I worked out all eventualities? I am not stupid, My Heart!'

'Then—then you had decided all along to—to stay with me?'

'Of course. Now, I will go to my room. Wait until I send for you. Firstly though, make ready to greet my lord father's messenger and then have him sent to me here.'

She found herself automatically stretching out her arms before her and bowing her head low on her chest. Khaleb had changed, had become distant, official, hard! At that moment he seemed to be a million cubits away. And the sick knowledge came, that he must have planned this escapade on the night he'd helped her get away from court.

Later, as ordered, she, Paihuti, Bebu and other servants went to the landing stage. The ship edged into the bank and the landing bridge was set down. The messenger, short, fat and pompous, accepted Paihuti's arm as he stepped ashore. Quiet, lovely, ladylike, Nefer waited. The messenger stretched out his arms, his hands palm downwards and made his obeisances, then he cleared his throat and said:

'My Lady Nefer, I bring greetings from the Big House. I bear a message from Pharaoh. It is for Prince Khaleb's ears.'

'I welcome you in the name of my father,' she replied. 'My man will lead you to the Prince and when your business is done you are welcome to eat and drink and bathe.'

'I thank you, Lady Nefer.' The messenger's eyes were stone hard. 'But I believe the Prince and I will be leaving almost at once.'

Nefer stepped back, allowing the man to pass. There was a terrible desolation sweeping through her. Even should she be allowed to live, she felt that she would not be seeing Khaleb after this day. She waited in the garden, sitting sadly at the edge of the lotus pool. And it was not the movement of the water but her own tears that made her reflection so blurred.

It was not too long before she was told by Paihuti that Prince Khaleb wished to see her. She went to him, her heart beating in a slow dull way. He was sitting before a table on which was set a papyrus roll bearing Pharaoh Thutmose's seal.

'I am recalled,' he told her flatly. 'It is an order and there is nothing that I can do.'

'Then—then I will come with you to face Pharaoh,' she whispered. 'We will—'

'No! I obey the order of the King, my father. You will stay here. It is over and done with, Nefer.'

She stood there, before him, crushed and forlorn. Then the tears in her eyes lost their warmness and tightened into little beads of ice. Khaleb was not grieving and he seemed to be quite unmoved by her own broken heart. Khaleb was as always being practical, easily accepting that Pharaoh's wishes must always come first. This when it suited him, of course. This when he was found out!

Wordlessly she bowed and like a small wraith, she backed out of the room. She went to the landing stage, followed by Paihuti and other people of the house. She stood, isolated, servants and slaves behind her, waiting to wish the Prince of her Dreams goodbye.

Khaleb left the house, followed by the messenger and there was wicked merriment in his eyes. Full of swagger and pride, he handed the servants presents of feathers and tiny carved figures of gods. He gave Nefer an emerald scarab set in gold. It was a large, fine thing, a million times more valuable than the little beetle that dear old Thickneck had given Zarah, her mother, all those years ago. Yet, looking down at the wondrous ornament, Nefer knew that Khaleb's present really meant a million times less.

'Be happy, My Heart,' Khaleb said brightly. 'With the gods on our sides perhaps things will fall back into shape. If they do, I will send for you.'

Looking into his eyes, Nefer knew that he was impatient to be gone. She felt no pain now, no anguish. She was in a vast frozen void, a silent plain that stretched into eternity. She watched in silence as he walked along the boarding bridge, and stepped with much laughter and joking on to the ship.

Oars splashed into the waters of the Nile. A wind caught at and billowed out the single red and gold sail. Nefer watched, dry-eyed, as Khaleb floated away, out of her life.

Amosis, Most Mighty stood in the central hall of his home and frowned. There was distaste and anger on his face. Tall, broad, known for his quiet strength and rugged good looks, he commanded respect wherever he went. One of Pharaoh's Most Trusted, it was his duty to ensure that order was kept in the area that had been won in battle by Egypt some years before.

Amosis had a proud bearing and his men obeyed him at a glance. He had fought alongside Pharaoh and also his eldest son Amenhotep during many campaigns. Amosis felt there were a good many battles left in him yet. Woe betide anyone fool enough to attempt to step foot over his part of the frontier. He would be ready, so too his men. They were fine, strong, well ordered and good fighters. Tough and hard—unlike the luckless messenger that had the ill fortune to cross his path. Amosis glared at the thin, weedy man, who nervously looked away.

Women adored Amosis who was large, powerful and masculine. He thought them to be pretty little things and accepted all that they offered with a certain charm and grace. Then he sent them away without a second thought. He was, as ever, a contented man.

He enjoyed his position of honour and had no aspirations to move higher in Pharaoh's affections. He was a soldier and enjoyed a good fight. He valued the rough comradeship of his men, the feel of the hot air fanning his face as he rode with them across the flat wilderness plain, else through the lush foliage of the further regions. It was all the same to him, North, South, East, West, he had ridden and fought in all directions, in the name of Pharaoh Thutmose. There was plenty in him yet. He was still a young man. This was no time to settle down. It would drive him mad, to kick his heels. But, loyal and dedicated, he had sworn to honour and obey My Majesty with the last drop of his blood. And it was this oath that was making him frown now. He glared at the man who was so small by comparison, and who dared to bring such a message from Thebes.

'There is no mistake?' he asked in his rich, deep voice. 'You are absolutely sure?'

The thin, weedy messenger, who had such a sallow, frightened face, crossed his hands across his breast and bent low.

'There is no mistake, O Mighty Amosis. As Pharaoh loves you, he gave tongue to his command and then ordered, "So let it be written. So let it be done." You are to return to Thebes for the wife that has been awarded to you. The pyramid of your honour rises even higher, Mighty One. You now own much property. You have risen to such a level that no less a person than the

Great Lord Per Ibsen has agreed that you are to become his son.'

'Why me?' Amosis asked simply.

'You have served with great distinction, O lord, all the world knows this. You were very young when you led troops against the hostile tribes in the Eastern Desert. Your brilliant management of campaign and resounding victories soon reached Pharaoh's ears.'

'Many men have done as well, if not better. Nothing I have achieved warrants the high office reserved for me now,' Amosis said pithily. 'I do not wish to take a wife, and I see no sense in this move at all. You have misread the papyrus.'

The messenger again raised the scroll and read in a clear, high but expressionless way.

'You did, in My Majesty's name, then face the Nomadic tribes of Nubia. You did bring them to heel. They were crushed by thy might. All hail to Amosis, Mighty Warrior.'

Amosis grunted and turned away, but Pharaoh's messenger continued ...

'There is even more! Because of your great valour and success on five different occasions, two of them under direct command of our Divine Pharaoh of Two Lands, and also the great and glorious Prince Amenhotep, you have been awarded by requisition from the Treasury the right to procure labour for the quarrying and transportation of a sumptuous sarcophagus for your own tomb!'

'Which is the zenith of all honours,' Amosis said bluntly. 'And to my mind, in that alone, Pharaoh has given me more than enough. There is a reason other than valour that has warranted Pharaoh's actions.'

'Not so, Most Mighty. Pharaoh has proclaimed, it is done. You have a great lady wife. With her there comes an establishment that is splendid, hundreds of cubits of land, many animals, servants and slaves and grain bins filled to the brim.'

'None of which delights me,' Amosis replied bleakly. 'I can only wonder anew, what is behind it all. Are you quite sure that Pharaoh has set his seal on his decree? It is an order?'

'It is an order!' the messenger replied. 'You must return for her as soon as you can.'

'Then go—and may thy nights be happy.'

'And may thine be happy and blessed.' The messenger made the formal reply. Then he bowed deeply, and took his leave.

The Kerma fortress at which Amosis was stationed was really a large, fortified township. Here in the heart of the arid land of Kush, garrisons lived with their families. The walls were massive, made of mud brick, more than thirty feet thick and strengthened with timber baulks. They kept out enemies, and even some of the dissenting people of Kerma, whose city had such a prime position for trade. Kerma, that lived, ate and slept under the proud citadel that was the ever watchful Eye of Ra. Outside the massive edifice there were dry ditches, elaborate curtain walls, fire-ports, loop holes, barbicans and drawbridges. The whole vast complex had been designed not only to control savage and war-like tribes, but also to act as Office of Documentation as well as a trading post. This for the collection of ivory, ebony, hides, gold, ostrich feathers, minerals and gums. Such goods were dispatched from the Kerma city base. Amosis and his men guarded all.

Amosis was angry, coldly, killingly angry. The whole business of Pharaoh's orders had made him feel a fool and he did not suffer fools gladly. He had to make his own way of life, since he'd been put in the army under a cloud. He had little time for sentiment. That emotion, so far as he was concerned, was for old women.

The old lady he had truly cared for had been his mother who had died when he had been so young he was still wearing his hair in a side-lock. He could not remember his mother's face, but he thought of her every time he saw cornflowers. She had always loved them. The only other female who had crept under his skin had been the little Nefer—who Pharaoh had now made his wife.

His mind went back over the years. He remembered how, upon first coming across her in the gardens at Ramose House, he'd been struck by the immensity of feeling in her large, soulful dark eyes. She had been nowhere near the edge of puberty, which was twelve. He had reached the official age of manhood, fourteen, some five years before and even though, according to the elders, he was still 'wet behind the ears', he had already proved himself. He had eaten at the scarlet table of passion in the Temple of Learning many times—and found being with an expert woman exciting enough to all but burn him alive.

A very different emotion had risen in his breast when he had come across the quiet, frightened, very sad little girl. For the first time in his life he had felt protective, had tried to help! Then the evil-minded Ese had put her own thoughts on the matter to his uncle and guardian. The upshot of it all being that he had been sent away. Not as the nephew of Pharaoh's Chief of Guards, but as a conscripted man as lowly as the dung at the officers' feet. He'd hated Ese, but realised now, that the Set saturated old She Devil had done him a favour. He had worked his way up through hard work and dedication to his calling—and he'd learned one all important lesson. Never to concern himself with young innocents again. He liked women of the world. Women who knew all the tricks, how to tantalise and make a man come alive—and who he could leave without a backward glance. All the same, he found himself hoping that the Black Dog had snapped at the heels of Ese. That Anubis, who inspired fear of Horus, the Dog of Death who for ever guarded the Northern Gate, would hold the soul of Ese in its sleeping jaws. Oh yes, Ese deserved to be held forever in the entrance to the swamps, to be covered in black slime and tortured for all eternity by snakes and ravenous crocodiles. He clenched his great fists and knew with utmost certainty, that he would meet up with Ese again one day.

'Amosis!' a fellow officer cried as he came up to him. 'You are recalled. How fortunate! I would give half my life to be going to Thebes to enjoy home leave.'

'And I would give half my life for you

107

to take my place,' Amosis growled and walked on. Then, as he returned to the barracks, to gather his few possessions together, he began to think of the capital, City of a Hundred Gates. Thebes, mighty, marvellous, magnificent to behold with its temples and obelisks glittering and gleaming under the weight of solid gold. And what of the river? In his mind's eye he saw the river-side markets with their displays of food, clothing and great earthenware jars. And Thebes itself, a city of beauty and grace. It spread along and away from the Nile and was laced with broad boulevards. Villas of the rich shrouded with sycamores and palm trees behind tall outer walls. And, on a different level, the small square, one-roomed dwellings of the poor. The sturdy, determined, toiling poor. But even they had god in their hearts and the bold, gold sun in their eyes—and more, in this beneficent age, they had their bellies full of grain.

Yes, Amosis thought, perhaps it would be good to walk Thebes once more. As to the 'Wife' business that was a very different matter. He would take the longest route back and by that time Pharaoh may have changed his mind. And it also might be worth having a word in his good friend Amenhotep's ear.

He strode along, powerful and magnificent, determinedly pushing the picture of the little girl Nefer firmly from his mind ...

Nefer stood at the gates of Ramose House childishly making bargains with Amun. 'If Khaleb sends for me today, I will make a great sacrifice to the temple and present your priests with bangles of gold. Please let Khaleb send for me. I promise to do good works in your name. O, god, hear me!'

No messenger came, just as deep down she knew he never would. She walked back to the garden. Sunlight dappled the ground with golden discs under the trees and a gust of wind scuffled little drifts of petals away.

Unable to endure her sense of loneliness, she walked back to the gate, through it, and down to the bank of the Nile. The rushes stood straight and tall, and from behind the rushes came Sebni's desperate voice.

'You are cruel, Twosre. You bedevil me, yet I am helpless. I will do anything you say.'

'Sebni,' Twosre's rich honey-gold voice sang his name, 'you are too slow, too staid, and I don't want you to do anything for me. Go away.'

'I will get you a necklace. A collar

more rich and rare than anything you have ever seen.'

'Ha! And earrings to match I suppose?'

'Yes, even earrings, Twosre.'

'Don't be stupid,' Twosre's voice was petulant. 'I do not want baubles, I have a great many of my own. Anyway, I only take presents from men, Sebni, My Brother. You are no man. You are afraid of that miserable old uncle of yours, afraid of my father, of me, and even afraid of yourself!'

'Do not be cruel, to me. Be kind.'

'How kind?' The rich voice became provocative. 'How can I be kind to you when you are afraid of me? Kiss me on the lips, Sebni.'

'Twosre,' Sebni said hoarsely, 'I would die for you, do anything, if you would just promise to be my wife.'

'Your wife?' The laugh was velvety, smooth and unrelenting. 'I have told you over and over again, that I'll be no man's wife. I take love as I want and need it, but I refuse to be tied to any man. Oh Sebni, Sebni, do I look like a creature willing to be caged?'

'I—I will love you forever, Twosre. For ever and a day.'

Again Nefer heard that teasing little laugh and her eyes filled with tears. She felt so sorry for Sebni, his pain was so evident, and akin to the agony cutting into her own aching heart.

Not waiting to hear more, nor caring to let them know she was near, Nefer began to walk along the bank until she was beyond the wide gentle sweep and the earth began to rise up, then swoop down in a wild and ragged way. The path faded into a track, then became non-existent and Nefer began to climb the bank that now stretched upwards, like a rearing snake. The banks at the water's edge becoming steep. Uncaring, she continued to climb. She reached a high point and stopped to look outwards, across the river, to that other bank, the Realm of the Dead. The place of family vaults, that were so rich in bright, coloured pictures of life, of statues, of gods, and hidden caskets of jewels. The secret, separate living place, of people who were never allowed across the river—to the worldly side. There were the priests, mummifiers, coffin makers, grave diggers and cemetery guardians armed to the teeth, ready at all times to keep grave robbers away. And beyond the living quarters of all these people, the still, lonely spirit places. The Left Bank wherein her real father, the Great Lord Ramose lay. He was at peace, dreaming in the world of Everlasting. How she envied him that.

Nefer's large sad eyes stared unseeingly

across the expanse of water. The river wind, frisky now, tugged at the turquoise and gold collar she wore and whipped her long dark hair so that it flowed behind her, leaving her heavy perfect profile in clear, uncluttered line, and too, showing that she was with child.

What does one do, she thought, when one's whole being dies? What happens to the spirit when one is so very unloved? Why has everyone that I have adored in my life left me in such agony and grief? She remembered that first her mother had left her, then Amosis. Sebni had preferred her own sister—and the most bitter truth was knowing the Khaleb had used her and left her without a second thought. He had not sent for her at all. The nights and days had gone by, endlessly, miserably, and she had never felt so alone.

Without realising what she was doing, she climbed even higher, then stood poised on the edge like a figure carved from stone. She was without conscious thought now, numb and empty. Then out of the silence about her a rich, deep voice said easily:

'I would not do that ...'

She turned slowly, gasping because the stranger had brought her back to the painful present. She saw a handsome man, well built, regal in his deep collar of red, gold and blue. His white kilt was pleated and he wore a wide belt fashioned from leopard skin in which there was looped a gold handled knife. He wore wide wristbands of gold. His dark hair was cut straight to just below his ears, but it was the magnificent pectoral he wore she looked at most. It was red and blue, turquoise and gold. It held the figures of the Holy Trio, then the Eye flanked by the falcon-headed Horus, and Set, with the head of the Typhonian animal. Then hanging below, gleaming, enormous centre piece, the pendant of Menthu. The god with the figure of man and head of a bull surmounted by the solar disc and two tall straight plumes. Menthu, the Theban God of War!

'I am perfectly all right, O Lord of Pharaoh's Might,' she assured the stranger in a small breathless voice. 'I know this place well and there is no danger at all.'

He smiled briefly and held out his hand.

'Of course there is not, Small Person, but for my sake, please come away from the edge.'

She shivered a little and drew back, wanting to hide from this high ranked soldier, indeed wanting to hide from the world. There was no escape. The large hand, tanned as was all his skin to the warm red of mahogany, had taken hold of her slim wrist. She was pulled, gently and firmly towards the man and had never felt so small, since her head barely reached up to his chest.

'I will walk with you,' he said. 'I know that you live in the large house by the river. I know also that your parents are in their home near the Palace. Your father is the great Per Ibsen?'

She nodded, wishing him further. He was an intruder and there was something in his manner, almost a familiarity, that she did not like. His hand still held her captive and she found herself being walked downwards along the path whence she came.

'Do you know that we have met before?' he asked her in a casual way.

Nefer looked at him blankly. He was staring down at her, searching her face. He was waiting for her to remember, but she could not. For a few moments, she could think of nothing to say, then managed lamely, 'I—I am sorry. I don't recall—'

'It does not matter. Tell me, are you always such a solitary little soul?'

'I am not so alone,' she answered him politely, hardly caring that he was being too personal and too inquisitive by half. 'I have servants by the score, some I value greatly as my friends.'

'And your younger sister?'

She began to feel a little uneasy. How was it that this great bull of a man knew so much? Was he after Twosre? She sighed inwardly because Twosre had no troubles where the opposite sex were concerned. Though perhaps—she sneaked a quick look up at the stern, arrogant profile—though perhaps Twosre had met more than her match this time.

'My younger sister is staying with me for a while, but she goes off on adventures of her own,' she told the man, then heard herself adding in a tired, dispirited way, 'And Sebni comes here sometimes too. When he is not working, or else visiting his uncle, of course. Sebni is my brother.'

'I had heard,' came the easy reply. 'Yet for all that, I found you alone and looking quite unable to deal with your life.'

'It is kind of you,' she said carefully, 'to concern yourself, but there is no need. I live my life the way it suits me best. I am a quiet, thinking person—and—' she was colouring furiously, but had to say what she felt, '—and I feel that you are being discourteous and rather too inquisitive in my affairs.' She rushed on, now quite unable to stop. 'I was standing up there alone because that is how I choose to be. You were kind to try and help me, but now—I will thank you to let go of my arm!'

'No. I don't think so.'

'I can manage.'

'Mm! Well, I would say that you don't manage very well,' he paused then added significantly, 'I think, Small Person, that I will take you in hand.'

He spoke with an air of familiarity and quiet determination and such was his size and demeanour that she dared not reply. He was of extraordinary high rank, he wore Pharaoh's personal seal of approval on one of his fingers that were so firmly clenched round her arm, so there was not much she could do. She bit her lip. Perhaps Pharaoh was going to punish her after all. Khaleb had not been able to convince him of the innocence of his stay. Perhaps Khaleb had been banished and she was about to be declared a wrong-doer. Perhaps she was to be stoned! Her eyes sparkled with unshed tears. It didn't matter, nothing mattered any more. There was only this sudden overwhelming weariness.

'You make no reply,' he said and since he was quite clearly waiting for an answer she said the first thing that came into her head.

'Thank you.'

He nodded gravely, seeming satisfied. Then the seriousness died away and his

116

face warmed under a slow, wide rather wonderful smile.

'Well, now we have established that, let me tell you my name. I am Amosis, known as Mighty Warrior, Keeper of Quivers and Chief of Southern Soldiers who are Pharaoha's Might. I was serving at the frontier of Kerma, but I have been recalled just long enough to collect something I own.'

He was watching her closely. She stared up at him, surprised and taken aback. The Amosis she remembered, who she had wept for and longed for all those years ago, had been not much more than a boy. How could her Amosis have changed and become this large, formidable, broad chested man?

'Amosis!' she whispered. 'Mighty Warrior, how you have changed.'

He looked her over in a slow, considering way, then said:

'And so have you. You are—more shapely.'

'Oh!' she replied and wanted to die. 'Yes, it has been a long time, Amosis. Such a very, very long time.' Her words trailed away. Then because he was silent and so evidently waiting for just one small spark of recognition and friendship: 'I—I have never met a real, living hero before.'

He shrugged, pushing her attempt to

117

compliment him away.

'We're a pugnacious breed. Ready to pit our wits against—well, practically everything.'

They had reached the downward track now, and he was still holding on to her arm. The reeds and other vegetation hereabouts grew so lush and tall that the river was all but hidden from view. Nefer felt, just for that moment of time, that she and Amosis were the only living people in the world. Again she glanced sideways and up at the strong, handsome profile. She had loved him all those years ago, loved him with all her heart and soul and every fibre of her being. Now he had returned, a stranger, a new and rather over-powering person. She did not want him in her life, not any more. She suddenly, very desperately wanted to tell him to go.

Then the rushes gave way and the world was open, clear and pristine in the sunshine again. It was all so perfect, so very beautiful that she felt miserable, the only misfit in it was her own pathetically stupid self. She must pull herself together. She must!

They reached the House of Ramose and Nefer made as though to wish him goodbye, but he walked firmly through the gates and along the path and finally into the house. Servants hurried forwards, holding pitchers of water in their hands. Wordlessly Amosis stood there while a serving girl undid his sandals, then she waited as he stepped out of them and on to the washing stone. The water, cool and scented, was washed over his feet, then dried on a silk-thin piece of flax linen cloth. Nefer, whose feet had been bare, went through the same ceremony. Paihuti appeared, crossed his hands over his breast and bowed low before them.

'May I know of your wishes, Lady Nefer?' he enquired. 'May I serve you in any way?'

'Thank you, Paihuti,' Nefer whispered, unnerved by the awe and hero worship she saw in the little man's eyes as he looked on Amosis. 'There is nothing I want or need.'

Dispirited the major domo turned away.

'Wait,' Amosis commanded. 'I am a guest in this house and I am hungry.'

Nefer looked up at him, her eyes deep wells of hurt. He took her gently by the shoulders and pressed her down on a chair.

'You will not believe this, Nefer,' he said quietly, 'but it will pass. The river recedes but it always returns with a different face the following year. So it is with our fortunes. We have the ebb and flow of good and bad. Nothing ever stays the same. You are sad now, but it is not possible to stay sad forever.'

She gave a dry, mirthless little laugh.

'You—know about Khaleb's stay here, Amosis? You understand that the Prince has let me down.'

'I do. And in that respect, he has not changed.'

'Oh!' She smiled in a shaky way. 'But at least you have not changed Amosis. You speak as you find, which in itself is a kind of—bravery.'

She meant ruthlessness but it was not in her nature to be rude. He had been a big, tall young man, she thought, and now he was a great bull of a man. She had leaned on his friendship once, and relaxed under the calm assurance of his eyes. Now she never wanted to be bothered by him again, not him nor anyone! And this in spite of all the family well wishers, their web of lies to keep Pharaoh unsuspicious and unaware of the facts.

Please Amun, she was thinking passionately, don't let Amosis know that my name was brought forward as his most desirable prize. I cannot bear the thought of him looking at me with contempt because Pharaoh was told that he has always loved me and wanted me.

There was a great deal of hustle and bustle as the servants came in and, under the watchful eye of Paihuti, began placing a feast on the table. The meal was sumptuous. Fowl, fruit and cakes. There was honey beer to drink or alternatively, the sweet juice of the grapes. Flowers abounded, for Paihuti had ordered garlands to be placed on the table. The servants, of both sexes, wore flowers round their necks. The girls' pert little breasts were naked. Men servants wore the usual white linen waist cloth. All had bare feet.

Paihuti had decided to make it an occasion, for he was over-awed and delighted to be serving such a distinguished guest. So it was that the house musicians took their places and soon, sweet and plaintive music filled the air. Amosis and Nefer were led to their places and pressed to eat.

Amosis needed no tempting. Nefer watched his quiet concentration as he ate. He sensed her gaze and looked at her and then again she experienced the wonder of his all embracing smile.

'We do not have such luxury at Kerma,' he told her. 'Soldiers never have been spoilt where ordinary every day living is concerned. I worked my way up through the ranks and I remember the early days very well. I live better now, but old habits die hard. I thoroughly enjoy and appreciate

121

good food since it's so opposite to water and dry bread.'

'Amosis,' she asked quietly, 'what made you—you come here to this house?'

He raised his brows and there was faint humour glimmering at the back of his eyes.

'You honestly don't know?'

'I can guess,' she whispered and looked at her gold platter in mortification. 'But you can find a way out of all this, I am sure of it. And as to what you saw, or thought you saw, I would never have—have jumped off the cliff, even though I do not think I will ever see Khaleb again.'

Amosis looked at her steadily, seeming quite calm but for the frantic little beating of a pulse near his temple. He is angry, Nefer thought wearily, he's coldly and furiously angry.

'I am sorry to tell you this,' he said evenly, 'but you are right you will not be seeing Khaleb again. He told me that he is to take a wife of Pharaoh's choosing and so keep the peace.' Amosis went on. 'I did not know that it was common knowledge that the Pharaoh wanted you for himself. I accept that your father allowed him to think that I had prior claims, for the reason being your peace of mind—but I find it very hard to accept that Khaleb came here, tongue in cheek, to get one over his father.

His father's punishment and perhaps even the banishment he might suffer should My Majesty find out, will very effectively keep the Prince away from you. Pharaoh will not enjoy the sneaky nature of Khaleb's particular game.'

'Game?' she asked piteously. 'So it really and truly was just a game on his part? I—I suspected it. No, I knew! I think I knew on the day he left this place.'

'Forget him, Nefer,' Amosis said quietly. 'You are a fine, serene and thoroughbred lady. You are not meant for the Khalebs of this world.'

'He—he called me, My Heart. He said that he loved me and that I reminded him of a little pet gazelle he once owned.'

'Such small creatures are doomed once the hunter gets them in sight, Nefer. You must shrug your shoulders and call upon Divine Hathor to wash what you feel for him out of your mind. The episode is over.'

Nefer hunched forward, her hands clasped desperately in her lap.

'O Mighty Amosis,' she said piteously. 'I am to have his child.'

'My dear, Small Person,' he replied evenly, 'whatever makes you think that I did not know?'

She threw out her hands in a helpless, hopeless gesture.

'That is why I have remained here—out of Pharaoh's sight. Out of sight of Khaleb's enemies, too. One look at me and it would be known that the Prince did not come here merely to examine temple plans. I—I do not think that anyone would believe the father to be anyone else. There are many servants and slaves here and even though they love me, there could be many moments where there'd be unguarded tongues. I have prayed at the Temple, to the great Goddess Bast, but I have received no sign. I do not know what to do.'

'Does Khaleb know you're with child?'

She shook her head.

'I never want him to know, Amosis. Not ever! For the sake of his child he would take me into his house when Pharaoh has simmered down.' She lifted her head then, proudly, and had no idea how lovely she looked. 'But I do not want to go into the house of a man who could so callously let me down. I believed—I had hoped that his ways had changed. Now I know that this is not so.'

She tried to laugh, but the laugh changed into a harsh sob. Amosis left his seat and came round to kneel at her side. Like a tired child she hid her face against his heart and could hear it beating in a steady rhythmic way. She

124

wondered what had happened in her own breast. It was so cold and frozen and still.

'You must forget,' Amosis commanded. 'Khaleb must be a shadow of the past.'

Nefer closed her eyes, but could not shut out the series of pictures that chased across her mind, of the lithe, springy, leopard-like man whose strangely hypnotic eyes had made her docile, eager to fall in with his slightest wish. Love had dropped like a sacred flower in her lap and she had been thrilled, ecstatic and swept off her feet. Too blind by adoration of him to protest at his unseemly haste. Quiet and shy for so long, she had devoured love, desired love in the same hungry way as Khaleb. They lived on the crest of a purple-misted pyramid it seemed, almost smothered by the cloud of mutual rapture. Playing, loving, quarrelling in quick succession.

And I knew all the time, she thought numbly, that he was selfish and self-centred and arrogant and demanding. No matter what Twosre said, I still loved him and lived and breathed for him. Now I feel as if my soul has died.

She was weeping silently now. And all the time Amosis held her against him, saying nothing, but occasionally his large hand stroked her hair. And Nefer derived a wistful comfort just knowing he was there and it was just as if he had never been away.

'It will be all right, Small Person,' he said at last. 'Just leave everything to me.'

'But if—when Pharaoh learns about me—when my parents find out they will have to turn their faces from me—or else be made to suffer for what I have done. I ran away from the Divine One only to fall for the charms of his son. My father and mother will be made to leave Thebes because their mere presence will remind My Majesty that it was a member of the Per Ibsen family who wanted nothing of him. The whole world knows how cruel he can be when things do not go his way.' She tried to laugh but it was a small panicky sound. 'I—I don't know what is going to happen to me. I—I am very afraid of being alone.'

'You could take me.'

She looked at him, the Mighty Amosis, Chief of Pharaoh's Might, and still could not believe that this was the same man as the tall, strong youth who had been so patient with her. But in spite of appearances the tone of his voice was the same, steady, calm, very sure.

'I thank you for the honour, but I could not do that. I—I still love Khaleb, you see.'

'No one can love a man so cruel. You

must have heard how he has let other ladies down. Ladies like you, Nefer. The servants and slaves were never quite good enough for him. He had to go for beautiful women whose very upbringing meant they should marry men ready to carry on their family name. We are a matriarchal society to a large extent, unlike in Persia where your mother was born. There women are slaves, chattels, pauper or princess it's all the same. Here, high born ladies head families as did old Queen Hatshepsut in her day. Perhaps Khaleb pokes his tongue out at that situation. On the other hand, perhaps it's just that he prefers the added excitement of the risks he takes.'

'He—he called me My Heart. He said—'

'When a man lets down one woman, there will always be a second and a third and so on until the end of time. Surely you knew that?'

'I do not want his child.'

'It will be your child.'

'It is almost as if—as if the awful Ese had laid a curse on me. I can hear her now, going on in her cruel neverending way about the sin of not living only for Amun.'

'She had a devil in her head. She was a fanatical daughter of Set. Forget her and all that she said.'

'I cannot,' Nefer said quietly. 'I have

127

tried, and I find that her face rears before me all of the time these days. I am being punished for my sin! Ese has won. I am sapped dry. I am cold, dead, fit only for the valley on the other side.'

Amosis stood up at that and towered over her. Suddenly his face was that of a stranger again and one that was coldly, furiously angry.

'The First Lady of my house does not talk like that. My First Wife has courage—else she is not welcome in my abode.'

She was staring up at him horrified.

'So—' she gasped. 'It has been done? Oh, Mighty Warrior, I am so sorry!'

'And so am I.' He smiled bleakly. 'But we must delight in Pharaoh's will. I asked you to take me a moment ago and your reaction was honest and sincere. We will do as we must—to the outside we will appear happy at the way things are. I knew of the child, as will anyone else with eyes to see. So—we will get you away from sight. Pharaoh has heard news of trouble brewing on the Border. My lady, you will leave this place and come to Kerma with me. Pharaoh already desires that I return quickly to stamp his enemies into the mud and stench from which they sprang.

'I—I am to go with you?' This is not happening, she thought wildly and dared

128

to ask: 'How long have I to arrange it?'

'We will be on our way at once,' he replied.

'But I must see Twosre, and send to my mother and my—'

'Nefer,' he replied coldly, 'we will begin our journey tomorrow at first light.'

He raised his hand, palm outward, breast high in a swift, courteous salute, then swung on his heel and left her too stunned to make a reply.

Amosis's face was grim, his figure taut. There was a saying of the wilderness soldier that a man who kept a clear vision of death inside of him would have no fear of it. But, Amosis thought grimly, there were many kinds of death. A man of the here and now was merely a being who had one part of him that had survived the traumas of the world.

He was himself no longer the eager young boy who had so hero-worshipped his warrior uncle. Who would have laid down his life for the iron-hard, eagle faced man. Who had so eagerly and willingly stepped into the trap.

'Go and stay with my old friend for a while,' the great man had said. 'It will do you good, and you will not be lonely at all even though you'll be living with a liverish old man. There's a child living in the mansion of Ramose. Be kind to her.

She is a sweetly pretty little thing. She's stuck with a She-Devil who talks only of god, and so her days must be grim. Take her under your wing, Amosis. Be a man, eh?'

What happened after that was a story he needed to forget, but never could. His banishment to the army had been like hell on earth. He had at that time suffered many kinds of death. Death to hope, to affection, to faith. And the most vicious torment of living had been his bewilderment, his desolation, and the slow tearing apart of his boyish young heart.

'My lord, my lord!'

He stopped and swung round to face Nefer who had hurried after him. The look she saw in his eyes made her falter and shrink back.

'Forgive me,' she said and her voice was calm for all her lip trembled. 'But I feel I must apologise for—for my momentary lack of dignity. This—this is all a shock, Amosis, for us both.'

'Yes,' he said coldly.

'And—and the only favour I ask of you now is to, please allow me a little more time. I want to say my farewells, and—' She bit her lip fiercely to stop her tears. 'My sister is most precious to me.'

He remained silent so long that she was conscious only of his strong jaw line, his

130

chiselled features, his piercing dark eyes.

'My lord,' she whispered. 'I cannot leave without seeing Twosre.'

'You do not seem unintelligent,' he said at last. 'Yet you are now acting stupidly. I should have thought that even you would have realised it's illogical to dismiss Pharaoh's wishes at this stage? Be ready by first light if you please.'

'You don't understand, Amosis. Twosre is—'

'Merely your sister,' he said coldly. 'On the other hand, I am Mighty Warrior, your Lord and Master. I am in my turn, subject to My Majesty's command, as are we all.'

'I beg of you, just a little while!' she cried wildly. 'I need to send messages to my mother and father. I desire to—'

'You will now forget that part of your life.'

'No!' She found herself hammering at his chest. 'I will not do as you say. They are all my loved ones, my dearest of dears. How dare you come here and treat me like a slave.'

He stood there, rock-like against her onslaught, his lips thin lines in his face. Then without a word, he picked her up and carried her back to the chair and set her down.'

'You are as light as a feather,' he told her

and now there was a faint gleam of humour at the back of his eyes. 'You are my wife and I will respect you as such. Please don't act like either a cheap river woman, or a hysterical slave come to that. If you do you will be treated accordingly.'

'Khaleb—'

His face darkened at the sound of the Prince's name.

'Treated you with about as much consideration as he'd give a river slut,' he cut in. 'Believe me, my lady, I will never treat you as such—nor in any other way.'

She gasped at his tone, which was now so crisp and cold that it sounded cruel. She loathed the way Mighty Warrior insisted on blackening Khaleb's name. He should not speak so of a Prince of the realm even if there was a spark of truth in what he said. As for river woman!

She leapt up from the chair, all the fear and tension that had been building up inside her now coming to the surface. She wanted to strike out at this cold-faced giant, she wanted to—'

'Sit down,' he said, and with two strong hands he pressed her back into the chair. 'And remember that like it or not, you are now Mistress of my House.'

'You are—' she began furiously ...

'No longer a boy,' he finished and now his tone was tomb-cold. 'It will do my lady no harm remembering the fact.'

He left her then, and she did not try to follow him because she knew that it would be no use. Amosis was too strong to fight, too powerful to deny and, by Pharaoh's command, he owned her, body and soul.

In her moment of utter despair she thought she heard a wild and ghostly laughing. Then dancing into her over-worked imagination there came the evil-faced figure of Ese.

'It is the will of Amun,' cackled the voice from far distant years. 'Your punishment has only just begun!'

Nefer found that she was, for the moment, quite unable to move.

CHAPTER FOUR

For a while Nefer sat where she was. It had all happened too quickly and she was confused, almost stunned trying to come to terms with Pharaoh's will. He Who Was God, had married her to Mighty Amosis, Chief of His Southern Might. Could Thutmose be acting out of very human spite? She found herself almost hating the King who was so strong and dynamic, who had such brains, vision and drive. Who had such a charming, ruthless, devastatingly wicked second son!

There was no doubt about it, she loathed Pharaoh who could make the earth tremble with a single look. She, Nefer, would have been on the side of the old Queen, had that been possible. Yes, the Great Hatshepsut who had successfully kept Thutmose under her thumb for nigh on twenty years.

Zarah, Beloved Mother, had spoken enough about the past to make clear how in the shadow of Hatshepsut the young Thutmose had been. The Queen had refused to marry him in spite of their mutual royal blood. Instead, she had taken the reigns of Egypt into her own regal hands and the land had been in peace.

Finally Thutmose had found the backing he needed. The old Queen was deposed. It was rumoured that she had been given the poisoned cup, but no one knew for sure. Safe on the throne at last Thutmose had spun the ship of State about and put it back on the course his grandfather had taken, which was that of foreign conquest. Her own father, the great and noble Per Ibsen, had been friends with Thutmose for all the days of his life. Now, to save her from the God-King, he had lied. But the plan had gone terribly wrong.

She was wife of Amosis and not of

Khaleb. She was to be banished to a garrison town on the wild Southern Frontier. She could not bear it! It was too awful for words. She must run away. She must get to—

Who could help her? she thought frantically. Now her pulses were pounding, her mouth had gone dry. There was no one. Even her father was helpless in this matter. What of Rekhmire, the Vizier? Yes, oh yes, perhaps he would help—if she could get to him of course. She had met him once and he had seemed quite approachable and kind for all he was the Chief Officer of State. He was the only person, other than Pharaoh, who could act in all civil affairs. He presided over the highest court of justice and—Nefer's heart sank like a stone—and he was also the Minister of War! Clearly then, he would side wholeheartedly with Amosis, Chief of Pharaoh's Might.

What could she do? Dear god Amun, she was crying in her mind, what must I do to escape this awful fate? Her frantic thoughts flew to Twosre. Yes, Twosre was wise in the ways of the world, she would know the best thing to do.

Nefer jumped up, her face working with grief and despair. Khaleb would never send for her now. He would never find some excuse to invite her into the warmth of his house. Pharaoh would never seek her out either. She was safe from both King and Prince—for she was Amosis's wife.

'Twosre!' she called aloud, heartbreak in her voice. 'Twosre, where are you? Sister, come here!'

Paihuti came and behind him, Bebu. Their faces sad and concerned. They know, Nefer thought, of course they do. They have been listening to every word and they know as much as I do. Oh dear God!

'She is not here, Mistress,' Paihuti told her quietly. 'I am sorry.'

'It was a very handsome young man,' Bebu tutted, 'and you know how she is. She agreed to go with him for a night and a day.'

'But why?' Nefer gasped. 'Tell me why?'

'Because she wanted to,' Paihuti replied. With great dignity he sank to his knees before Nefer. 'My sweet lady,' he said, 'allow me to travel with you.'

'And leave the wife of your heart, Paihuti?'

'With your permission, I will come too,' Bebu's voice was rich and warm. 'How could it be otherwise, my little love?'

'Then who will stay and care for Twosre?'

'Why Abu and his wife who have been trained to take over from us.'

'But Twosre may—'

'Mistress,' Paihuti's distress for Nefer

made him throw caution to the winds, 'your merry little sister will follow us in her own good time.'

'She may not—I need her.'

'Divine One,' Paihuti answered. 'A garrison town? For the Lady Twosre, that will be enough.'

'Hold your tongue, else I'll have it cut out!' Nefer shouted. 'Rouse everyone in this house, every servant and slave and make it your business to find my sister. No! Do not dare to argue. Do as I say!'

Grieving, frantic, Nefer washed the paint from her face and brushed her long hair till it shone. Then, she went in search of Twosre herself.

The moon was round and pure and it lit the world. Nefer walked quickly, trying to remember all of Twosre's favourite haunts. Most of all, she knew Twosre loved the river bank. Unheeding, Nefer searched. Her bare feet racing over hard and soft mud.

How could the gods be so unfair, Nefer thought. I have had just one lover and there is to be a child. But Twosre! She is in love with love, she indulges in love. She all but eats lovers! Yet she is still slim, her eyes glow, and she looks quite untouched. She is happy and free. I am trapped and were it not so, perhaps Pharaoh's anger would be great enough to have me killed.

The honest part of her knew that Mighty Amosis was a man far too good for her now. She should feel relieved that difficult decisions had been taken from her hands. She was grateful to Amosis, her Lord, truly! But she so needed Twosre to be with her now. However, Beloved Sister had gone off on adventures of her own. She would return when it suited her, happy, glowing and quite unabashed. There was no time to spare! Amosis had given his command.

We set out at dawn, Nefer thought desperately, for Kerma, a remote frontier town. How shall I fit in? How will they see me, a lady who has never known much about soldiering families and their way of life? There is a war going on at the frontier, and—a new thought struck her. Perhaps I will get killed. Yes, that would be a way out all round. If I meet my end at the frontier they will be free of the embarrassment I have caused. Pharaoh will be able to dismiss his suspicion, that I rejected him in favour of his son, and that my lord father helped in my first escape of all. Yes, I will go to Kerma and there, for their sake, I will die. The immensity of the thought startled her.

'What am I doing!' she asked herself aloud, shocked out of her mood of despair at last. 'Who am I to be thinking so? Why am I not more deeply concerned for my child?'

Then the need to survive, the utter and absolute determination that her unborn baby should take in the sweet breath of life rose so suddenly and strongly inside her that she felt surprised. Her lips trembled as she thought of the little brother who had died. He had had no choice!

She drew in a deep breath as she decided what she would do. She must assimilate everything. She would stand as tall and as proud as a great warrior's wife should. Amosis would learn to respect her, for she would become a new dignified person under the mantle of his name. There would be no more hiding away. She would live for her child and be a wondrous mother. In that way she would find fulfilment and joy.

Nefer turned away from the bank of papyrus and began to make her way back to the house. She remembered that her Lord Husband had chosen to name her Small Person. She would show him that she might be tiny against his tremendous stature, but she was the length and breadth of the universe when it came to measuring the size and courage of her soul.

In spite of her determination, her treacherous heart jumped nervously when she saw the far away pearl-like glow already lightening the eastern sky. Soon the birds would waken and the waters of the Nile would be tinged with red and gold. Amosis would come for her and she would have to leave her father's house.

As she neared the Ramose residence she saw the gathering of men, slaves, oxen and drovers. Then, followed meekly by a group of conscripts, taken from the fields, the imposing figure of the Mighty Amosis himself.

Hesitantly, she moved towards him. His face was stern when they met. His eyes roved over her taking in her dishevelment and the mud on her feet.

'Why are you not ready and waiting?' he asked. 'Did I not tell you that we were to set out at dawn?'

'Forgive me, my lord. I—I have been looking for Twosre, my sister.'

'She is to come with us?'

His tone was so granite hard that she felt despair. She turned her palms upwards and shrugged in an uncertain way.

'Yes—no—my lord, I do not know.'

'But you do know that you are coming with me?'

'I do your bidding, yes, O Mighty One. But—'

'You will learn,' he told her sternly, 'that when I give an order, it is to be obeyed. The consequences of forgetting this can

140

be grave. Since I am ready now and all arrangements made, you will come with me—just as you are.'

'No!' All her pent up frustration and anger came to the fore. 'I will wash. I will be anointed with oil. I will be dressed in fresh linen and—'

'You will do as you're told,' he cut in smoothly. He raised his hand and beckoned. Bearers trotted forward. With no further word, Amosis lifted Nefer and put her in the carrying chair. 'I will leave a message for those who will come after you,' he said crisply. He turned and ordered the bearers, 'Move on!'

She rose from her seat, determined not to let this man have his own way so easily. But with consummate ease he held her there.

Once the bearers were on the move she had to remain still to keep safe.

While she was being taken to the landing berth, Nefer's feelings of anger grew. She was being ordered about and treated like a witless slave. She was Lady Nefer, daughter of both the Ramose and Per Ibsen house. She was—Amosis's wife!

Tears sprang to her eyes and she angrily brushed them away. Then, at last, the cocoon of nervous fear that had surrounded her since Ese's day, was stripped away. She felt naked but stingingly alive. Her fine giant of a husband would soon learn that he was dealing with no menial. She would show him. Yes, she would show him if it took her the rest of her life!

The great four-master ship riding at anchor was splendid with its banners and pendants and blood red sails. There were other craft, many of them imposing, filled with men-at-arms. The great barge was crammed to overflowing with stables for horses, camels, oxen and cattle. There was food for the men and food for the beasts. Oil, wine, beer and water was contained in giant earthenware jars, as were the bushels of grain. There was a buzz of excitement and much activity.

There were men everywhere. Rough, tough men with a glow in their eyes. This was adventure, the way stalwarts should live—and die. Cut and thrust, noise and smell, bread and wine—and over and above all, the might of Pharaoh's good will.

Nefer's chair was set down. She was helped out with the deference due to her as a woman, but the litter bearers were drinking in the scene with greedy expressions on their faces. They were looking at heroes. Men ready and willing to defend the name of their king. Men who would be blessed by Amun and whose souls would go straight to the joy and delight of Elysian Fields should battle finish their earthly lives.

She was taken to the great ship and was helped aboard by courteous but impatient hands. She stood there, tired and dishevelled and utterly unsure. She was a woman among a legion of men. At that moment in time, she felt she was the loneliest person in the world.

What must she do? Where should she go? No one seemed to care. Where was her Lord Husband? What a devil he was!

She inhaled sharply, her anger returning. She fixed a passing youth with her eye and commanded imperiously:

'You will come here!'

He obeyed at once and bowed low, his hands with palms facing the ground.

'You will lead me to my place.'

'My lady,' he murmured and remained in his lowly position, waiting for her command.

A field peasant and very quiet and patient, she thought and felt sympathy. He has been taken from his work and he had no choice but to obey. He knows about as much of all this as I do.

'You may hold up your head,' she told him in a milder tone. 'Do you know the place set aside for Mighty Amosis's wife?'

He straightened his spine and she took

143

a long look at his nice rounded face and black berry eyes. At his full lips, tanned skin and his very brief but river-clean loin cloth. She smiled, liking him and her expression made him brave enough to admit:

'My lady,' he said in a soft pleasing voice. 'I am only newly arrived. I do not know your place.'

'You will find it for me?'

'Yes,' he replied, and turned and left her, relief on his face.

She stood there wondering about the captain of the ship, about Kerma, but most of all she was wondering about Amosis. He who should have been here to greet her, to introduce her to men of rank, to tell them who she was and to make her position clear.

He is detestable, she thought and her anger at his arrogance and pomposity grew. Perhaps, she thought coldly, I have been seen as a sad and lost creature for a long time now. Now everything had changed. One day I will show the world—and most particularly Khaleb, that I am a woman of great account!

The youth returned, his face happy and relieved.

'You will follow me, my lady?' he asked diffidently. 'Your place is magnificent and nowhere near this stinking spot!'

It was not stinking, only full of muddle, of great jars and woven baskets of grain, and all manner of necessary things in the game of taking men to war. But the youth's words pleased her. He was in fact accepting her as a personage of some account in spite of her muddy feet and reed stained dress. In spite of her lack of noble facial paint! He smiled at her, nervous and rather shy. She found herself liking him even more.

'What is your name?' she asked him as he began carefully leading the way.

'Uronarti, my lady. I was born near that place.'

'Would you like to serve me rather than be with the others?'

He looked uncomfortable and she smiled in swift understanding.

'It is all right, Uronarti, I realise how it is. You will be a fine soldier. I am quite sure. I did not mean to take away your pride.'

He did not reply and she followed him past the men, the animals, the clutter of the cargo, to where at the further end of the ship was a large fringed canopy with woven linen sides. Under it she found a reed woven couch, cushions, and everything she would need for the journey. There was even a bead threader and boxes of pretty gleaming beads and semi-precious stones for her to amuse herself with. A board game and a little musical instrument with strings.

My Lord Husband has seen to my comfort after all, Nefer thought wryly. I must forgive him a great deal for this.

'My lady will permit me to leave now?'

'Yes, Uronarti,' she smiled. 'You may go.'

He turned away then froze as a big ugly brute of a man strode forward shouting and waving a whip.

'What are you doing here, eh? I gave you a job to do, fool! How dare you waste time talking to serving girls when I ordered you to fetch the rope.'

'Lord, I am sorry.' Uronarti fell to his knees in supplication. 'I will fetch the rope.'

'It is done already, the fixing complete and now you will learn what happens to vermin reckless enough not to heed my words.'

He raised his whip and brought it down with all his strength across Uronarti's quivering shoulders. The young man did not cry out. The man raised his whip to deliver a second blow as Nefer ran forward and stopped him.

'Enough! This man was helping me.'

The man glared, his eyes wicked.

'He should obey orders,' he snarled, 'not

toady up to serving women.'

'He was obeying orders,' she said in a tight furious voice. 'Mine!'

'And who do you think you are?' he bawled. 'A servant of a lady, that's who you are! And one who's not so wholesome as she should be by the look of things. By Set and all devils, the Lady Amosis must be blind to take someone like you into service aboard this ship.'

'You are unspeakable,' Nefer gasped, furious at the man's insolence and hating the glinting cruelty she saw in his eyes. How sadistically his type treated servants and slaves! The whole world hated an evil master. This creature was not a man of honour, she could tell. Perhaps a tradesman of the lowest kind. Poor Uronarti! How terrible to be at the mercy of a beast such as he.

'I am Seshat, Master of Supplies,' the man snarled. 'And people under me know what happens if they don't do as I say.'

He ruthlessly brushed Nefer aside and raised the whip to beat Uronarti again, but she cried out and leapt forward to hold on to his arm. By now, men of lowly position were watching, had fallen back, their eyes wide. There was not one who dared to interfere. To defy a master meant that one courted death. No one wanted to sail on the Black River before the correct time, nor come face to face with the Jackal of Embalming.

Beside herself, loathing the bestiality she saw in Seshat's eyes, Nefer leapt at him again. He shook her off and as she cried out, a cold voice snapped:

'Hold!'

At that everyone froze. Panting, feeling ashamed at her lack of dignity and grace, Nefer kept as still as everyone else. She was breathing heavily and felt utterly distressed—then seeing the look on Amosis's face—ashamed. He was coldly, killingly angry. Even so, his voice was level as he spoke to Seshat who was now in position of supplication, his hands outstretched before him.

'Master of Supplies, what is the meaning of this?'

'I was going to punish a disobedient servant, lord. This young woman tried to interfere.'

'And you laid hands on her?'

'I merely pushed her away.'

'You are a foolish man,' Amosis said, his voice tomb cold. 'You are also an animal to treat a young lady so.'

'Lord, she is a serving wench with dirty dress and dirty feet—and she tried to obstruct justice.'

'She is a young female and, no matter her rank or state, she deserves a certain

148

amount of respect. Had she been a lady, Seshat, she could have your hide. Indeed, she could ask for, and receive your death.'

Master of Supplies was beginning to realise the enormity of the Lord Amosis's anger. A much deeper fury than the committed crime warranted surely? The girl was merely a servant—one treated servants kindly, contemptuously or cruelly. Either way, it was of no great account. Even so with a terrifying certainty, Seshat knew that at that moment his life was in deadly danger. Then he heard the girl, and quite unmistakably, there was mercy in her voice.

'Forgive me, my lord,' she pleaded. 'I did not know that I was taking this young man away from his duties—and in turn, Master of Supplies did not know about me.'

'Then,' Amosis asked flatly, 'what is your wish?'

'That the Master of Supplies returns to his own business.'

'That is all?' He was staring hard at her now. 'There is nothing more?'

'I would like Uronarti to stay in my service.'

'I was speaking of this disgusting jackal who calls himself Seshat. What punishment shall he have?'

'Your anger is punishment enough, my lord, and—'

'Not so,' he cut in imperiously. 'This animal laid his filthy hands on your person. He will have those hands cut off.'

'No!' She was now as angry as he and her eyes held the fire of defiance. 'The man was determined to see that his orders were carried out. He must do this work correctly. I presume that this boat must leave at a certain time?' Small as she was, Nefer took a step nearer to Amosis and stared up at him, adding pointedly, 'Had my Lord Husband allowed me a little notice before leaving my home, other arrangements could have been made. My own servants would have been here, and I, in clean linen, would have been recognised.'

'And had My Lady Wife allowed me a little integrity,' he replied smoothly, a faint quirk uplifting the corners of his mouth, 'she would have known that all she needed was a little patience.'

Nefer looked beyond Amosis, then gasped and felt abashed. Coming eagerly towards them were the dear familiar faces of Paihuti and Bebu as well as several favourite servants and slaves. As Amosis turned away Nefer asked quickly:

'My lord, Uronarti may stay with me?'

Amosis looked at the quietly venomous Seshat and then towards the still totally unnerved youth. He made up his mind.

150

'I give you Uronarti,' he told her distantly. 'Let us hope that he shows rather more alacrity in obeying your own commands than he did with his previous master.' He looked coldly at Seshat. 'You may go. However, be warned, do not dare to even step into the Lady Amosis's shadow from now on. Should you ever be unfortunate enough to do so I will have your hands and feet cut off and then you shall be boiled in oil.' He strode away without a backward glance.

Now that Nefer could not see, his lips curved upwards even more. His eyes were full of laughter. There was more to his wife than he had at first thought. He realised that now. It had taken courage to stand up to Master of Supplies. How diminutive she was, and how very sweet. He had almost given himself away just now. He had almost let her see that already the years were fading from his mind. He was seeing a little girl half hidden among the flowers again, and feeling the protectiveness that had risen up so fiercely that he'd all but choked. Amosis pulled himself together and went in search of his men.

He is cruel and ruthless, Nefer thought. He is a soldier, a man without the gentle sensitivity that I so loved about him all those years ago.

As she gave herself up to Bebu and

151

everyone else's fussing and fretting, she was thinking regretfully of days gone by.

How she had adored Amosis, how earnestly she had looked up to him. How wise he had been, how gentle and kind. Her heart had sung like a bird on that morning when he had impulsively taken hold of her hand. How safe she had felt then, how warm and secure.

Then Ese had come upon them. Her eyes had widened, like a cat hypnotising its prey. Right after that, she had begun to question, to ask what had been going on? What indecencies had occurred.

How Twosre would have laughed at the woman and lipped her, Nefer thought, and found herself wishing very desperately that her sister was on the ship. She said as much to Bebu who helped her wash and dress in clean clothes.

'My lady would be unwise to wish for Twosre's presence,' Bebu said flatly. 'That is, if my lady wishes to keep the full attention of her lord.'

'Bebu!' Nefer said quickly. 'There you go again! I will have none of your innuendoes and—'

'My lady,' Bebu insisted, taking her life in her hands, 'your pretty little sister loves you as deeply as you love her. But she gets mischievous pleasure from making men—all her men—as wax in her hands. It

152

happened—even with Sebni, your brother. Is that not true?'

'Don't!' Nefer said wearily. 'You take too much upon yourself, Bebu—and I still want Twosre here even though I accept that all you say is true. Twosre is as complex as the Nile—and as necessary to me as the Great River is to our land.'

'Hail to Hapi, God of the River,' Bebu replied.

After that she followed Nefer to the ship's side and there they looked in silence at the glinting water that travelled the length of the narrow nation of Egypt. The Delta was the only place where the country was wide and there the Nile's seven arms provided a web of waterways. There in the North were the silent marshlands, endless reed beds and holy, hungry crocodiles. A place very different from the wild, vast, red and rocky, heat laden area of the South, where they were heading now.

The warship Nefer was on was steered by a large bladed oar in the stern. It had a wooden hull. Its massive sail was made of cloth, the rigging of papyrus fibre. Its crew numbered two hundred soldiers, there were also servants and slaves aboard and like all water borne troops, oarsmen, whose heads were barely visible. They could always be identified on land by a leather patch on the seats of their kilts.

In spite of herself, Nefer felt proud of the men around her. They were brave fighters, and mostly were archers. Neither by look nor deed had any man shown distaste, that she, Nefer, Lady Wife of Mighty Amosis was aboard. Even more unsettling, that a canopied shelter had been erected for her, whereas their own lot was rather more harsh.

Amosis's vessel was not the only ship on the river. There were others, each carrying up to two hundred and fifty soldiers. There were also galleys and skiffs and cargo transports filled to the brim with supplies. It was a sight to terrify all enemies, Nefer thought, and felt frightened herself.

She half turned, nervously, for Amosis was striding towards her, sure-footed for all they were afloat. His figure was outlined against a blood-red sky that would blacken with a great swiftness as the sun took its mighty leap into the Underworld. Soon now the Moon God Chons would reign.

'What are you thinking, Small Person?' Amosis asked as he came to a halt at her side, pretending not to see Bebu discreetly slipping away.

'Nothing important, lord,' she replied gravely. 'I was being a little fanciful just then, that is all.'

'In what way?'

'I was thinking how opposite Ra and

154

Chons are. Red and gold, black and silver.'

'And your choice?'

She looked up at him and smiled in a faintly apologetic way.

'Against the red and gold of day, I think I prefer the gentleness of Chons. His realm holds the pure clean whiteness of the moon and sprinkled everywhere, there are untold millions of smiling stars.

'And what are your conclusions about these two different worlds?'

'I—I was thinking that people are rather like that,' she said unsteadily. 'They are either fiery or cold.'

'Oh? And to which of the two extremes do I belong?'

'My lord, you are a strong and determined man and you have fiery red blood racing through your veins.'

'And you,' he told her. 'Are cool and gentle, and as beautiful as the night.'

'No,' she corrected him sadly. 'You see, my heart is not dancing to the rhythm of the stars. I am merely a pale imitation of the person I was while in Khaleb's arms. I seem to be living in a nothing land of perpetual grey. That makes me angry.'

'At the Prince?'

She shook her head and her hair swirled round her face like black silk.

'At myself!' She stepped closer to him

and took hold of his arm. 'I owe you a very great deal, my lord. You are protecting me with your name. You have rescued me from the morass of self-pity into which I had sunk. Pharaoh's command must have been as distasteful to you as it was frightening to me, yet you have not openly despised me, not let the world see the real truth. I will always be grateful for that.'

'And if gratitude is not enough?'

'Then it shall be as you wish,' she said proudly. 'It has been decreed that we are man and wife. So it is written and so it shall be done. I will bed with you, if that is your choice.'

He was staring down at her, perplexed. He saw that she had changed somehow and become strong. He felt an unwilling admiration for her, which was unexpected, and for a moment he was almost wishing to take up her challenge. Instead he smiled coolly into her defiantly upturned face and said:

'Well spoken, Small Person. You are not such a lost cause, after all. Indeed, I go so far as to say that you had just cause for being depressed. That you are pulling yourself out of it brings you much credit. How strange!'

'My lord?'

'There was once a time,' he said, 'when

I loathed and detested the sound of your name.'

'Oh!' She was shocked and her hand fell away from his arm. Her moment of new found confidence, gone.

'How is it that you are still on your feet?' he asked her. Then because her stunned expression made him uncomfortable, he looked away from her and stared at the waters that were now so dramatically outlined by shadowed black banks.

'I—I could not sleep,' she replied quietly. 'I—just could not!'

He turned to her again.

'Because you are afraid to dream?'

'My dreaming is ended.' She was herself again. 'I am now coming to terms with stark reality.'

He was relieved at her about face and said easily:

'Wouldn't it be easier to do so sitting down?'

'Am I to be allowed a choice?'

For the first time since he had reappeared into her life, she heard him laugh. It was a pleasing sound.

'My dear Nefer, it seems we progress. But I really would prefer you to be more comfortable. Come, sit down with me and we will talk.'

He led her to where there were coils of rope and waited in silence while she sat down, then he took his place at her side. There was silence between them as the order rang out to pull close to the shore. As the ship neared the banks, landing men jumped overboard and waded on to the land, pulling ropes held over their shoulders. The ship shuddered a little and settled in the low water. It was made secure and at last the men were able to relax. Some closed their eyes and slept where they were, leaning over the oars. Others leapt ashore, laughing and shouting out jokes. In a very short time fires made pyramids of light on land and there came an appetising smell of cooking food.

'Soon, very soon now I'd say,' Amosis said easily, 'the oarsmen will wake to a man. There's nothing like a meal to galvanise people into action. Are you hungry? Would you like to go ashore?'

'I would prefer to stay here, my lord,' she replied. 'I am curious to know why once you loathed and detested me.'

He shrugged, then asked:

'How much do you know about me?'

'Very little,' she replied, then floundered on: 'Except that you are a very brave soldier and held high in Pharaoh's esteem. And—and that you are now my Lord Husband—even though you deserted me when I was a mere child.'

He nodded slowly, then asked:

158

'What do you know of my family, Nefer?'

'Nothing I'm afraid. I—I am sorry.'

'Don't be sorry,' he told her and now his tone had become harsh and cold. 'Now I shall tell you a story and you will listen and perhaps understand. I am the only son of Rahotep, who is the younger brother of Ramses, who was once a Chief Guard of Pharaoh. It was during Court duties that my uncle saw how close to Pharaoh were certain men. Among them, Per Ibsen. Then my uncle Ramses, a greedy ambitious man, conceived a plan. To marry his only nephew to the daughter of Ramose, who also had the good fortune to be the first daughter of the Per Ibsen House. Such an alliance, he felt sure, would bring him a step nearer to Pharaoh and through him, great fame, fortune and grace.'

'Oh!'

'My father, Rahotep, did not want this thing. My mother cried, but even so, I was sent away to stay with people near your place. Our meeting, Small Person, was arranged from first to last. This I did not know.'

'Oh!' she said again and wondered wildly why she could think of nothing else to say.

'We became friends I think,' he said

evenly. 'I must confess that I found you a sweetly pretty little thing.' He looked at her and she felt her cheeks go pink. 'Indeed,' he went on, 'you are not much different now. I like the stylish way you wear your dress, the colours in the collar you've chosen, your hair flowing free and the way you have outlined your eyes. And also, being with child suits you.'

'Thank you, my lord,' she replied and felt unnerved. He smiled wryly.

'How greatly time has wasted all that was so promising. How could my powerful uncle have guessed at the fanatical poison running through the blood of Ese? How could he have foretold how filthy were her thoughts and how greatly she could lie! Did you know that she told priests that I had tried to violate you? That you were meant for a life in the temple as a pure, untouched servant of god?'

'But I still do not understand—'

'You were to be matched if my uncle could arrange it, and by all accounts he had a good chance of success. Ese put paid to all that. She was believed and I was banished—and yet, here I am now. How the gods must be laughing at their joke!'

'Was—was my father Per Ibsen a party to the match?'

'He knew nothing. The plot was all very clever really and simpleness itself.

160

My uncle relied on you and I becoming close to each other. So close in fact that your parents would find themselves agreeing that our names should be written side by side in Temple Files. But Ese lied about our innocent holding of hands. I was banished to the lowest position that could be found for me in Pharaoh's army. I was spat on and reviled and I could not understand why. As you know, Nefer, Per Ibsen was not the only one not party to my uncle's plan. And so, for many years, the only one I felt I could blame for all my troubles, was yourself.'

'Then,' she whispered, 'then when was it that you learned the whole truth, my lord?'

'My uncle was killed in battle. It was not until then that my father told me the whole story. Had he spoken before he would have been thrown off the family lands. There was my mother to care for, and sisters. There was nothing he could do.'

'It—it must have been very hard for you,' she began. 'And you—'

'It was harsh and cruel for me,' he told her stiffly, 'but I was young and strong and needed only to have concern for myself. My father on the other hand, had to live through the shame. Had to hear the name of his only son reviled.

And not once did my uncle seek to defend me.'

'My lord,' she was almost weeping, 'how deeply you must hate the sound of my name.'

'I do not hate you now. I am merely a soldier who does his duty as he sees fit. A person who recognises that for the second time in your short life you have been used as a pawn in a man's rotten game. You shall be secure from now on. I will ask nothing of you and you must accept nothing from me. As my lady you will be safe from Pharaoh—and from Khaleb.'

'Please,' she gasped painfully, 'do not speak of the Prince, I cannot bear to hear his name.'

'If you have a boy,' he told her starkly, 'the Prince will follow you. Khaleb has fathered three daughters by Palace Women—one of whom is a Princess. He is fond of his children and they are much loved, but he wants a son.'

'I did not know,' she said faintly, and wanted to die. 'He never once said—'

'It is all in the past now,' he told her firmly. 'And Son or Daughter your child shall be known as the light in the eye of Amosis. Now allow me to carry you ashore. I have already ordered that a meal shall be prepared for us. I have also made it plain to your people that you and I will eat alone.'

His tone was authoritative, but she had no desire to argue. The tale he had told was so stark and obviously true. Now she understood and everything had become clear.

Suddenly Nefer was remembering Amosis as he had been. So young, so wonderful and so good in her eyes. How he had suffered—physically far more terribly than she could ever visualise. Mentally, perhaps far worse because he had found it in his heart to hate. She had never hated him, she had only been impossibly sad.

As Amosis lifted her into his arms, she felt a new emotion. It was a mixture of poignancy about lost youth, a compassion for that proud, tough, but terribly vulnerable young man.

I will try and make it up to him, she vowed. I will make him forget to hate the name of Nefer. He will learn that I can be an asset rather than a thing of shame.

Amosis dismissed the servants who rushed forward to help him disembark and waded ashore with her cradled in his arms. Proud, dominant, he carried her through the shallow waters like a king. She snuggled against him and relaxed.

CHAPTER FIVE

The camp fires were ablaze, glorious. There were game birds roasting, and onions, lentils and savoury cakes of grain. There was fruit piled high, honey-bread and wine. And the lights from the flames made the shadows dance. Those illusive reflections hinged on the feet of men were considered to be their visible, but untouchable souls. People were in awe of their shadows, some even felt fear.

Nefer, resting comfortably on piled cushions, felt that her shadow looked serene. She was at peace for the first time in months. This because she had a purpose in life and knew exactly what she wanted to do. She was sitting next to Amosis and in the sudden flaring of light his shadow joined hers. She was surprised and turned to see that he had moved closer. It was not unpleasing and she smiled. She was rewarded to see his lips curve in a wide lazy grin.

Because music played and the lord master smiled, spirits were light in the men. So it was that their shadows twinkled, grew short, then long, jerked and leapt and were as merry as the humans to whom they belonged.

'They know that from tonight there will be nothing left but hard work with perhaps death at the end of it all,' Amosis said in a calm matter of fact way. 'As their commander, I felt it my duty to allow them this night—and the promise that when victory is ours, there will be many more times just the same.'

'Then you are a man among men,' she told him. 'For you have feeling in your heart.'

He raised his brows at that.

'I would prefer to call it common sense,' he replied. 'A happy man is a loyal one. It is as simple as that.'

'My lord!' she said softly, unbelieving, and smiled again. I do not love this man, she thought, but my admiration grows by the hour. He is my husband and I am proud of the fact.

A picture of Khaleb leapt and contorted in the heart of the fire like a little red imp. With deliberate firmness Nefer pushed the picture away.

'You must enjoy every moment that you can,' Amosis told her. 'Kerma is quite isolated and beyond the Third Cataract. We travel over land for six days to reach it. But for now, we continue up stream.'

'May I know a little more about Kerma itself, my lord?'

He shrugged, but his expression was kind.

'It is a town of considerable size with the citadel overlooking all. We call our citadel Walls of Amenemhet. Within it we are self-sufficient. You will happily make friends with officials and their wives. Scribes and their families have quite an easy time of it too. Soldiers bear their lot as stoically as is expected of them the world over. When I left, we were all co-habiting quite peacefully with the local African populace. It's the outsiders that are our concern.'

'And—and are you the Most High of this place?'

'I am not,' he told her. 'I am first and foremost an army man. Of the Southern army, I am Most High. But we are all subject to Governor Khonsu. It is his task to trade for and expedite the many shipments of goods to Egypt, and we give many goods in exchange. I believe that much was being gained by all. Now something seems to have gone wrong. We are in the heart of the Sudan, Nefer, and so we are extremely vulnerable. There are spies and evil-doers abroad.'

'And the news Pharaoh received was very bad?'

'Bad enough for him to order my return

166

and to send reinforcements, but not so terrible as to bring about an all-out war. You will be safe enough in the citadel. But from now on, I cannot allow any Egyptian to walk alone in Kerma itself. However, I have no doubt that will all change quite soon.'

His voice held all the calm assurance in the world and she heard herself saying:

'I feel safe with you, Amosis.'

'Really?' His strong tanned face was very near hers. Then came that wide lazy grin again. 'Not too safe I hope, My Lady Wife. That would seem to be a very damning message—to a full-blooded man.'

She felt her face grow hot and her eyes were very bright as she told him:

'Mighty One, I am very well aware of the fact that you are a full-blooded man and I also understand and accept that I am indeed your wife.'

'That is as it should be,' he told her and turned away to accept wine, clearly dismissing the meaning underlying her words.

Piqued, Nefer refused wine but accepted a sizzling, well-cooked portion of quail. She watched the people round her, but she was very aware of the man at her side. She turned to watch as he laughed at something one of the men in the group nearest to him said. He is a man's man she thought, and they rate him as highly as he rates them. Any woman in his life will always have a rival—Egypt's Army! How mighty such a rival is! And how formidable.

Relaxed, with his most trusted and high ranking officers near, Amosis was good company. His conversation was lucid and to the point. His laugh was a rarity, but when it did occur he threw back his head and gave a delighted roar. More intrigued than she would admit even to herself, Nefer continued to watch him.

Much later the fires were banked up and night watches began.

'You will return to the ship now, Nefer,' Amosis said.

'Will you, my lord?' she enquired.

'I will stay, as I must, with my men.'

'Then I choose to stay on land also,' she said quietly.

He shrugged, but allowed her to have her own way.

That night she slept under the stars, on a bed of rushes built under the trees. Near her, Bebu. The serving girls, Yati and Kanes were curled up like kittens at her feet. The air was sweet with the smell of damp earth, crushed grass and wild flowers. The moon was milk-white and serene. Nefer closed her eyes. Amosis's warning of forthcoming danger banished as effortlessly as chaff before the wind. She felt safe sleeping, with the Pharaoh's men not too far away. There was also darling Paihuti, with him Uronarti and somewhere unseen, the giant man who had married her at Pharaoh's command.

'Mighty Amosis will guard us,' she whispered and her hands rested gently on the child nestling inside her womb. 'And you will live, My Sweet Precious. You will learn to laugh and sing and play in the sun. Your face will be beautiful, your form perfection itself. I will adore you, my little baby, and my adoration will make you survive.'

It was then that she remembered the small brother that she had never seen. She was able to understand her mother's heartbreak and sense of loss. Her eyes filled with sorrow for the tiny woman she loved.

'She must have gone almost mad, My Sweet Precious,' Nefer whispered to her unborn. 'Thanks and praises to Amun, that Mother had Father at her side. They must have wept together but at the same time drawn comfort from the fact that they did not have to suffer alone. I am alone, and Khaleb your father did not care. I am alone and I—'

Nefer stopped then and for the first time truly believed what she had once thought inconceivable. She was not alone as she had been in Ramose House and so often elsewhere. She need not be covered in fear, guilt and shame ever again. She had a protector, husband and friend. As wife of Amosis she could relax and forget her previous stress and care.

Amosis, Mighty Warrior, she thought and fell asleep whispering his name.

When she awoke the sun was already preparing the world for his coming, for red banners were already flying in the eastern sky. The camp was awake and lively. Women were grinding grain for bread, men took their animals to the water to drink. Cooking fires were blazing away.

Bebu and the others were smiling.

'Hail and good morning, Lady Nefer,' Bebu cried. 'You slept well and long. You will have a good day!'

'As will you, my friend,' Nefer replied and yawned and stretched and felt at peace with the world.

The women gathered round, anxious to help her to wash, and to anoint her with sweet smelling oil. The birds were fussing and fretting in the trees and from the rushes there came the harsher cries of water fowl. Uronarti approached and shyly offered her a Sun-Blossom he'd picked. She accepted it and had Bebu fix it in the dark shining of her freshly brushed hair.

170

'My lady, your wishes?' Bebu asked. 'Shall we walk together and exchange pleasantries while we wait for our first meal? There is still some time before we embark. Lord Amosis has ordered that the journey to Kerma will be taken as carefully as possible for your own sweet sake. That shows his concern for you. We must hurry like the wind. But the journey must be as easy as possible. Just think of that!'

Nefer was touched at this, but had to comment:

'That was kind. But foolish. A great soldier should not have been saddled with a weak and stupid Theban woman. He needed someone fine and strong, a frontier wife perhaps.'

'Which, by your tone, you intend to become, Lady Nefer?'

'Yes, Bebu! Now I will walk.' She held up her hand as they all made to join her. 'No, I mean to go alone.'

'My lady,' Uronarti pleaded, 'let me come with you. Let me keep watch.'

'There is no need,' she pointed out. 'Look how many of us there are. There can be no danger. No one would dare approach.'

She had her way and left them. For the first time since Khaleb had said goodbye, Nefer found herself feeling happy as she walked to the river's edge. The banks were a riot of Sun-Blossoms. They were like a golden carpet everywhere. The air was filled with their pungent odour.

'You are beautiful!' Nefer was unable to contain her bubble of pleasure. 'You are rightly lovingly called Sun-Blossoms. Never, in a million years, will I use your official title "Tooth of the Lion". How sad and just because of the shape of your leaves! It is the sunny smile of your faces that I see.'

She began to sing as she gathered the flowers, forgetting everyone and everything in the pleasure of the moment. Then Amosis found her.

'Come, my lady,' he said in his quiet, proprietary way. 'A meal has been prepared and we will eat it together as man and wife should.'

She smiled up at him and held out her flowers.

'Aren't they beautiful, my lord?'

'They're very nice,' he dutifully replied. 'And the leaves are good to eat too.'

'I—was thinking of their loveliness rather than their usefulness, Amosis.'

Her tone was almost frosty and the edges of his mouth quirked upwards as he remarked:

'Flowers are not usually a soldier's concern. However, I confess that those look very attractive in your arms.'

'Oh!' Her eyes were shy. 'A compliment, my lord?'

'Indeed,' he replied. 'My dear Small Person, there were times, many years ago, when I thought you to be something of a flower yourself.'

'Thank you,' she said, absurdly pleased. 'And my memories of you, Mighty Warrior, are and always will be entangled with the vision of the Ramose gardens and their wealth and bloom.' She sighed a little. 'How sad it is. We grow up so soon. Our little delights and secret passions are stripped bare in the light of reality and yet our sweet memories hold on fast. I loved you so, my lord.

'As I love you now,' he replied courteously and her cheeks burned because he was so clearly merely being polite. 'But I must explain to you how different your life will be from now on. The security of Ramose House is behind you. Kerma is not at all like Thebes. There will be danger abroad and you will have to take care. If our enemies are strong they will lay siege.'

'I am determined to learn,' she told him. 'I promise to be a good wife, Amosis, I will try to make you proud of me. I will never willingly let you down.'

'I know,' he replied and was very serious now. 'And from now on, you must never

173

be so rash as to wander away alone. Have I your promise?'

'Of course, my lord.'

'That is good.' He looked her up and down, rather as he might a prize mare and noted how she was growing, then added: 'I was against the idea of all this. Now I am not so sure.'

'Then, I am glad,' she replied and meant it because she saw Amosis as her saviour. He was frightened now because his air of authority made him very remote, his character almost too strong. But he had taken her with him, had publicly accepted her as Pharaoh's great gift. In her eyes therefore, he could do no wrong.'

'Taking a wife held no attraction for me at all,' he told her. 'But I have often considered that it would be a pleasant experience to father a child. The one you now bear shall be mine.'

'I will give you a child of your own one day, Amosis,' she told him quietly. 'One who owes his beginning direct from your loins. In this manner I will pay back the great debt I owe.'

Again his lips quirked as he looked down into her earnest upturned face.

'I will hold you to that, perhaps,' he told her. 'But I rather think you and I will have to wait a while. You have enough to contend with right now, don't you agree?'

Her cheeks flamed, but her eyes were steady and sure.

'Nevertheless, my Lord Husband,' she replied. 'Good practice never comes amiss. I would choose to spend my nights in your bed from now on.'

He raised his brows at that.

'My lady, without love?'

'I can manage very well with—respect, my lord.'

'Respect, Small Person?'

'If you respect my need to pay in full for the bargain Pharaoh made; if you respect my body when you use it, it will be enough.' She laughed then, a shaky, broken little sound that rustled against the pale blue forget-me-nots and made a little paean of pain in the morning air. 'After all, my Lord Husband, respect is far more than the natural father of my unborn ever gave.'

His eyes were searching her face very carefully. He seemed angry and she wondered if he was annoyed at her for her forward ways. He was silent for so long that she heard herself stammering:

'Forgive me. I—I did not mean to make you angry. It—it's only that I am now so very determined to grow up.'

'And you believe that coming to my bed will help wash away the humiliation you received at the hands of Khaleb?'

175

'Yes.'

His growing anger was the more terrible because it was so cold.

'I speak words I should not. Even though the Prince is son of the Divine One, I would like to grind his face in the mud. If you are so hurt to grasp at straws, if you feel that coming to my bed will help assuage your pain, you are welcome, Nefer. But remember, I shall not send for you. I will not even wait for you. You must come to me in your own good time and of your own choice. Is that perfectly clear?'

She nodded and stepped towards him, full-blown and lovely in her white flax linen dress. The gold collar with its design of red and green stones, the flowers and the sunlight, all reflecting in her eyes.

'My lord,' she said quietly, 'I will come to you. I belong to you. I am content that this is so. Being your wife has given me back my own sense of self-pride and—and I am grateful to you.'

'A beggar is grateful to pick up a crust that has been thrown in the dust,' he told her stiffly. 'But who are we to argue over crumbs and wonder why they are thrown? At this moment crumbs are sufficient. Who knows what the future may hold? Come, we will go back and eat. After that we will get ready to board ship.'

'And we will hurry to Kerma,' she said,

trying to please him. 'For bargains are only bargains and not half so important as duty, my lord.'

His stare was so hard that she was taken aback.

'My lady,' he said stiffly. 'It will be wise to remember that I am and always will be Pharaoh's soldier. This first and last.'

'Forgive me. I did not mean—' she began. But impatient now, he turned away. She walked disconsolately, two steps behind him, the Sun-Blossoms already wilting in the heat of the new day.

That night, aboard ship, Amosis stayed in the company of his men. He lay on the deck, with no cover and no pillow, sleeping rough and ready, and clearly at ease. Nefer heard this from the lips of Paihuti, and also, a little later from Uronarti, who she had sent to see if the situation remained the same.

Not quite sure whether she was relieved or wretched, to have been so effortlessly set aside, Nefer lay in her own perfumed shelter and finally closed her eyes. For a while she listened to the music of a reed pipe that Uronarti so plaintively played.

The river journey continued, the oarsmen following the pacemaster's quickening beats on the drum. There were cool starlit nights and hot, but dustless days as the ship made its way to Semna on the Second Cataract and way beyond. They were still to travel more than a hundred miles to Kerma, that was situated so importantly beyond the Third Cataract. High above the sprawling buildings of Kerma stood the great citadel which the Egyptians held.

Technically, Kerma was in the land of Kush, the vast area inhibited by dark skinned peoples. A land that was wild and silent and remote. The place where once, long, long ago, old Thickneck had been born.

Now the ship made its way between cliffs of rock and then, as the valley widened out, past occasional palm-groved villages, where women and men grew crops. All being irrigated by water-wheels or lever-bucketed from the river. These cultivations were set like green jewels against stark, dead rock, or lay under some golden, wind-rippled sand dune, curving to a sharp edge at the top of an incredibly precipitous face. The lead ship went on, the proud, dignified head of a flotilla of Egypt's might. And the people on the banks saw the armada, watched how strong in fighting men the land was. Then they sent up prayers to the gods. For in Thutmose the Third's hands, they were safe.

To Nefer the journey was like living in Elysian Fields. The Second Life, she reasoned, could never be better. She was fussed and fretted over by her own. Her Lord Husband remained kind and attentive and made no nightly demands. Her thickening figure made her a little clumsy, but all was as it should be, she knew. Her feeling for the child she carried grew. She felt filled with love and longed to hold him in her arms. Yes, somehow she was sure that she carried a son. A little boy, her Most Precious, who would, one day, make up for the child Beloved Mother had lost.

She waited to deliver with sweet and tender expectancy ...

On an early hour when the green dawn was breaking over the bleak, jagged masses of rock, Nefer's son arrived with little or no trouble at all.

And Bebu, who had been a wonder in her nursing and love, laughed with joy as she handed the linen-wrapped newborn to Nefer.

'My lady,' she said, 'he is beautiful. He is all that the heart could desire.'

Yati—she of the Merry Smile, and Kanes—she with the Dreamy Eyes clapped their hands together and cried out thanks-giving to Holy Hathor and all of Egypt's gods, for the safe arrival of the beloved child. Then Nefer remembered Amosis's words and she whispered urgently:

'Kanes, go and tell my Lord Husband that his son is born.'

And while she waited Nefer cradled her baby in her arms and held his tiny face against hers. Tears of joy and wonder streaming down her face.

'Hello, My Precious,' she whispered. 'Welcome to this world. You are the light of Re to my eyes. I love you, my life. You are the song in my soul!'

Such was her adoration that she neither saw nor heard Amosis come into her shelter. He watched her and thought what a picture she made. Then she looked up and he was startled at the glory he saw in her eyes. She held the baby out to him. He felt strangely moved.

'My lord,' she said, 'here is your first son.'

He took the baby and stared down at the minute puckered face, then he smiled.

'You have done well,' he told Nefer, 'and from this day he shall be known as Nesmin, son of Amosis and Nefer.' He handed the baby back to her, bowed his head in polite courtesy and went away, to stand thoughtfully at the prow of the ship.

She is still the wide-eyed Small Person I knew all those years ago, he thought, and again felt strangely moved. How helpless she is and how brave. What is more, she is kind. Servants and slaves love her, yet it is true affection that makes them act towards her as they do. I see no false fawning in the eyes—even of the field boy and he is new to the game. Perhaps Pharaoh was wise after all. I will protect Nefer and at least be the guardian she needs. As to the child, he is mine and may Amun help any who try to say otherwise.

Back in the shelter, Nefer kissed the tiny face and felt her heart reaching out love in a great golden glow.

'Nesmin,' she whispered tremulously, 'so that is your name, My Sweet Precious. Nesmin, how nice!'

Three days later, the ships reached the flourishing trade centre of Kerma. The journey had taken over two months. Nefer watched as all the hustle and bustle of disembarking began. Vessels, great and small, were being unloaded. Animals neighed, screamed, bellowed or squealed. Men shouted out loud, ordering, heaving, working, their limbs gleaming brown with sweat and oil. Every so often there came the sharp crack of a whip as it seared across a slave's toiling back. And high above, overlooking the sprawled out hotchpotch of Kerma itself, could be seen the great red-yellow walls of the Egyptian fortress. Herein there lived a small part of

Amun's Kingdom, rigidly holding on to ancient traditions, determined above all, to keep intruders out of their land. It was for good reason that the frontier guards saw to it that no foreigner was allowed to pass the fortress to Egypt, except for trade in the river side city itself of course. And even then the foreign trader had to tranship his goods in Egyptian craft. Pharaoh Thutmose had decreed it and great was his might. Never would the uncaring days of Hatshepsut return, he swore. Enemies would be crushed into the red dirt of the desert before they were allowed to step on to Egypt's black soil.

The Infantry filed off the boats, close, ranked, hardy, tough. No army, merely a company to set fear rearing into the hearts of those who watched. A corps of charioteers followed. Strong, yet light, the vehicles were made of wood with metal strips and leather bindings. Light spoked wheels and rear-set axles allowed drivers to make tight fast turns. The High Officer of the Charioteers was a tall, lean, hawk-faced man. His two horses were black and beautiful, adorned with ostrich feathers and they wore necklaces of little gold bells.

Amosis strode to where Nefer stood, drinking it all in. She was cradling Nesmin in her arms. Amosis's eyes were bright, his expression pleased. Now he was on his own ground, an army man, carrying out duties as familiar to him as his own hands.

'My lady,' he said, 'it will be expedient for the men to travel up to the citadel in a slow and certain leisurely way. The people will see our strength, and then will beware. Undoubtedly there will be spies among them—and they will tell of our numbers to the enemy outside.'

'Then—then Kerma is not against us?'

'The city itself, no. But beyond, there is a man and his millions who must be reckoned with. I wish you to go ahead of us, guarded, of course. It is my intention to make the journey to the citadel last at least one night and one day. You can make the journey much quicker than that.'

'If I am with you,' she replied carefully, 'would it not show that Amosis, Mighty Warrior's Woman of the House is not afraid? Wouldn't it be less trouble if Paihuti, Bebu and I went in line with the rest?'

'It is of no consequence—whether you stay or go ahead,' he told her, exasperation in his tone.

'It is to me,' she said fervently.

He gave her a quick impatient grunt and walked away.

It took time and patience but at last

the great column set out on the leisurely journey to the citadel called *Inebuw Amenemhat* (Walls of Amenemhat) and it was exactly as Amosis required. All who witnessed the numbers of men, the animals, the corn bins, oil jars, food supplies, women and slaves, wondered at the might of Egypt and marvelled at Mighty Amosis who rode so proudly ahead.

Nefer was being carried in a curtained litter by four strong men. Bebu walked alongside. Kanes and Yati followed demurely behind. Paihuti and Uronarti had set themselves to guard the litter and strode, eyes alert, one on either side.

'We are enough to put the fear of Amun into the heart of the devil himself,' Bebu said stoutly and wheezed as she laughed. 'I can see nothing but peace in the region now.'

Nefer, holding Nesmin, his face shielded against the red dust by a fine mask of gauze, nodded her head.

'I am proud to be carried in a litter bearing the personal banner of Amosis,' she said. 'He is a very great man.'

'As so will be your son,' Bebu replied. 'For he will follow in the footsteps of our lord.'

'And—and not in the ways of—'

'The Prince?' Bebu's eyes narrowed in a

184

mock angry way. 'I know of no prince, my sweet Lady Nefer. And if we know what is good for us, we will never think that way again.'

'Oh Bebu, you are so wise!'

'No, only determined to keep the skin on my back,' the plump lady replied and pulled such a woefully funny face that Nefer heard herself laugh.

'Bebu, your sheer good spirits and unflagging strength make you worth your weight in gold!'

'Then let us hope and pray the Lord Amosis thinks the same. I could do with new bangles and beads.'

'Oh Bebu, how wicked. As for treasures I will weigh you down with them if that is what your heart desires.'

Bebu laughed disparagingly.

'My lady, if I were a native of these parts, I would ask for camels instead. Out here they are worth more than grain, or women, or slaves.'

'It is the same all over I understand,' Nefer replied. 'And perhaps it is fitting that we lesser beings should remember our own lowly place. Oh, look over there, how superior they are and too bad tempered by far.'

There were lots of camels in Amosis's train, for the region they were in now was hot and dry. Here the camel really was valued more than gold, grain, women, servant or slave. For his master it carried all burdens, he furnished flesh and milk for food, and his hair provided material for weaving cloth. At night in camp the little children drank cups of the camel's thick cheesy milk mixed with water. Herders wore turbans and robes of brown camel-hair cloth. The camel master slept under a camel-hair tent.

Nefer was thinking of camels simply because she had seen a nurse camel with the helpless young swinging in a hammock on one side.

'Do you know about camels, Bebu?' she asked. 'Is that young beast very sick?'

'No. He is just weak on his legs because he is newly born, my lady. He is as helpless as the young Lord Nesmin in fact.'

'The baggage camel is his mother?'

'No. A nurse animal, that is all.'

'Why is the baby not on his mother's back?' She held Nesmin close to her heart. 'I could not bear to be parted from my child.'

'My lady, camels are so stupid that if the mother could not see her baby, even if it were on her own back, she would think he had been left behind. But now she can see him on the nurse camel and follows contentedly enough.'

Nefer was satisfied, but she kept a look-out for the baby camel after that.

'He is new-born, like you, My Little Lord. And to his mother, as sweet. Oh, how I wish Khaleb could have seen you. How great would be his joy. But he rejected us, My Precious and we have a mighty warrior for our lord. We will learn to love him, you and I. We will make him learn to love us!'

After the day's march, when the dark blue velvet dome of the sky was hung all over with little golden lamps of stars, they came to the great gates of the citadel. Beneath them, the flares from the streets of Kerma seemed to be almost as far away as the sky.

There was a great deal of noise and confusion. The gates swung open to let them pass. It was then that Amosis left the head of the column and the camel he had been riding all day. He handed the reins to one of the foot soldiers and strode towards Nefer. He pulled the blue flax linen litter curtains to one side and stared at her.

'You are well, Woman of my House?'

'I am well, my lord,' she replied, blushing because he had so firmly given her the title of first lady wife.

'You will be taken to your home,' he

187

told her. 'And there you will rest. I have sent runners ahead of us so you will find all preparations made.'

'Thank you,' she replied steadily. 'That was very kind.'

'My kindness is nothing against your courage,' he told her. 'I have said very little, but I have noticed a great deal. You gave birth to Nesmin with little or no fuss. You have acted with great restraint during a hard journey. Small Person, I am proud of you!'

She was so taken aback that she could think of nothing to say. He gave his wide, lazy grin.

'Nefer, you look well with your son—'

'No! Our son,' she cut in swiftly. 'Your son and mine Amosis. That is how you said it would be and I am well content.' She laughed, a small wistful sound. 'I too, have a father not of my blood, remember? The Great Lord Per Ibsen. If you are to Nesmin as Per Ibsen has always been to me, I will thank all of Egypt's gods.'

'My lady,' he said quietly, 'if you continue to look up at me as you are doing now, as soon as you are over your waiting time, you will find me in your bed.'

'My lord?' she whispered uncertainly, and thought she heard him chuckle as he strode away.

CHAPTER SIX

Inside the imposing and quite enormous fortress walls there were many people. Reed canopied baiter centres lined the walls. Sections for workers stretched in a straight line. Flares gave light. A section of the tall tower bearing Pharaoh's emblem stood proudly over all. Soldier barracks, long in line, flat and uncompromising, outnumbered all. Beyond them, stables and even further on, livestock pens. It was the place to make a last stand should Kerma fall.

Almost a city within a city, Nefer thought, and it is a strong, rather comforting place.

The establishment to which she was taken was more substantial than most. It was fashioned from mud bricks, was columned and had a quietly gracious air. As she entered the rush-lit reception area, servants ran forward crying out welcome. Some held long stemmed, blue lotus flowers in their hands. Nefer smiled her gratitude, handed Nesmin to Bebu, and accepted the offerings then made a gracious speech of thanks in reply.

'This is not a bad base for a military man, my lady,' Bebu said. 'We will soon make you feel at home.'

'Yes,' Nefer replied quickly, 'we must! For this is my place while my Lord Husband stays. I swear to stand at his side for all the years he breathes the sweet breath of life.'

They entered the central hall which led to smaller rooms. Clearly these were where all business was conducted or visitors entertained. Everywhere oil-lamps gave out their pale yellow light and so, on being led to the third area of the house, which was set aside as the private living quarters, Nefer was able to declare all that she saw to be plain but good.

Bebu lay the sleeping baby on a wide bed that had golden painted legs and a mattress of thin woven leather.

'You will be comfortable here, my lady,' Bebu said, then, having lifted the lid of a large carved wooden chest, 'and there are plenty of good linen sheets.'

Nefer felt her pleasure growing. She turned to the two girls.

'O She With a Merry Smile,' she said to Yati, 'find the bathroom for me. Tell me how it is. And you, my Kanes with Dreamy Eyes, see how we fare outside.'

'The servants of this place could have done just as well,' Bebu remarked tartly,

190

when they had left. 'Why send your own on such a menial task?'

'Because from Yati and Kanes I will hear nothing but the truth,' Nefer replied serenely. 'I have come to trust them almost as greatly as I love and trust you. Where are Paihuti and Uronarti, by the way?'

'Gone to the cook and to oversee the kitchens,' Bebu laughed. 'You know how Paihuti is, how fussy he can be. I swear by Set, he'll finish up with having Uronarti as bad as he is. That young man and my husband seem to really get on and—' here Bebu's eyes twinkled and she laughed in a merry knowing way, 'my lady, have you seen the lovelorn looks Kanes keeps sending Uronarti's way?'

'No,' Nefer had to admit. 'I have not.'

'You will give them permission?'

'I will have their names written together on papyrus if that is what they truly wish,' Nefer said and felt suddenly very tired and rather sad. 'Love is not easy to come by, Bebu. And it is often very swift to go.'

'And sometimes it returns through a different window,' Bebu replied.

Yati came rushing in, her face wreathed in smiles.

'My lady,' she gurgled, 'the bathroom is fully lined with good stone slabs on the floor and the walls. It has a lavatory suitable for all needs. But, over all, it is all very manly and bare.'

'Ha!' Bebu sniffed, 'then it is good that I bought jars of sweet perfumed oil and many scent cones, lots of pretty linen cloths and other gentle feminine things. There will be no problem there.'

Shortly after that Kanes came back and said in her quiet, gentle way:

'There is a chariot house outside, my lady, and in the light from the flares, I saw three silos so the Lord Master will have no shortage of grain to grind or to mash for beer. I saw a well, a garden area where sadly no flowers grow. There are horses in the stables. I think I heard cattle. I did not go far enough to see more even though My Lord Amosis has spared no expense where lights are concerned. I—I have come to the conclusion that—' she faltered into silence. By even hinting at having an opinion she had gone too far.

'Go on, Kanes,' Nefer encouraged.

'This is a good place, my lady, but—but run very much for—for a man.'

Yet there were blue lotus flowers waiting for me, Nefer thought. Lots of sweet smelling flowers! Amosis must have had them sent on ahead. He must have bartered for them along the river bank. Yet—yet he told me once that soldiers had little time for flowers. The thought should have charmed her, but she felt tired and dispirited and hardly knew why.

Nesmin awoke and began to cry. At once, four pairs of hands reached out. It was Bebu who handed him to Nefer and said:

'My lady, if you intend to be busy throughout the days, turning this refined barracks into a warming and loving home, should you not consider employing a nursing mother?'

'I will think about it,' Nefer replied. 'But if I do decide that way, the woman's own child must be alive. Breast-mothers without their own young become too possessive by far.'

'I will see to it, my lady.'

'And the child must be a boy, Bebu. It will be nice for Nesmin to have a breast-brother to grow up with. My son will follow in Mighty Warrior's footsteps, I have no doubt of it. It will be good for him to have a beloved companion at arms.'

'Then shall I begin to—'

'No more now, Bebu! I am tired and I will rest.'

Having been bathed and refreshed, Nefer lay on the bed. The night was hot and she was glad of the cool linen sheets. The wooden head-rest was well polished and more comfortable than cushions by far.

It enabled what air there was to swirl against the back of her neck. She lay with Nesmin held jealously in her arms. He was the most precious thing in her life—and quite unmistakably, he looked like Khaleb. She would never be able to forget the Prince while she held his child against her breast. She had tried so hard, had been so desperate not to see Pharaoh's second son in her little baby's face, but the likeness was there and could not be disguised. She felt the hot blood surging to her cheeks. She wanted to run away, hide! But she knew that it was impossible to escape from one's own weak self. She had sinned, and for a little while Khaleb had been the light of Re in her life. He had shown her how to be a real, full-blooded human being. Made her realise for the very first time that perhaps she and Twosre were alike. It was just that her sister could enjoy passion without affection, whereas she, Nefer, needed warmth. Needed the emotion of love as surely as flowers needed the sun. And she had thought Khaleb had felt the same!

A thrill of horror went through her as she remembered Ese's never-ending tirades—and yes, the monstrous woman had been right! She, Nefer, really did prefer a man's devotion, care and desire. God was omnipotent, she accepted that, but she was human. Unlike Ese, she could not live fully and devotedly for Amun. She needed to enjoy all the days of here and now, not wait for ever in the hope of a delicious After Life.

She looked down at the baby in her arms and felt adoration for him. She knew that Ese's god could never reward her enough. Never give her the precious gift that a mere mortal had. Khaleb had presented her with a treasure beyond price, Nesmin. Khaleb had given Amosis a son. In that moment, Nefer knew that her lord husband was the far finer man. A man who forgot to be cold and hard when the baby's minute fingers curled round his large hand. It was her fault that he had now become a man who showed the world a character that was hard and cold. Yes, it was all her fault!

Unbidden, hot tears came to her eyes. She fought them back. Life was too short for regrets, she told herself, and she was a million times more fortunate than most. She must and would count her blessings. But, oh, if only Twosre were here!

She fell asleep and dreamed that she saw Twosre in Lord Amosis's arms. She heard herself calling out from vast distances, 'Sister, please come to me. I have a need of you here. Bring my brother, Sebni with you. I die for the sight of his shy and delicate smile ...'

When Nefer woke the morning had already turned the world red and gold.

Beyond the citadel walls the sun seemed implacable, the silence profound. Barren lands stretched into eternity and to the strange lynx-eyed old woman riding her one humped camel, there came the awesome feeling that she was the only living creature left in the world.

'Amun,' she cried out in a harsh, mad voice. 'If I heard truly, and she is the same Nefer out of Ramose, I know the way to return her to you for Everlasting. In thy name, I swear, I will help her on the way. I have a plan—a good and righteous plan. But first, I must make sure that it is the creature who brought shame on our heads, when she was old enough to know better. God, how I will make her pay!'

The wild high-pitched laugh of an unseen jackal echoed eerily over the rippled waves of the sand. And Ese's mad cackle echoed out to meet it, while the camel continued in its soul-weary, mindless gait ...

The Nile lazily licked the feet of Thebes. Landing stages were piled high with flowers and shrubs, marvellous trees and foreign pottery from the Mediterranean area. There was copper and turquoise from Sinai, lapis lazuli from Asiatic areas, gold came from Nubia and the Indus, silver from Asia

Minor as did perfumes. The marvellous purple dye came from Tyre and wood from the Lebanon.

Ananias, whose name meant, the Cloud of the Lord, knew all about these things and made good use of them all.

Ananias lived in splendour and he owned many silos of grain, fat cattle and slaves. He was a proud and artistic man, and beloved by all the rich and noble women. The work of Ananias was an ever increasing source of wonder and delight. Each full moon Ananias opened the door of his house for the ladies to come in. There, in the light from a window was the stand that held a single, magnificent bejewelled collar. Sometimes the marvel would glow against white linen so fine that it seemed like a cloud. On other occasions, creations would twinkle, sparkle and beguile, against black. Usually, then the collars would hold the exquisiteness of rubies, and lace patterns of gold. Mauve the most valued colour of all was usually reserved for the milk-white deliciousness of pearls.

To be the proud owner of one of Ananias's collars was to be one step away from the delights of the Second World. If you were rich and important, a somebody, male or female, then you wore one of Ananias's famous collars of jewels. It was unwritten law in the high society

197

of Thebes, and the wily Ananias, who had fostered and nurtured the law, chuckled richly and searched for even richer and rarer things.

Sebni did not think or know much of this as he stood looking at the closed door of Ananias's house. He saw only that the collar Twosre had desired must have gone. An instinct so strong that it was almost a physical pain, told Sebni that the closed door was an omen, an omen of the shutting out of Twosre's love for him. Because he knew she loved him, he told himself so, over and over again. It was just that she was wild, that her hot blood made her cruel as well as a thing of fire. Yes, the fire of Re, she burned so at one's heart and soul.

Once, many years ago, his hateful, irascible uncle had said that the daughters of Per Ibsen's house had the power in them to destroy him. Sebni had shivered and felt afraid and he had known that rend and wound and tear and beat, crush and destroy though she might, Twosre was the goddess in his soul and he was as helpless as a child in the spell she cast.

Unexpectedly the keeper swung open the gates and a small, merry, rotund little man came through and saw Sebni disconsolately kicking his heels outside.

'Can I help you?' Ananias asked, his

large, soft brown eyes alight with smiles.

'Oh—er—the blue collar—it is gone?'

'To a young prince out to impress his best ever love,' Ananias laughed. 'But I have other splendid things inside.'

'The same as the blue?'

Ananias shrugged.

'Where would the pleasure be in acquiring of a collar that could be duplicated? But come inside, do! I see by the pectoral you wear that you are a member of the Per Ibsen House? A noble seat, lord. Very noble indeed.'

'Yes. I am the Son of that establishment,' Sebni replied proudly.

'Then I will show you something very special,' Ananias told him. 'And you are honoured, for you are the first person to set eyes on this piece. The gemstones are from far distant African lands. To be honest, from deep inside the Earth Goddess herself. The Star-Stones have been worked on, and magic has been performed. Come. You will see.'

Sebni, who had followed this man into a large and gracious room was not listening, he was looking at the collar nestling against a cloth of soft cornflower-blue. Diamonds like minute tears, diamonds that glittered and glistened and twinkled and sparkled. Diamonds that held the red of fire, the green of the great oceans, blue of the sky, and the arc of the rainbow. Every conceivable irradiance that could flash and reflect the rays of light, the gold of the sun.

'What would you ask?' Sebni's voice was little more than a whisper as he stared as if hypnotised by the baubles that would buy him Twosre's arms and lips and love.

'I would need an estate,' Ananias laughed. 'And I would need a house full of servants and slaves. These stones are a great rarity. Pharaoh would snap at them for his Great Wife were it not for the expense of the wars. However, it does not matter. You must be a person of property, a man owning animals, grain and slaves. Offer me an estate and a bargain might be made.'

'Why a whole estate?' Sebni faltered. 'Are you not already a wealthy man?'

'I can never be too rich, nor own too much,' Ananias replied. 'Because, you see, my fine young man, I was once a mere slave. I was given my freedom by a good mistress who loved the fine collars I made. Every day since, I have breathed a solemn oath. It is that I will not die surrounded by the dire poverty into which I was born.'

'I—I will think of your words,' Sebni said quietly and the sweat came out on to his forehead and glistened there. Then he was outside and walking away from the house that held within its walls a magnificent collar worth more than all he had in the world. He walked blindly on until at last he reached the house that belonged to his horrible uncle, through the wide hall and to his room that was the sanctuary and shrine of all his hidden dreams.

And once he was alone, Sebni gave himself up to thoughts that scorched and withered and repelled almost as much as they enticed, seduced and tempted. And over and above all, there were thoughts of the blue stones that Twosre could not have and the white Star-Stones that he wanted her to possess. Then he made up his mind. He knew what he must do. He picked up the long, lean very heavy statue of the Holy Cat—and like a sleepwalker, he left the privacy of his room ...

Sebni shivered as he waited by the river and still Twosre did not come. He became absorbed at looking across the water, to the distant West Bank that shimmered like a land of ghosts in the haze. Valley of Kings, he thought, Valley of Queens, City of the Dead. A picture danced in his mind, of bodies soaking in natron, waiting to be dried and to be bandaged, then entombed.

'Amun!' Sebni whispered to himself.

'What is it that makes me see things and feel things like this on an evening by the sweet peace of the river?' And even as he asked the question he knew the answer. It was the need and desire to be with Twosre again that was driving him slowly mad.

Then he heard her singing and he began running towards her, almost sobbing in his self-abasement. He reached her and thought the sunlight had turned her to gold.

'Twosre!' He breathed her name, and felt his heart squeeze because she was so beautiful.

She tossed her black mane out of her eyes and her dark eyes were pools of bright anticipation.

'The blue stones?' Her voice was a coaxing whisper. 'Did you get your little sister the collar of beautiful blue stones?'

'No!' he gasped. 'They had gone.' Even as the words left his lips the suspicion rose in his mind like a lecherous green cloud. He felt himself shaking and the suspicion was so real and malignant that he felt momentarily sick. 'But you knew they had gone, didn't you?'

She pursed her lips and began to whistle, a light, high, teasing tune and he stood there and the suspicion grew until he forgot himself long enough to find the strength to grasp hold of her arm.

'You've been with Prince Khaleb, haven't you? Answer me. You've been with Khaleb and he bought you the collar you desired.'

She was laughing at him now and he stepped back. The ripple of her laughter made the nausea in him rise and recede and rise again, and all the time he was picturing Twosre with Khaleb. And all the time too, he was picturing the collar that was above value, even that of blue stones.

'You won't laugh when you see what I have acquired for you,' he said and his sickle-shaped eyes were glittering with hurt. 'You'll wish you hadn't been so cruel to me, then.'

Suddenly the laughter stopped bubbling in Twosre's throat and she was angry.

'I am not cruel to you, Sebni. I have never been cruel or felt cruel. From the beginning I have refused you, My Brother, and from the beginning you have tormented yourself. You want all of me, Sebni, and I am not prepared to give that much away.'

'You have always been wild and wilful— and cruel!'

'Think what you must, Sebni, but this I will say. Other men are happy to accept only what I am prepared to give. They leave me content, happy and free. You

203

want me to be your Woman of the House. To have our names linked together forever on the temple papyrus. You want to own me, Sebni. I will only be owned by myself!'

Before he could beg her, plead with her for forgiveness, she had whirled round and left him alone. Twosre's eyes were bright with love and need, hurt and hate, desire and the sense of being damned as she ran away.

She was meeting Khaleb again because she felt she must. Knew she must. Accepted that he needed only to raise one brow and go to him she must. He treated her as he treated any female, high born or low, as a slut. She always gave as good as she got. She played with men as he played with women and left them as easily, with no further backward glance. She threw back her head and lipped him, treating him as she would a peasant, and gave him not one ounce of servility or respect—as his position deserved. He could have her killed. He could kill her himself. He let her live—and suffer.

We torture each other, Twosre thought. And have done so since we played in the palace gardens at our little childhood games. Khaleb is cruel to me—and I am cruel to Sebni. Though I am now being wicked I will continue to pretend that I do not know that my adopted brother is following me.

Khaleb was waiting for her, in a reed filled world of sunlight and shade and she ran to him, her face alight with pleasure, her eyes full of pain.

'O Prince!' she cried. 'How is it that you send for me yet again? Wouldn't a river woman do just as well?'

'As whores go, you're the best.'

'And ladies?'

'You are better than any lady I know.'

'In what way?' she cried, playing his game for all its worth. 'Tell me how it is that I am better than any high born woman you know?'

'You can play the game my way.'

'Only because your way also happens to be my own. I relish my feelings, Khaleb. I enjoy my needs. I am not drawn to you as a person, O Mighty Prince. Only as a great and powerful bull that has the strength and stamina to satisfy a herd of holy cows.'

'Be careful,' he laughed. 'The goddess Hathor might be displeased at what she hears.'

'How can I fear Hathor when what I am saying so greatly tickles the fancy of my lord?'

'Do it! Do it to me now.'

She fluttered her lashes and pretended a coyness that, she knew and he knew, was quite foreign to her.

'Do what, my lord?'

'Tickle my fancy.'

She laughed and then, because she knew that Sebni was hiding quite near and watching her with fever bright eyes, she stepped towards Khaleb and began to make a great play at teasing and fondling him.

'You know how to get to me,' he told her and there was already a hotness in his glance and his hands reached out to begin some fondling of his own. 'Indeed, I believe that you are the only one who can make my heart beat too fast.'

She was leaning against him, teasing him with her ripe warm body, gazing up into his face with her large velvet-soft eyes.

'My heart is beating too, O Khaleb,' she said huskily, 'because you are a bull and I am beloved of Hathor. Will you serve me?'

'Right now!' he said, arrogant and sure.

'Oh no!' she laughed and turned from him and ran through the reeds towards the river. At the bank she stopped and turned to face him, taunting. 'I am not that anxious, my lord. I like to play first. I like to be teased and I like to be coaxed. And only when I am good and ready will you serve me.'

In swift deft movements she pulled her

shoulder straps down and stepped out of her fine linen dress. She stood there, poised before him, naked apart from the jewels she wore.

There was an excitement tearing through her because she knew that her body was the object of desire for not one man, but two. She pirouetted before Khaleb, turning so that she knew Sebni could also get a full view. And she felt like a goddess in her power, as with fluid grace she arched her body and dived into the river.

She laughed up at the sky, to the sun, to the silver crested tongues of the river, and as he caught her, Khaleb. The water swirled round them, enclosing them, embracing them as they began their passion play in the womb of the Nile.

After a while Twosre forgot Sebni and the thrill her power over him gave her. She saw, felt and needed only Khaleb. Her desire took over and she returned the Prince's passion with one greater than his own.

Sebni stood under a palm tree until the moon had taken over the sky and a million dust flecks became pin-points of light in the strong silver rays. Sebni was only half aware of the tight band of pressure in his head. His mind was full of thoughts, torments—rivers of thoughts and they were a repugnant reservoir of rage, frustration and jealousy. And the thoughts were so strong, so stinging, that they made dull sounds in his head and the sound was a desperate requiem for Twosre's love.

A picture kept dancing before his eyes. A picture of Twosre in the arms of Khaleb, and yet every so often the features of the Prince contorted into the full bloated face of his own uncle. Sebni knew that he would one day kill the Prince and shout with joy at the thing he had done.

Twosre, safe in the comfort of Per Ibsen House, stirred in her sleep and smiled and curled herself round like a kitten. And the moon that streamed through the windows showed that Twosre's smile was a sad smile and two tears trembled on her long dark lashes. Twosre dreamed of the only man she had ever loved. The man who had been as ruthless and cruel to her as he had been to Nefer. Yet, in the very earliest of times, she had beaten the Prince hands down. She had paid him out, simply by going to his elder brother, Amenhotep, the Heir Apparent, and telling tales.

Oh how Khaleb had paid her back! He had seduced her beloved sister and now he used her, picking her up and putting her down when he chose. Every so often he threw down a present, paying her for the favours, just as he would a courtesan, neither knowing nor caring that now the colour of the blue stones was like so much wasted chaff in her hands. But she should not take it out on Sebni, nor worry Beloved Mother and her Lord Father with her wild and wilful ways. No she really shouldn't.

Per Ibsen sat on his chair and looked as fine and noble as a king. He was listening to what the hard faced Law Official had to say. It seemed impossible, but it was true.

Sebni's uncle was dead. He had died horribly from multiple vicious blows. His murderer was undoubtedly deranged—and there was growing suspicion that the killer was in fact Sebni, adopted son of Per Ibsen himself.

'I cannot believe this thing,' Per Ibsen said. 'My son is quiet. He keeps his thoughts to himself, but he is not mad.'

'He is now a man of property, my lord,' the Law Official said. 'Or was! I understand that he signed over his inheritance to Ananias. Ananias has made haste to take up residence there. Understandable perhaps? Many people act with great haste where property is concerned. If they do not, Pharaoh's Scribes will list them among those taken over by the throne now. O lord, can you please tell me where I can find Sebni? Who are his friends? What of your daughter, Nefer? Were they not close?'

Per Ibsen shook his head.

'Sebni was once going to take my daughter Nefer as his wife. However, nothing came of it.'

'Where may I find your daughter?' the Official insisted.

Per Ibsen did not like this tone and replied haughtily: Sebni will not be with Nefer. She married someone else.'

'Perhaps that is why Sebni went berserk?'

'No! It all happened many months ago. Find my youngest daughter and then perhaps you will also find my adopted son. My daughter Twosre will tell you nothing but the truth.'

'And where may we find your youngest child, my lord?' the cold eyed man asked, his impatience held in stiff control.

'I do not know,' Per Ibsen replied in all honesty. 'But I will send for the Lady of the House, and my servants and slaves. Someone will know.'

But the lovely Lady Zarah did not know, nor did the servants or slaves. How could they know? Was not Twosre the wild one, the naughty one, the one who listened only to her own heart? How could they tell who Twosre was with? Twosre told only that which she wanted to tell—and she came and went exactly as she chose.

'Then I will tell you where I myself can be found at all times,' the Law Official said coldly. 'When Twosre of Per Ibsen House returns, I wish to see her. I also wish to see Sebni, your son.'

He left walking stiffly, his air of authority making all the servants bow low.

Lady Zarah's eyes were wide and afraid and she clung to Per Ibsen.

'My lord,' she said frantically. 'There is the ownership of property at stake here. Pharaoh's advisers will have an interest in this.'

'We will have to wait,' Per Ibsen replied bleakly. 'But of them both, our beloved Twosre will know best what to do.'

'My lord—what of Sebni? My heart is sore, afraid for him. The Law Official is wrong, wrong, wrong!'

'Morning Light,' Per Ibsen groaned, 'the boy has seemed very strange of late, but I did not believe him to be mad—and I refuse to accept such a thought even now.'

He held Zarah close as she began to weep ...

Sebni's feet swished through the dry reeds that edged the bank of the river. He felt triumphant, and the anticipation of Twosre's lazy almost condescending sensuality made the wild beat of his heart begin its echoing in his head. There was that other experience, too! The swift strength, that moment of utter and absolute power—that exquisite erotomania and the excessive reverence he had felt before, that moment of complete potency. Now he was like a god. He had life and death in his hands—and the collar!

Sebni smiled through his bright half-moon eyes as he looked down at the precious package he carried. This then would be his ticket to the wonder of Elysian Fields. He began talking to the package and chuckling until the reedy echo of his own voice reached into his sensibility and he stopped, frowned and felt lost.

He came upon Twosre as she lay in her secret place in the tall, seeding grasses, and he went on his knees and gave her the collar. The magnificent creation that she had known nothing of until Abu, He Who Had Taken Paihuti's Place, had crept from the house to warn her.

As Twosre looked into the now very anxious sickle-shaped eyes, she felt a deep anguish. She had learned what he had done to acquire the collar and she accepted that the guilt of this thing lay on her shoulders alone. And she put out her slim tanned hands and tenderly cupped his face between them and kissed him gently on the lips.

'Sebni,' she said and her voice was crooning and incredibly gentle, 'Dearest

Brother, you must listen to me. I am going to get my things and we are going away. You will come?'

He nodded and knew that heaven was his.

'You promise to stay and wait for me here, Sebni, my love?'

He nodded again, and lay down in the rushes and closed his eyes.

Twosre ran, silently and quickly, keeping to the loneliest places, until, unnoticed, she reached the Law Officer's place. She handed a servant the unopened package.

'Please give this to your master,' she said. 'And ask him to return it to the one who is named Ananias, Cloud of the Lord. Explain that Sebni, Son of Per Ibsen's House has decided not to go through with the agreement he made. He has agreed to Pharaoh's wishes instead. To leave his uncle's land and property under the auspices of the throne. Master Sebni is going away from this place, to join the wandering peoples, among whom his own father was born.'

Before the servant had a chance to reply, Twosre had whirled round and run.

'Where are we going?' Sebni asked, a long time later. 'Not that I mind, so long as I am with you.'

'We will follow the road by the river bank,' she told him. 'Until we reach the

213

place of the old man, Pepi. Remember him? How dear a friend he is to beloved Mother and Thickneck? He is a fisherman as you know with three strapping sons. I am hoping that, when it is safe, they will take us on a journey by boat.'

'When it is safe?' he asked, puzzled.

'Yes, but do not worry, Sebni. Everything will be all right if you leave things to me. Will you do that?'

He nodded, frowning a little.

'But you will let me look after you?' he asked at last. 'You do not mind?'

Her dark eyes danced and swam with a myriad of unshed tears.

'I want you to look after me, Sebni,' she said. 'And I want our beloved Nefer to look after us both.'

'Yes,' he said. 'That is good. Nefer is kind and wise and understanding. I did not realise that we were going to visit her.'

'You love her as I do?'

'With all my heart,' he replied and suddenly he was smiling and holding her hand.

They walked together, along the river way, just as they had done as children. And the thought of Nefer, who had always been so sweet and quiet and gentle made them both feel happy and secure again. Twosre began to sing the Song of the Nile and Sebni joined in.

'It is a long journey,' Twosre said after a while.

'I do not mind,' Sebni replied. 'With you I would happily journey to the end of the world. But I think you know that.'

'I never knew just how much, how deeply you felt and—Sebni?'

'Yes?'

'I—I wish that I had not been so unkind.'

His face screwed up as he smiled.

'You never were,' he told her. 'It is just that you were always more adventurous than Nefer. And—and you did not always stop and think.'

'I wish I were more like my sister,' Twosre said wistfully. 'She is beautiful inside and out. I am very wicked, you know.'

'Everyone can see that you are a goddess,' he told her. 'A wonderful feline daughter of Bast. I cannot live without you, Twosre.'

'Yes, I know that—now,' she whispered and her heart went out to him because once again there was so much anguished uncertainty in his eyes. 'And Nefer shall know too. She will understand how it is, Sebni, and she will help us. Her Lord Husband is all powerful. At Kerma we will be safe.'

'And together,' Sebni spoke quietly.

'That is all that really counts.'

'Yes, we will be together and with our beloved Nefer,' Twosre whispered and smiled through her tears.

CHAPTER SEVEN

The moons waxed and waned and Nefer was happy and relaxed. Nesmin's progress was good, and with each passing day his awareness grew. He was a happy, contented baby with dark hair, rosy cheeks and a face usually wreathed in smiles. Everyone adored him. Nesmin was taken to see Amosis's pride and joy every day. Four especially splendid war chariots decorated with rosettes and bars of silver and gold. The four horses, Ra, Horus, Sphinx and Duat were magnificent. They were pampered and spoiled and had their own army of slaves who cared for them and acted as guards.

Sometimes Minya, the governor's wife would tease:

'I swear that Amosis loves those animals and chariots above his own life. Though I grant you when they are on parade, they are a most impressive sight.'

Minya, a tall, charming woman, had

taken to Nefer. It was she who found a suitable breast mother for Nesmin. The name of the young woman was Oyahbe—The Moon Flower. She was pretty, round faced, with eyes as soft and gentle as those of the holy Hathor. Nefer loved her on sight. Pepy, her son, was good, quiet, round faced and had solemn eyes.

'We shall be as sisters, Oyahbe,' she said. 'Tell me the name of your sweet baby boy?'

'Pepy, my lady, the same as his Lord Father, who is a scribe in the army.'

'Oh?' Nefer laughed and kissed Nesmin who she was cradling in her arms. 'Look at my child, Oyahbe, see how he smiles! A scribe you say? I did not realise that the army needed to have scribes writing down words.'

Affronted the young woman replied:

'They are always very necessary, my lady. They log the storing and despatching of supplies. They enlist recruits and tabulate mercenaries. They send communications into the field and back to Pharaoh in Thebes. They are royal record-keepers and do a very important job.

'But of course, dearest Oyahbe,' Nefer replied quickly. 'I was not meaning to decry. Oh, just look at the boys! They are smiling at each other. I am sure that they are going to be very close friends.'

Oyahbe nodded happily at that. Just then, Bebu came in. She was frowning and looking worried.

'My lady,' she said, 'I am puzzled. When the gates were opened this morning there was a strange old woman among the crowds. A matter of insignificance one would have thought. But I overheard gossiping slaves. It seems that the old woman was making enquiries about you. She asked your name, and your title before you became Chief Lady of Amosis's House. When she learned all that she could, they said she laughed in a wild, frightening way. She said that by having your names written together on the Holy Scarab, you had proved a point she made many years ago.'

'How strange!' Nefer was mystified, but most of her attention was on Nesmin who was chuckling at the sound of the little silver bells he was waving in his hand. 'Where is the old woman now?'

'Back to the desert, my lady. It is all very odd.'

'Perhaps she wonders about the wife of the Chief Soldier of the South, Bebu. After all, our Lord Amosis is a very important man.'

'I made a few enquiries myself,' Bebu admitted. 'And my puzzlement grows. The old woman is believed to be in contact with the Spirits of God. She talks to them, and sees what we do not. She is a relative of one of the Kushite Kings named Hapdjefi, and has his sympathetic ear. Hapdjefi's realm is by the oasis beyond Abu Simbel. The King is a very rich and powerful man. He has often spoken out against Egypt's rule over his land.'

'Then Hapdjefi is my Lord Husband's enemy, Bebu, is that it? And through him, the old woman is our enemy too?'

'It means that you must be careful, my lady,' Bebu's tone held fear. 'It is all too peculiar!'

'While I live under my Lord Husband's roof, I am safe, Bebu. Of all people, you should know that.'

When she was alone, Nefer's thoughts turned to Amosis. His attitude towards her was puzzling and left her feeling piqued. He spent far too much time with his men. A man's man, rough and tough, he exercised with them, practised with them, laughed and joked and was at one with them. Then, when he left the men, he'd go to the stables and make a fuss of the animals there, especially Ra, Horus, Duat and Sphinx. On returning to the house he'd usually be accompanied by high ranking officers. He was particularly interested in the timing and planning of the directions to be taken of armed patrols. Special hand-picked warriors were always on full alert outside the citadel walls. On the rare occasions Nefer found him alone, he would smile and reply to her courtesy talk, but he had distanced himself from her. He made her feel shut out and this affected her, in a cold tomb-like way.

One evening, Nefer found him thoughtfully looking down into the woven reed basket that held the sleeping Nesmin. His expression was kind so she was encouraged to approach and said:

'My lord, our son grows more strong and more beautiful by the day. He recognises his friends, and he laughs out loud. He is very active, and he loves the little wooden horse you gave him. He will be a skilled charioteer, or at the very least, a great horseman one day. I take him regularly to see your prize horses and the gold decorated chariots that you use for ceremonies. He loves them all.'

'He is a fine child,' Amosis's tone held affection. 'He is a son to be proud of and I am well content.'

Nefer's heart sang. Amosis clearly adored the happy, contented, quite delightful baby boy. Also, Amosis was kind and generous to Pepy, the little breast-brother. But it was Nesmin who gained his full attention and care. Neither by look nor deed did he give way anything except true love for his adopted son. This even though Nesmin's likeness of Khaleb was more pronounced the older he grew. Nefer had the courage to continue:

'He—he usually is a little charmer,' she said carefully. 'He knows how to get his own way.'

She waited uneasily for his reply.

'Which will stand him in good stead when he's a man,' Amosis acknowledged and grinned in a wide wicked way. 'Personally, I was never blessed in that direction.'

'I—I would not say that!'

'Oh?' His smile was wryly humorous.

'There is more attraction when a man is truly masculine, my lord,' Nefer pointed out in a quietly determined way.

He was looking at her very intently now. She was vaguely conscious of the velvet look of the sky through the window behind him and the silky, silvery sheen of the moon. There seemed to be a great stillness in the world, only the muted breathing of two baby boys who lay sleeping in their separate reed baskets. Such sweet breath, like the gentle whisper of innocent prayers. It was a hushed, emotional moment and suddenly Nefer felt near to tears.

'Come,' Amosis said quietly, 'we will leave them in peace. Shall we talk, Nefer?

Shall we spend a little time together? Indeed, shall we be very private—and go to my room?'

Her heart was thudding against her sides, but her smile was serene.

'It will be an honour, my lord,' she said quietly and felt that she was on the threshold of one of the most mysterious and personal experiences that would ever happen to her.

She walked at his side, tiny against him. She felt that she needed to talk, but could find nothing to say. Her throat felt tight, her mouth dry. Her heart was hammering even more wildly, and she found herself silently praying to god that she did not displease her husband, did not let him down.

They reached his special place. There was very little in the room. An outsized bed, some chairs and a stool with leather plaited seats. There was also a stand on which stood a wine jar. A statue of the war god stood in his niche on the wall. Against plain blue wash, war shields were arranged, and standard poles bearing Pharaoh's Emblem. Also there, was the emblem of the South. Very impressive too was the Mighty Warrior's own flag bearing his name interwoven with that of Harmachis, the God of the Rising Sun. Intrigued out of her self-consciousness Nefer asked:

'Why Harmachis, Amosis?'

'Because he rises triumphantly out of the darkness,' he replied. 'There were many years of my young life that seemed exceptionally grim.' He sat down on one of the chairs.

'I am sorry,' she whispered. 'I feel that it must have been my fault.'

'Yours?' He raised his brows in surprise. 'How can that be?'

'You—you were sent away in shame because of me.'

'By Ese!'

'You were treated very badly.'

'By the army!'

'You have good reason to feel anger and to rail at your fate.'

'I have even more grounds for shouting out in triumph and feeling great joy. Like Harmachis, I have survived the night. Like him I feel anticipation, for I await with confidence, for the full glory of the day.'

'Amosis, how grand you sound—and proud.'

'I have a high position and I have the respect and regard of the men. My home is comfortable. I am rich in friends, property, animals and slaves. The honours I have won in many battles of war are piled up high enough even to warrant Pharaoh's delight. And then, Nefer, I have Nesmin. Also, I have you. Because of all these things, yes, I am proud.'

'You put me at the very end of your list,' she said wistfully. 'Am I of so little account?'

'You are of very great account, Small Person. I have grown accustomed to having you here. I am accustomed to your face.'

'And that is all?' she asked, feeling rebuffed.

He leaned over her and she wished that she was taller. He was so imposing, so awe-inspiring, so strong! He was watching her, examining her and even though she wanted to, she dared not look away. At last he said softly,

'It must be your choice, Nefer. There will be no going back.'

'My lord,' she whispered, 'there was no going back from the moment Pharaoh made me your wife.'

'Then you are quite sure?'

'Yes,' she murmured and trembled as his large hands reached out to lift her up into his arms. He was holding her close now and she could feel the heat of his body, the power and the desire.

'Quite sure?' he asked again and he cupped her chin in his hand in order to tilt her head so that he could stare directly into her eyes.

'I am certain, my lord.'

He frowned at that.

'One day you will forget to call me "lord", and you will say "I love you, Amosis" but until that time your acceptance will do. You are very beautiful, Nefer. I have wanted you for some time. Now I will take the reward that Pharaoh so graciously gave me and glory in his name.'

His voice had changed, become hard and angry. With a sinking heart Nefer realised that this then was no game of love that her Lord Husband played. King Thutmose had presented Amosis with a ripe fruit and he was now about to imbibe. It was as cold and as matter of fact as that. She wanted to laugh and she wanted to cry. She did neither, merely lay in his arms in silent obedience. Then he pulled her against him, hard. There was no escape from his mouth. His lips bruised against her own. His hand was tearing at her dress.

'You're beautiful.' His voice was almost guttural against her mouth. 'And you are mine.'

He effortlessly lay her down on to the bed. Then he was above her. His arms were like cruel bands as they arched her against him. He seemed to be driven by a kind of madness. Whether he was angry, or guilty, she neither knew nor cared. All she was conscious of was the domination of the man and of how helpless she was.

225

She was unable to keep her mood of calm acceptance. She was drowning in her own awakening senses and tears of shame came to her eyes.

Her Lord Husband took her with power and expertise. She felt that she had been overwhelmed by a vast plain of heartbreak and pain. He was large and strong and the rhythm of his body fitting into her own held an agony. Yet she knew that it would be an even greater hell if he stopped. Gradually her responses became as fiery as her Lord Husband. She gasped and cried out his name. He took her to a realm of passion such as she had never experienced before. No, not even with Khaleb.

His movements grew more powerful, more demanding, more intense. She was reaching upwards, gasping, flying higher. Then it seemed that the world exploded and she was part of an eternity composed of shooting stars. There was a stinging moment of suspension, then the slow, feathery return, back into the hard reality of Mighty Warrior's arms.

They lay there, together, in silence for a long time. Nefer was too afraid almost to breathe. Please, she thought wildly, Oh please god Amun, do not let him be contemptuous of me. Do not let him throw me into the dust of cold disrespect.

He cleared his throat and she felt her heart lurch in fear.

'You are the Lady of my House,' he said coolly. 'I am well pleased.'

She could not speak, dared not, and having looked at her long and thoughtfully, he went on:

'Well, Nefer, perhaps it will be better for you if you now return to your own bed.'

Dismissed, she gratefully slipped away, unable to bear the knowledge that Amosis had taken her out of passion and not romantic love.

Amosis lay very still. He should be at peace but was not. He thought of the girl his wife had been, and of Ese's curse. It was working, oh yes! Unhappiness was all around them, like an almost physical thing. Worse, he was being moved emotionally in spite of all the power of his iron will. He could not dismiss the picture Nefer made as she walked like a sliver of light and loveliness through his house. He thought again how she looked while holding Nesmin in her arms. How shy she seemed, how ready to run away, just like a little fawn. Yet she had tried to be brave for all that. Had sparked up to him at times and, may the gods help her, she had tried to do her wifely duty. Had even gone so far as putting on an act just for his sake.

227

His thoughts made him angry. He left his bed and walked to the room where servants had left platters of food. He put a lamp flame against blackened wicks. Fresh lights glowed like fireflies in the shadowed room, but the expression in Amosis's eyes became more bleak.

He turned his attention to the meal and broke off a thick chunk of honey-bread and took a strip of cold meat. Through the great open window he could see the sky and found himself remembering how Nefer had once spoken about the difference between moon people and people of the sun. He was a full blooded day person, she had told him and there had been a wide eyed innocence about her.

He clenched his fists together and groaned. Well, he had shown her that he had no time for all her fanciful sort of stuff—even though he'd proved how red blooded he could be. Where was the harm in that? By Set and all devils, the girl was his wife!

He remembered how she had looked at him when he'd sent her away. Her face had been pale in the faint starlight. What a weary little face, so wistful and worn. She'd been like a child who'd been slapped and was bewildered and wondering what she had done wrong. As she crept away he thought he'd seen the glint of tears on those long, dark lashes. Yes, tears!

At that moment Amosis hated himself.

Later that day, Nefer walked into the garden area of the house. Clearly it was very true that Amosis had not time to spare on flowers. Suddenly it was desperately important that she put her own ideas into being. There must be fine linen hanging, glowing with colours, on the walls. An artist must come in and paint gracious frescoes where there had been only plain wash before. And most dear to her heart, there would be a garden. There would be trees and shrubs and flowers. The house had its own well, which was good. She would give one of the slaves the honourable duty of watering and continuously caring for all the new and lovely growing things.

She tried to concentrate but her husband's face kept rising in the air before her. A strong, quiet, granite face that held the timeless nobility of the giant carved statues of the kings. Where had the fine, quiet youth gone, the boy she had so adored all those years ago? The boy had loved her, she was sure. Not so, the man.

Remembering his love-making made her face flame. She had responded to him, cried out his name, and he had told her in a stiff distant way that he was well pleased! Then he had sent her away, back to her own room. Had he rejected her? Had he merely used her because she had been there in his house and—available?

Unable to bear her thoughts any longer, she fell to feverishly making her plans for the garden. It would be, must be very beautiful. It would be a garden fit for the gods. There were trees and shrubs for barter in the banks of Kerma, and, too, Lotus flowers. But there must be seeds, she would have to ask the governor's wife. Minya's garden really was like a desert jewel, full of colour and light.

Nefer suddenly felt too restricted by Amosis's rules. The garden should be a lovely, very personal thing. She wanted to choose what was to be grown, herself. There were no enemies about, all was calm and peaceful, she felt. Perhaps she would risk the journey down into the city and make her way to the warehouses there. She would barter with her own jewels and with her own gold bands. Then, when the garden was a creation of living beauty, the Lord Amosis would look at the Lady of the House with new eyes. Perhaps see her as more than a mere creature to be enjoyed in bed.

She was busily thinking and planning how she would set out her garden when

230

a messenger came hurrying towards her. He stopped before her, crossed his hands over his chest and bowed.

'My lady, a message for your ears alone.'

'Yes?'

'The message is from the second youngest son of Pepi the Fisherman. He sends Health, Strength and Sweet Breath of Life to the Lady Nefer. He says that when it is safe, in just over two full moons from now, he will arrive with special visitors, a man and a woman. They need your help. It is very necessary that they stay out of Thebes for a while. That they remain out of Pharaoh's sight.'

'Thank you,' Nefer replied calmly enough, but inside she felt a terrible fear. A man and a woman needed to escape Thebes and were coming to her for refuge? So! Pharaoh had finally come to realise that her beloved Mother and noble Father had gone out of their way, not once, but several times to keep her away from Pharaoh's gaze. Now in all probability, the Divine One, Thutmose the Third, had come to learn of her affair with Khaleb. This in spite of all the subterfuge! Pharaoh would punish her parents most terribly if they stayed in his sight. So within less than three full moons she would be welcoming them with open arms.

Afraid for them, but utterly happy for

herself, Nefer, clapped her hands together. At once a servant appeared.

'Please,' she said, 'take this man into the house. Look after him well. See to it that he wants for nothing. Also send a message to Lord Amosis, who is with his men. Tell him that the Lady Nefer asks him to please return to the house. Say that she wishes to speak to him of a matter of utmost importance.'

The man servant bowed and led the messenger away to where there was food and wine, beer, fruit and a place to rest. Also a woman slave to lie with him should his passions need to be assuaged.

'My beloved Mother, my dearest Father,' Nefer whispered when she was alone. 'How greatly I have missed you and how anxiously I will wait for the return of each full moon. Amosis will welcome you with open arms, I know it. And you will see your little grandchild for the first time. How you will adore him! How greatly Nesmin will be spoiled!'

Amosis was instructing his officers when Nefer's message came. He inclined his head in his usual polite way, but was inwardly furious at the interruption. He tried to get back to the business in hand, but a hard core of anger and frustration knotted his insides.

He could see Nefer in his mind, feel her, smell the sweet perfume she wore. She had been like fire and flowers in his arms. She was not only a gift from Pharaoh but, too, a gift from beneficent gods. He tried to drown his thought, determined that this one Small Person would never get under his guard again. Never make him feel fresh from torment.

'By Set and all Devils,' Amosis swore under his breath. 'I will never open myself up to the schemes of women. This no matter if they are small and sweet and infinitely beautiful with big sad eyes. Or if they are mad old hags with poison in their veins.'

He remembered Ese and felt murderous. If he had her in his power now, he knew with evil certainty that he would have her stoned to death by the hordes. Indeed, he would be the first to take aim! Ese had ripped away his own little-man happiness, the security of life and love and he had accepted it. Ese had seen the flower of his youth shrivel and die. As for his wife, Nefer, never again would he weaken his own position because of her. He had climbed his way up to a trusted position, wealth and power against almost impossible odds and he'd die before he stepped down again.

Just remembering his early, unformed

years in the army made him sweat. He had arrived, confused by the swift and ruthless banishment from his home, not knowing why! He had been cut to the quick by his mother's tears and his sisters' enforced retirement to their rooms, his father's tight worried face.

'The Lord Per Ibsen's punishment could be terrible. You must go,' he had said—and that had been all. There it was again, something to do with Nefer. He had ground his teeth together and said nothing, his heart torn and bleeding because no one had bothered to say goodbye.

After that he had tried. By god, how he had tried to fit into his slot in the army, to do what his superiors asked.

His mind went back to how he had been then. Enthusiastic, young, desperately eager to get things right. All the new recruits' lives were hard, but his was worse. He was picked on, bullied, humiliated before them all. Puzzled at his lot, cut to the quick because the others were ordered to treat him for the pariah he was, he pressed on. Never complaining, never crying for mercy, and that had seemed to make things even worse.

He was put on duties, the hours and endurance tests which would have killed many lesser men. He was cruelly punished for errors that in others merited no blame.

He was whipped and kicked and made to do things considered to be almost too menial for slaves, shut up in isolation too often to count. But solitary or not, he was almost always miserable and immensely alone.

Gradually his puzzlement and grief was replaced by an ironhard resolve. He would never give in. Never! He would survive their unwarranted punishments, their bestialities, and one day, he swore, he would beat them all at their own game. So he had grimly gone on through the long lonely days, beaten but unbowed. Then one night, when the purple night was ablaze with stars that were the world's living tears, a scrawny little man had crept out to the solitary post where Amosis had been put in punishment yet again.

'May the gods be with you,' the man said. 'Open your mouth and drink. Later there will be bread.'

'You—you risk your life—for me?'

'For a dog that has suffered as much as you, my son. Drink!'

And at last, he had found a friend. The wizened little man was a scribe who held much respect. He was called He Who Writes The Truth. One day, He Who Writes The Truth said:

'Young man, I have made it my business to learn many things. You are

235

accused of trying to seduce a child, the accuser, a woman named Ese. Your uncle also accuses you of bringing great dishonour to his house. Living, you are an embarrassment to him. He wants you dead.'

'I did not do this thing. I swear it!'

'I believe you, my son, and I feel there is a dark secret your uncle bears in his heart. He has the name of a proud and brave warrior, but I feel that he has been up to something very underhand.'

'You are mistaken in this!' he had replied and felt stunned. 'And if it is true that my uncle wishes me dead, tell me the reason?'

'No one knows why, but I am sure that I'm not mistaken,' the old man replied. 'But, take heart. You are young and strong and you have the will to survive.'

'My own father,' Amosis murmured wretchedly, 'has turned his face away from me. My mother weeps. My sisters do not speak my name. I will suffer, yet it feels as if I am dead.'

'You are not alone, my boy. There are many who feel much as you do now. I have written some words on papyrus, and, too, they will be painted on walls and chiselled on stone. In years ahead, when we are all but distant whispers in the wind, my words will be accepted and understood. I am sure of this, because I know that men will never change.'

'Tell me the lines, He Who Writes The Truth. I want to hear.'

In his thin old voice the Scribe recited the lines that peoples in the far away future would read.

'Come I will speak to you of the ills of the infantryman. He is awakened while there is still an hour for sleeping. He is driven like a jackass and he works till the sun sets beneath the darkness of night. He hungers and his belly aches. He is dead while he lives.'

Amosis had nodded, his expression bleak. 'Death might be preferable to some of the treatment I have received,' he murmured, his young voice now harsh with misery because of the ruthlessness. 'I cannot believe that Ramses, who I looked up to—my own uncle? I do not understand? Why have I been sent to the most loathsome of places and received treatment usually reserved for criminals? I could bear the torment more easily if I were anywhere else but here.'

'You do not wish to be an infantryman?' the old man enquired. 'Can there be any easy road for the poor, ordinary man in the army? Of course there cannot!'

'I was sent here as helpless as a trussed goose. I was reviled and, deepest cut of all, my own father did not come to wish me goodbye. Oh Scribe,' Amosis had said earnestly, 'I would never have chosen this! But I would cheerfully shovel dung to be with the horses. I find them such magnificently noble beasts.'

'I will do all that I can,' the old man had promised. 'I will try.'

It had taken two years of toil and misery, endurance and stoicism, but at last the young Amosis had been granted his wish. By that time he had become a trained fighter, a winner, a champion in the game of war. Several successful campaigns had made him a hero. He had his choice of the good things in life and he indulged with vigour. He was courteous to the women he took, but thought of them as chattels. He had come to the conclusion that they were all like the pretty child whose treachery was still making him pay. Oh yes, Nefer, that was where the cause had to be. She had caused mischief of some kind, been vindictive and cruel to have made his own uncle treat him so. He had loathed and detested the memory of her and had sworn to the gods: 'One day I will make her pay. I will make her wish that she was dead!'

Many, many moons later, with his uncle killed in a battle in the West and his dear old friend the Scribe long dead, he had learned the truth. Nefer of Ramose House had been as innocent as he. He had mentally forgiven her long since, but his distrust of women remained unchanged.

Now, Nefer had become the Woman of his House, his First Lady Wife! Already, he found that she was getting under his skin. He was finding it almost impossible to get her out of his thoughts. He kept seeing the sweet beauty of her face. No wonder Khaleb had gone out of his way to seduce her. She was like a child in the ways of the world. She loved Khaleb and probably always would. Amosis clenched his hands together. He would fight off her charms, keep her in her place. He had to, for his own peace of mind.

It was late when Amosis finally condescended to return to the house. Nefer hurried to greet him. She was wringing her hands, pale and distraught.

'Amosis,' she said urgently, 'I have received a message from an old friend of my family. My parents are in grave danger. They are coming here. They need your help.'

He frowned.

'What trouble, what danger?'

'I can—can only assume that Pharaoh has somehow found out how often my Lord Father has forgotten his loyalties to

239

the Throne in order to help me.'

'Ah!' he said coldly. 'The pattern remains the same it seems. You are like a poison to those who try to help you, my lady. I tried to help you once, when I knew no better and look what happened to me!'

She cried out in shock and alarm and shrank away from him, hardly able to believe her ears. He was a cold and furious stranger. In spite of telling her that he had since learned the truth, and accepted the fact that it had been none of her doing, he was still looking at her with loathing in his eyes. What had gone wrong? Why had his attitude changed?

She felt the blood rushing hotly to her face. It was because of the happenings in the night? Yes, she was sure! Her Lord Husband must have enjoyed her. It made him feel beholden to her, or perhaps even ashamed—of whom? Of himself—or her? Either way, it did not matter. Beloved Mother mattered and her noble Father mattered. Amosis must help them—he must!

'They—they will arrive two and a half full moons from now, my lord,' she said urgently. 'And if you do not help them, I will know that you have nothing but cold stone for a heart. I cannot and will not accept that you are as stiff and as without emotion as you appear.' Then casting caution to the winds, she stepped closer, her cheeks twin poppies. 'Mighty Amosis, I will not accept your negative reply.'

'No?' He raised his brows. He felt his reserve fading, for all he wanted to distance himself from this small female who had so complicated his life. 'Aren't you forgetting your position in my house? Have you forgotten where your loyalties should lie?'

All her pent-up emotions broke free. How dare he!

'I mean it!' she said furiously. 'And I know my position in your house very well, my lord. Indeed I shall never forget how very royally you dismissed me from your bed. I meant what I said. You have the hide of a crocodile and you are as cold as—as—'

Words failed her as her eyes brimmed with unshed tears, then a sense of unreality came over her. Amosis, her Lord Husband, had folded his arms and was looking at her in a very proprietory way.

In spite of himself, he smiled, slowly and widely, so that the smile somehow seemed to take over his face and twinkle in little laughing lights in his eyes. And the smile stayed and made him look young and rather mischievous because he found it amusing that such a very small lamb was daring to so openly confront a lion.

Nefer saw that, just for one brief moment, Mighty Warrior had become a different person, a breath-taking, marvellous man whose sex appeal was almost tangible. He was a lion of a man, powerful, one who could and would kill, but who at that moment was almost lovable. But she was beyond caring now, frantic with worry. The safety of her loved ones was at stake.

'You are as immovable as a stone ram,' she flared. 'And you have no heart! You are tomb-cold. Yes, you really are tomb-cold!'

His voice was heavy with meaning as he replied suavely, 'Cold? Even though that might be true, my lady, I have red hot blood running through my veins.'

'It does not matter, Amosis,' she brushed his words away. 'Your blood, hot or cold, cannot have any bearing on this. I beg of you, hold out a helping hand to my parents. They come in secrecy. No one outside of Kerma will know of their arrival. And those already here do not have to be told just who our visitors are. It could be so simple!'

'And what will I gain for all this, Nefer?'

'What have you in mind?' She was fighting to keep control now. All she knew was that Zarah and Per Ibsen had to be saved.

'I will have a second son.' He paused, his smile gone as he added, 'One who will perhaps bear the likeness of myself?'

She reeled against the harshness underlining his words. He was reminding her of Khaleb, being deliberately unkind! She lifted her head proudly then, and stared directly into his eyes.

'Mighty Warrior,' she said with quiet deliberation, 'that will be no problem at all. As from now, I will so arrange it that I sleep permanently in your bed. It is as I have already told you—a personal debt of gratitude that I have to pay. One that I must and will discharge.'

He was examining her face and now there was exasperation in his tone.

'And that is all? A debt you have to pay?'

She eyed him with the same kind of contempt that she felt he had given her.

'That is all, my lord,' she told him with a coldness that matched her looks. 'Now, if you will excuse me, I will make arrangements for Bebu to take watch over my son. Oyahbe will be there as always, for Pepy's sake. I usually like to be near Nesmin myself as you know.'

'From now on your first duty will be to me,' he reminded her sharply. 'I hope I make myself clear? To me alone!'

'As you will, my lord,' she answered

him and then with ice-cold dignity, walked away.

Amosis watched the Small Person and wanted to swear and rail against all the gods. There had been a certain amount of satisfaction in the fact that momentarily, he had a sense of power over her. Though curiously enough, it now left him with a desire to go and bury himself. She would not descend to grovelling, not if he cut her to pieces bit by bit. She was the Lady of His House, his Chief Wife—and last night he had gloried in her, been almost like a young, untried youth in his passions for her. He had been quivering and alive—and vulnerable. Yes, it was for his own moment of vulnerability that she must pay. Even so, there was a very tender look about Mighty Warrior's mouth as he watched the small lovely young woman walking steadily along the large columned central hall. He had a mental picture of a little girl sitting amongst a galaxy of flowers. She had been wearing gold ornaments in her hair, and holding a blue, sweetly perfumed lotus blossom. There had been something about her, a certain look in her wide, hurt, innocent eyes. She had had the same expression just now.

The greatest temptation of his life confronted Mighty Warrior then—to go after the Small Person he called Wife.

He wanted to hold her against him and tell her that he was there, her Guardian, the Protector of her life. But in such action weakness lay. Nefer had adored Khaleb, it was the Prince that she still loved. As it was, his own taking of her person should come under the heading of out and out theft. He was taking advantage of her—and had every intention of continuing to do so. A thirsty horse drank its fill when confronted by water. Well, Nefer was a cool, wonderful pool, of intoxicating wine. She was Pharaoh's gift and so, he, Amosis, was determined to drink his fill, then leave without giving a backward glance. He felt guilty just the same.

With wonderful self-control, Amosis turned his face away, knowing quite well that he would fall if he watched that receding figure much longer. He could almost forget his own rule, never to allow his heart to rule his head. Then he remembered Khaleb and was a man of metal once again. It was the Prince that she loved. He must never forget that.

That night Amosis took his wife with a ruthless determination. She lay there, passive now, obeying him, submissive, but withdrawn. She did not respond as she had previously and Mighty Warrior knew with angry frustration that although winning physically, mentally, he had lost.

When it was over, he felt more angry than before. He turned his back and said no word. In a little while he slept.

Nefer lay beside her Lord Husband, her eyes wide and sad. She was thinking of Khaleb and thinking of Nesmin, his son. With Mighty Warrior, she thought, I will lead a life-time of safety and security. I will be a good army wife. The sons of Amosis will tread down strong well-worn pathways. They will be well behaved and follow the rules. Soldiers, fine and strong like their father, proud and beautiful to behold. They would be like young gods!

Then she thought wistfully of Khaleb's children. Of how they must be, in the Palace, and her breath caught in her throat. Yes, Khaleb would father many children. Thankfully, he would never know about the little one sleeping in the reed basket in the room next door. Oh yes, Khaleb would have sons; laughing naked little imps playing in the sun. They would be strong and tanned and charmingly self-willed. They would make friends in an easy open way. Then they would leave those friends without regrets, knowing in their childish wisdom that there would always be other friends, other guardians and other slaves.

Khaleb's children would all be like

Nesmin. Sweet, smiling Nesmin who was so wonderful to look upon, and whose great dark eyes were so reminiscent of shiny dark Southern grapes.

What of the child who might be conceived even now? Would he be large and strong and quiet? Would he have a slow, warm, very wide grin, rather than Nesmin's quick ready smile? Would he have the angry eyes of her Lord Husband? Would he ever look upon her with suspicion and contempt?

'Holy Hathor,' Nefer whispered frantically, 'Isis, Great Wife and Mother, forgive me my sin. I do not want to bear Amosis's child. I do not wish to have a son born out of passion with not even one faint breath of love.'

Then Nefer fell to thinking of Beloved Mother and of the baby boy she had so tragically lost. She began to pray in earnest then, for Nesmin, and for all the unborn young in the world. Her thoughts were suddenly very, very sad. She fell asleep at last, feeling lost and alone. How she loved and missed Twosre and Sebni, her brother. Her last waking thoughts were of Zarah, her mother, not of the man asleep at her side.

'I will save you, My Mother,' she murmured. 'I will save you no matter what the cost. To this I swear.'

247

She woke early. Even so, Amosis had gone. She clapped her hands and waited for Yati, Kanes and Bebu to appear. Then suddenly and inexplicably she thought of Twosre, could almost see and feel her sister. Such was her own sense of premonition that she felt a great upsurge of fear.

'Twosre,' she whispered. 'Little sister, where are you? Now what trouble are you in? Twosre hurry to me here!'

The servants came in and Bebu and the girls. There followed the fussing and fretting, the choice of delicately dyed, fine linen clothes. Wide collars of precious metal and stones were set out and Nefer chose one of faience beads and silver strips set with lots of red, blue and green gems. Long matching strips hung from her ears. Round her arms, wrists and ankles she wore bangles of silver finely plaited with gold.

She painted her lips and nails red, her lashes and brows were accentuated with khol. She wore red, blue and green beads strung on silver, in her hair.

Nefer listened to all the lively chatter, joined in the laughter and fun. When Oyahbe came in with Nesmin and Pepy chuckling and kicking, one under each arm, her joy in the new day should have been complete. But though Nefer smiled and made a fuss of her son, she still felt the dread.

Twosre, she was thinking, what is it? You must be in trouble of some kind. I sense it, feel it, like a shroud of foreboding deep in my heart. Twosre—my dear!

She tried to fight her sense of impending doom, her premonition that the future was blood-stained and unclear. And, as was happening quite frequently these days, the awesome vision of Ese came cackling and dancing into her mind ...

CHAPTER EIGHT

Twosre was standing alone by the river, deep in thought, then she smiled and dismissed her worries. Pepi, the fisherman who had now become a gentleman, was an old and trusted family friend. Pepi's sons were going to help get her and Sebni to Nefer. She need think of the problems no longer. They had been banished, and she could think of more pleasant things—like her own fine land. Egypt which she was soon to leave, perhaps for ever if that was how the gods decreed.

Egypt was a land of great, rather strange beauty. The river was shining in the intense

249

sunlight. The cliffs of Western Thebes, that edged the desert, became the living glory, glowing with indescribably lovely colours. This every time the sun rose, and also when it set in a fiery blaze of red and gold. In the sudden cold of darkness, the stars shone with a brilliance that was extraordinary in a purple-black sky. They glittered even more than the collar that should, by now, be safe back in Ananias's hands. Twosre shivered and began to walk along the bank, the rippling river dancing and sparkling at her left. She must find Sebni. It was not wise to leave him too long alone.

Sebni whistled as he walked among the rushes. He was living in a new, free world, and also he had Twosre. The hours they spent together now were long and sweet and Sebni was happier than he had ever been before. He breathed in the hot river sweet air and was at one with this pulsating isolated world of head-high reeds, and green watery channels.

Here there were no questions asked, no confidences given. Above all, there were no officials near and one felt safe. Sebni whistled again and let the dark mud squelch through his toes. This was a good life, he thought, the old one merely a bad dream. The most wonderful thing of all was that somewhere, not too far away,

Twosre was gathering flowers and thinking only of him.

Twosre's eyes were troubled as she walked. Two more days to go, she thought, and then we leave. What will happen to us? How will he be? Oh gods of the air, what shall we do? She turned her head from side to side, as if searching for answers, and then with half a sob in her voice she said aloud:

'He killed the old man. Killed him in a terrible way, but he scarcely understands! He is not himself! Dear gods, what can I do?'

'My lady?'

She stiffened, terrified that she had been overheard. Then shocked when she saw who it was approaching her. Gusts of air lifted dark hair off the strong forehead and, as Khaleb smiled, his teeth shone, even and white.

'You are so lonely these days that you need to talk to yourself?' he asked as he fell in step beside her. 'What happened to the lively, laughing Twosre I knew?'

'She is here as always,' Twosre replied and smiled archly, trying to hide her nerves and fear. 'What brings you here, lord?'

'You.'

'You have followed me this far? Are you off your head, My Prince?'

'Are you?'

'Now you speak in riddles, Khaleb!'

'And you act in riddles. Sebni has committed a crime, you know it and so do I. I accept that there is no proof! The Star-Stones are now back with Ananias. My Lord Father has his hands on his uncle's estates. Everyone is happy—except the Law Enforcer, and he must be looked out for. But I want to know why you, of all people, are so concerned with an adopted brother. And why is he so dependent on you?'

Her eyes widened with fear. 'How did you find us, my lord? Are you going to give us away?'

'I have come to offer you my help.'

'Why?' she asked, suspicion in her tone.

'Why not?' he parried. 'Don't you trust even me?'

'I do not need your help, my lord! Leave us alone. Allow us to go our way in peace.'

He stopped walking and, grasping her by her shoulders, swung her round to face him.

'You must not be left alone with him. You are asking for trouble and you know it. Twosre, can't you understand what I am trying to say?'

Twosre's eyes were burning with anger. She made as if to swing away, but Khaleb was strong and he too, was angry.

'His obsession for you is unhealthy and I don't think you're safe with him. Don't you see, Twosre, can't you understand? I have had to skulk out here after you like an animal on the prowl, keep out of his way, and all I want to do is talk. Don't you realise that this is the first time you have been seen without him in tow? Old Pepi is afraid for you and having seen what I have seen, so am I!'

'Your concern for me is touching, Khaleb,' she said in a tight angry voice, 'but it has come too late. My only concern now is that Sebni needs me.'

'Because he is mad?'

'No! He is sick, that is all. He is sick and he needs to be left alone. Not even my parents know where he is. I think I almost hate Pepi for breaking his oath of silence and telling you.'

'Pepi loves you like a daughter. He was afraid for you. Sebni is dangerous.'

'He's a child! He needs care and he is the same as you or I, nearly all the time.'

'And the rest? What happens then?'

She shook her head.

'It's only when he hears strange noises in his mind. He is afraid then. He—he cries like a child, Khaleb! So you see he is not dangerous, only very, very sad.'

'He is like a rope round your neck.

Where will you take him, what will you do? Leave him!'

Twosre's eyes blazed.

'While he needs me, I stay!'

'I cannot understand you.'

'Really Khaleb?' she teased, her dark hair swirling away from her pale, scornful face. 'Then I shall tell you just this once, and after that, I want you never to mention my attitude towards Sebni again. He really loves me. Unlike you, who have wanted me, taken me, humiliated me and thrown me away when you've finished with me. Sebni wanted to *marry* me, that's how he loved me. He is ill because of me. He did—he did what he did thinking it would please me. So you see, Khaleb, the one person who I should have revered above all others, I have destroyed.'

'He destroyed himself. And I still don't see what you can do to drown your own totally misplaced guilt. Twosre, you are—'

'I have done the only thing that I could to make him happy, Khaleb.'

He laughed shortly, angrily.

'You have taken him to your bed, Twosre? That should make any man wild with joy.'

And then Twosre threw back her head and laughed.

'My Prince, you still do not understand,

do you? Of course I have taken him to my bed, but before he could or would accept, I had to give—' She laughed again, as if seeing some great irony in her joke. 'You see we went to the Temple. Our names are written together, and a holy scarab inscribed. You see, O Prince, I let Sebni marry me!'

'You are mad,' Khaleb's eyes narrowed and his lips were drawn back in twin thin lines. 'You will have the priests destroy the record. You will smash the scarab.'

'I am many things,' she flared, 'but this is a contract made before Amun and therefore a contract I will not break.'

'I am your Lord Master. I will not allow this monstrous thing.'

'It is done! And the only punishment Pharaoh metes out to us—of death—will finish it. Goodbye, Khaleb.'

Then she left him, running like a wild thing to where Sebni waited.

'Here I am,' she cried on seeing him. 'And we are in luck. Pepi's son has found us a new place, a secret place in which to wait until the boat comes to take us away. Are you hungry?'

'I am a little.' His soft voice was suddenly pleasing to Twosre.

'Sebni,' she said gently, 'you are a cut above the rest. Now come along, you must eat.'

He followed her along a half hidden track to a small mud and straw hut. Inside there was only a rush bed and a tall blue water jar. Outside, a pot bubbled and boiled and gave out very appetising smells.

Twosre broke a loaf of unleavened bread into pieces and ladled out two bowls of meat and onion stew. They began to eat the meal in silence. Sebni smiled suddenly.

'You are an extremely beautiful wife,' he said and there was deep pride in his voice. 'I love you, O Woman of the House.'

She jumped up and taking a cloth of linen, she began to wipe the grease away from his mouth. And then his rather anxious brown eyes were looking into her own sparkling ones. And she melted. She ran her fingers through his hair.

'As Lord Masters go,' she said softly, 'you are very, very nice. By Amun, it's getting so I don't know what I'd do without you.'

The look he gave her was one of such utter adoration and trust that her resolve to stand by him was doubly strengthened. Two days, she was thinking desperately, we have just two days here. Khaleb must never know. Khaleb never gives without reason. He has offered to help us. That means he wants something in return!

Then her eyes flew wide open in shock and horror as realisation came. Khaleb had heard about Nefer! He had found out that Nefer had been with child, could that be it? If so, he needed an excuse to leave Thebes for Kerma. What better reason than that he had been chasing a criminal, one who had tried to evade loyal duties to the Crown?

What of Nefer? What of the child? He wants to see if she had a son, Twosre thought desperately, and if she has, he will take it away from her. He is the son of the Divine One, second Prince in the land. His word will be obeyed, no matter what the command. We are helpless. Oh, my poor darling Nefer. What will she do? How will she feel? And how will Mighty Warrior react to having the Woman of his House die of a broken heart?

All that day and through the night, and on through the further sun-drenched hours until dawn on the third day, Twosre felt barely able to breathe. But at last she and Sebni were safe aboard the vessel that belonged to Pepi the gentleman who, from a humble fisherman, had risen to be the owner of several fine crafts.

As the boat pulled away from the shore, Twosre sighed with relief. They had made their escape, their destination unknown. She was about to turn away from the side and go in search of Sebni when her

257

heart lurched and seemed to leap into her throat.

There, just behind them, was a large, imposing ship, bearing Prince Khaleb's banner and the emblem of his House. Khaleb himself was standing in the prow. Legs astride, arms folded, his blue and white striped linen headdress blowing crisply in the wind. Khaleb was smiling triumphantly, victor of the day.

Twosre knew then that the Prince would follow her. Follow her to the ends of the earth if need be.

She had failed Sebni, failed Nefer, and she failed her parents whom she adored. They were all in Prince Khaleb's hands.

She looked up, beyond the billowing red sails, to the vast world above, the blue immensity of the sky.

'Holy Hathor,' she cried, anguish in her voice, 'how is it possible to love, yet to loathe a man so much?'

There was no answer from the gods. All was serene in the heavens. Far below the Nile rippled on its journey. One that had its beginnings thousands of miles away, and by its own origin, had given birth to the narrow strip of fertile land known as the Nation of Egypt.

'Forgive me, Nefer,' Twosre wept. 'I had no idea that he would follow me here.'

'My lady,' Amosis said to Nefer one deep purple evening. 'In two days from now our presence is requested at the Governor's residence. We have received a message that King Hapdjefi is to pay us a visit. We find this surprising. Hapdjefi's men have openly attacked us over the years. He is the enemy of Egypt, he has to be forced to pay tribute—not this! A State visit. It does not make sense.'

'Perhaps he is bending his knee at last, wishing to talk peace?' Nefer replied. 'There has been no sign of trouble since I have been here. Perhaps this king has had a change of heart?'

'He is up to treachery of some kind,' Amosis said darkly. 'Make no mistake about that. We will be on the alert, my lady, never fear.'

'Amosis—' she began hesitantly, then stopped.

'What is it?' he replied not unkindly, but with very little warmth. 'If you have something on your mind, please speak.'

'My lord, I would like to go to Kerma.'

'Go down there?' he was frowning, then: 'No!'

'But Amosis, my—'

'You are doing very well already. The Governor's wife has made many gifts of shrubs and trees. You have ordered flowers. This place is altered beyond all recognition

259

already and I am well pleased. But you may not go to barter for more plants. I feel that the peace you so fondly believe in, is about to be shattered. If it is, there are plenty in Kerma who would willingly side with Hapdjefi, believe me.'

'I—I was not thinking of flowers, or shrubs and trees,' she insisted. 'I was remembering that the time draws near for the arrival of my parents. I—would like to be there to meet them.'

'Out of the question, Nefer. I wish you to remain here.' He added sharply, 'Here, where you are safe inside the citadel.'

'But we can see for miles from the top of the walls!' she pointed out. 'The desert is empty, there is nothing but barren rocks and sand and stones.'

'You will not argue,' he told her. 'Allow me to know what is safest and best for you, Nefer. As for empty deserts, I can tell you that you are mistaken. And at Hapdjefi's approach, behind him every inch of the wilderness will be alive. We must be on guard!'

'Amosis? My lord?' Her tone was humble now. 'I very much wish to go to Kerma!'

'And stay in one of the filthy hovels they call inns?' He laughed angrily. 'And do you intend that you and your servants should hang about waiting for a ship that might never arrive? It will not be safe in Kerma.

You may not go. That is an end to it.'

'Paihuti and Uronarti have made friends in Kerma,' she persisted. 'And Uronarti, who loves Kanes to distraction, took her with him last time.' Then defiantly, 'It must be really hard to be a soldier.'

'Oh?'

Her head lifted even higher and her cheeks flamed, but she went on: 'You trust no one, my lord! I would not want to live, if I felt about people as you do.'

'I see. So you trust, do you?'

'Yes,' she flung at him. 'Of course!'

'Because people love Egypt?' His voice held a frosty derision now. 'Do the vanquished ever adore their conquerors?'

'Perhaps not, my lord, but they bow down before her, and recognise her might. And here in the South, Mighty Amosis, *is* Egypt. There is none who would dare to stand against us now you are here.'

'Your faith is touching, but misplaced.' He held up his hand and effectively stopped her from arguing. Then went on in his own quietly ruthless way; 'So! You believe there is no one in Kerma who would dare to defy me or attempt to harm you? You are certain that you and the servants would be safe because they travel with the Amosis banner held high?'

'Yes!'

'Tell me,' he said smoothly, his eyes

261

snapping, 'do you remember a man called Seshat?' He stepped nearer to her and although she stood her ground, she felt nervous before his strength, humiliated by his coldness, his aloofness. 'Think about it.'

'I—I do not remember!'

'Well, you should. You stood up to him in defence of Uronarti, the peasant you so adore. Seshat was Master of Supplies, remember? A brutish man with snaky little eyes, who travelled with us aboard ship?'

'I—I remember,' she whispered and felt herself blush. Her Lord Husband's reaction at that time had almost made her believe that he cared for her. Only a little perhaps, but, yes, cared!

'Seshat and his cronies tried to cut me down a few nights ago.' Amosis's tone was matter of fact. 'Before he was himself put down for good and all, he cried out—"In the name of Hapdjefi you'll all die like the dogs you are!" Tell me, does that sound like love and loyalty towards Egypt—does that sound like peace?'

She was barely listening to him now. She was staring up at him, horror in her eyes.

'They—they tried to kill you? How? Why? Oh, my lord, the mere thought of it makes me feel ill!'

'Had they succeeded, I dare say I would

have felt worse than you do, my lady,'
he replied and grinned in his wide slow
way. 'As to how and why—the "why"
is no secret! How they were able to
set on me is simpleness itself. I must
have been watched. They learned that it's
often my habit to ride out to meet the
men returning from late patrol. Morale
can get low at the times of shadows.
So what of your talk of divine safety
now?'

'If anything happened to you,' she
whispered, shaken to the core, 'I—I—'

'Enough!' he cut in. 'I told you merely
to make a point. The incident occurred in
line of a soldier's duty. That is all.'

She held her words of concern back, to
hide how shocked and worried for Amosis
she was. Then a new fear rose and this
she could not hide. She stepped forward
and clutched hold of his arm.

'My lord, under the circumstances, isn't
it even more imperative that my parents
are met and escorted safely back here?'

He laughed disbelievingly.

'I know of your worry where they are
concerned. I have agreed that they shall
stay here for as long as they like—no
matter what trouble they are in. But do
you honestly believe I'd send my men into
what can easily turn into a cauldron of
hate, on a domestic cause?'

'Amosis, they will walk into a hot-bed unknowing. My mother will step ashore smiling and in innocence. Oh god! Hapdjefi's men might set on her. They'll certainly go for the great royalist Per Ibsen. Don't you see? My father could be captured and held for ransom at the very least!' She was openly weeping now. 'Amosis, you must do something!'

'Be mindful of who you are and try if you can to be more realistic,' he said. He was getting contemptuous of her now. 'We here, are on the defence. We need to place our men with great care. We will be outnumbered, three to one I would say, should Hapdjefi make an all-out attack. Frankly, your people will be safe if, when they arrive, they stay on board ship. The citadel must and will stand.'

'Forgive me, I—I am still puzzled,' she persisted. 'All this talk of enemies, of men trying to murder you and yet—yet you say that our enemy is to come here on a peaceful mission!'

'Ah! Now you can see how complex this situation is? We'll know more when we actually come face to face. Hapdjefi is cunning. The more friendly he seems, the more carefully we'll have to watch our back gates. We will welcome him, and put on an act as good as his own. At the end of it all, we may have found out what he's

264

after, and what, if any, are the terms he wishes to make.'

'But mightn't that a be a misjudgement on—'

Amosis stood up very tall, his expression cold and impatient.

'I find it irritating that the Woman of my House dares to question and argue with me. I am feeling mortified that, by her every word and look she deems me to be a fool!'

'I am sorry, my lord,' she said quickly. 'I beg forgiveness if you thought that. Oh Amosis, My Husband, don't you know even now, that nothing could be further from the truth?'

'Oh?' He raised his brows in a supercilious way.

'I admire and respect you more than any other man,' she wavered, tears springing unbidden to her eyes. 'It's just that—that I miss my mother so much. I am so anxious to see her again, and—'

'And so you shall,' he said crisply. 'But at the right and proper time. Now if you will excuse me? There is much to do. Above all else, we must show them our strength.' He paused, then added significantly, 'We must *all* show strength!'

He turned and left her and she watched him with sorrow in her eyes. She had not been the sort of woman she had determined to be all that time ago. No, quite the reverse! She had kept on about missing her mother, about the desire to meet her beloved father, to make much fuss and joyous celebration in their name! And he, her husband, had listened, and tried to explain. She had dared to argue and—only in a little while before that, he had been set on. Had nearly met death!

Shaken, wretched, sick, worried and feeling totally ashamed, Nefer went to find Nesmin. He sat in the garden playing with his favourite toy, the wooden horse Amosis had given him. He chuckled and held out his chubby arms and Nefer held him close. Pepy crawled towards her, his face creased in a two-tooth smile.

'My lady,' Oyahbe said, 'such excitement! What will you wear to meet the visiting king? The affair is to be very grand.

'You—you know?'

'But of course,' Oyahbe teased. 'Doesn't the whole world?'

'It is a marvel to me how the news gets round,' Nefer said quietly and felt unease. 'And as for meeting the Hurrian. The idea does not please me at all.'

'But it will be a great chance to make a good impression, my lady. The Lord Amosis will be so proud of you. So adoring!'

'I hope so,' Nefer replied and thought how well her own secret was kept. She was in the Lord Master's bed as a woman to be enjoyed, but not as a wife. Sweet goddess Isis, wife and mother, she prayed, don't even let them find out! I could not bear the humiliation and shame.

'You looked sad then, my lady,' Oyahbe said. 'Is there anything wrong?'

'Of course not, I am puzzled, that's all. Oyahbe, tell me all that you know about the Hurrian King.'

'I only know what I have heard, my lady. Gossip is not always the pitch of truth.'

'Tell me anyway,' Nefer said.

'They say Hapdjefi is now very old. His son Hapu was brought up with Egypt's Divine One's own children in the Great Palace.'

'Then perhaps I should remember him,' Nefer said and frowned. 'But I do not.'

Oyahbe laughed merrily at that.

'It would be very surprising if you did! After all, there must have been dozens upon dozens of children there.'

This was true since in the course of his wars, Thutmose found it expedient to remove the sons of local rulers to Egypt as hostages for their father's good behaviour.

'Hapu was anointed by Pharaoh himself,' Oyahbe said, her voice filled with awe. 'Now he has come back to rule his State.

He awaits, in deference, for full control until his father dies. But in the meantime they reign together, and are mighty in strength.'

'Yes, yes,' Nefer said impatiently. 'I gathered that.'

'Hapdjefi had a favourite daughter. Her name, Sitamun. She was placed in Pharaoh's harem. Her lady-in-waiting went with her and it is said that Sitamun and all the women with her came to learn about and love Egypt's great Unseen One, Amun.'

'Where is Sitamun now?'

'She died, my lady. Her women mostly stayed where they were looked up to, and given respect, in Egypt. It is said that Hapdjefi never got over Sitamun's loss. She was his favourite child.'

'That is very sad,' Nefer breathed. 'All very, very, sad. I would lay down and die if I lost Nesmin—or Pepy who is dear to me.'

'And I also, if I lost either the young lord or Pepy,' Oyahbe replied. 'But let us speak of more pleasant things. What will you wear for the royal visit? It will be a grand and glorious affair. Minya swears that she will blind the Hurrians with many fine jewels. What about you?'

'It must be something very special,' Nefer said quietly. 'Something that will

268

greatly please my lord. But the visit is not to be yet. I think I would like to be alone for a while. I want to think and plan.'

Nefer left the garden and entered the well lit courtyard, which even in this short space of time had blossomed. Minya had given her tubs of flowers and there were vines and young palms, even vegetable plants that Paihuti, accompanied by Uronarti, had bartered for in Kerma. The place was full of shadows and blacknesses. Flares and torches burned great in number, but there was still something awesome and mysterious, Nefer thought, about the night-time world.

She felt nervous apprehension, and the warning of Amosis's words was impossible to forget. So the Hurrian King Hapdjefi was coming to the citadel on a visit—for what? It was all some kind of terrible trick, if they were overrun by desert hordes, they'd all die. Nesmin would be killed, all of the little children would! The women would be thrown to the men and after usage, very few would survive. Egypt's soldiers would be cut down, Amosis would be tortured. They would cut off his head. They would—

A tear coursed down her face and fell with a splash on her hand. This brought her to herself. She squared her shoulders resolutely and walked on into the eerie, whispering gloom. She made her way towards a stone seat. There was already someone there before her. She hesitated, and her small feet stumbled over an unnoticed tub.

'Hello again,' Amosis said. 'You came, as I thought you would. You know, you are a young and unusually pretty girl to be found in a desert fortress at night. Aren't you tired to death of stewing in this oven-hot hole?'

'My lord!' Nefer whispered quietly as she sat down beside him. Despite all her good intentions, she wept.

Amosis cursed and felt helpless, more moved than he cared to admit by her tears. He clumsily put his arm round her shoulders. It was not until he felt her trembling that he knew exactly how frightened she was. Her poor heart was thumping to such an extent that it made her shake from head to foot. Her glorious hair tickled his cheek as she drew near and lay her head against his shoulder. He cursed silently and fought his desire to be like Khaleb and put on the same air of false charm. Babble a lot of cheerful, meaningless nonsense just to allay her fears. Yes, that was what her beloved prince would do!

He felt a sudden unreasonable fury and just for a moment wished that Khaleb was near. He wanted to choke the life out of the man who, he felt sure, his wife dreamed of every time, he, Amosis held her in his arms. But now? This moment? He was not quite so sure. She was cuddling against him, was feminine and frail. Amosis sternly repressed his inclination to take advantage of her vulnerability and kept his voice religiously calm as he asked:

'What is the matter, Small Person? Is life with me here so intolerable?'

Suppressed sobs were the only answer.

'I frightened you, didn't I? I am sorry, my lady. It is just that you must learn the truth of our situation here.'

A tear stained face was laid against a massive chest and one tiny hand reached out to clutch another that was almost twice its size.

'They—they might have killed you!'

'That is usually a soldier's lot. You should know that no fate can be better than that of marching gloriously into the Other Life. One's duty having been well done of course.'

His tone held rebuke. Her small hand was hastily withdrawn.

'I know that,' she replied in a low broken voice. 'But my life would be empty without you, my lord. And—and it is just the same for me, Amosis—I—I have grown accustomed to your face!'

He said nothing. All was silent, save for Amosis's quick drawn breath. Nefer got up unsteadily and stood facing the rock-like figure who had married her. An arm was slipped round his neck and a soft cheek laid against his.

'Forgive me for being so very unlike a proud hero's wife,' she whispered. 'I am not very strong, I do not relish a battle, nor victory for Egypt and Amun, if it means losing you. I like planting flowers and listening to the music the flute players make. Stories of campaigns, of combat, butchery and massacre merely terrify me. I like watching the moon, and its star children dancing in the sky. I—I am one for fine and gentle things. I—I like playing with babies, which I suppose is not the kind of thing with which I should be concerned.'

Amosis's throat moved convulsively. His stern face became more gentle. Two arms went round her in a hug that took all her breath away.

'Nefer,' he said quietly, 'I believe that you speak the truth. You don't care that I am a great hero in Pharaoh's eyes. You see me only as a man! I am proud of you. Believe me, I am. You are all that is sweet and feminine. You are like Goddess Isis, wife and mother. Stay as you are. Always be that little girl I found in the garden at

Ramose. And Nefer?'

'Yes?'

'When we meet the Hurrian, will you do me the honour of wearing pink? It is the colour you wore on that day and I cherish the memory still.'

All of her gratitude and emotion rose to the fore. Her Lord Husband had actually let himself go sufficiently to say something nice! She turned and stretched her arms upwards and wound them round his neck.

'It will be my honour to please you,' she told him steadily. 'I always want to please you, and my heart aches when I make you cross.'

'I left you, intending to go to my men,' he told her roughly. 'But that can wait. I feel like having your company—in my bed. I grow fond of you, Nefer. You are desirable and I am very conscious of being a man.'

He stood up, towering over her and, still holding her, led her back inside the house. She went with him, for the first time, willingly, some of her humiliation fading away. He grows fond of me, she was thinking, and he shows it by the look in his eyes. Yes, he really is fond of me—and for now, that is enough.

That night the citadel standing on its great mound and fortified by its walls and towers, was for Nefer, the gardens

273

of Ramose. Amosis was the steady-eyed strong looking young man who had so trusted and loved.

Next morning, Amosis Most Mighty, Chief of Pharaoh's Southern Power, had returned. The eager youth had gone.

'My lord,' she said unsteadily, and felt absurdly small and shy. 'I beg you to take care.' She stepped towards him, her arms outstretched.

'Thank you for your pretty speech,' he told her and gently disengaged himself from her intended embrace.

He bade her goodbye quite kindly, but already there was a distance in his eyes. Clearly, he was thinking of the forthcoming duties. Mentally already at one with his horses and men.

All men are the same, she thought as she watched him walk away, proud in his army clothes. The Badge of Honour was emblazoned on his shield. He had the ceremonial fly-whisk in his hand, a sword glinted from the belt at his waist. But just then a picture of Khaleb jumped into her mind. She frowned at the intrusion and hastily pushed the image away.

The day was spent quietly in a delightful manner. Nesmin was now able to make his desires and needs known and did so joyously. His lovely little face almost always wreathed in smiles. He and handsome baby

Pepy were as one and cried if they were parted even for a few moments. They seemed to have a mutual understanding, and for Breast Mother, Oyahbe a deep love. Both babies would reach out adoring arms to Nefer the moment she came in sight. She would kiss them and tickle them, her eyes soft with laughter, mingling with their own. Still laughing and playing, teasing Oyahbe, and begging Bebu to comb the whole citadel for new pots of rouge of the palest shade, Nefer was thinking all the while, Pink! And all the time I believed Amosis preferred blue. I shall wear my colour of a blushing new morning. My collar shall be gold with rose coloured stones. I will wear dawn-lilies in my hair. I will hang like a misty sunrise on my Lord Husband's arm. And though I am not brave for him, I will try to be beautiful.

'What is it?' Bebu grumbled. 'You are going on as if it is time of the New Year. I have never known you to fuss and fret so. You want to wear pink? Then pink it will be. Goodness, I hardly think the Lady Minya will worry so much over a mere Hurrian King!'

When the brief moment of dusk fell over the land, Amosis returned to his home. The servants washed his feet, then bathed him, and anointed his weather beaten skin with oil. Usually unbearable at such times,

275

normally impatient of the efforts of slaves, content to wash himself with his own hands, he allowed their ministrations and made neither rebuke or comment. Then wearing clean linen, refreshed and free of the hot dust of the day, Amosis found himself going in search of Nefer. Once again, he discovered her, sitting in a large gilt covered chair, the sleeping Nesmin in her arms. Her expression was gentle, her lips upcurved as she looked down at her child.

'He grows quickly,' Amosis said and sat on the ground at her feet. 'You made a fine son. You must have a perfect way of carrying the unborn in your insides.'

'Yes, lord,' she said softly. 'I feel that is true.'

'I want to fill you up with my seed,' he said firmly. 'I want to know that I have many sons to continue my name. Is the idea hard for you to bear?'

'I will melt with joy on the day I learn I am with child by you,' she replied. 'For when that happens I know that I am on the way to keeping a promise I made.'

'You will hand Nesmin over to Oyahbe now,' he told her, awareness in his eyes. 'I wish to know the sweetness of your breasts and the glory that your pretty dress hides. Come to my bed, Nefer. Make it soon. I feel a need a burning in my flesh. My bones are on fire. You excite me as no woman has before. I will take you now, since I cannot stay the night.'

She went to him and the passion in Amosis ran untamed. It was as if by will and strength alone he would sire a son. And Nefer found herself whispering to the gods to answer her Lord Husband's prayers. Then she gave herself up to the sensation of such ecstasy that she felt she must be flying through the sky.

When he was through and he was dressed as Mighty Warrior again, she watched until his large figure disappeared in the darkness. The slaves on duty along the way, and also at the gate, relaxed. Relieved that they were no longer under the threat of Mighty Warrior's eagle eye.

On high, the stars continued to play hide-and-seek round the skirts of the moon. The great citadel stood on its haunches above its high mound. It was like an ancient animal, quiet, still, watchful, an old guard dog sleeping, but with half opened ear and eyes. Totally unaware that there were traitors in its heart.

Below the citadel lay the lower town of Kerma with its grid plan of straight streets and baked brick houses. Its stores, its merchants rich and its sore ridden poor. In one inn, that was noteworthy only for its air of desolation and filth, enemies of

Egypt had gathered like vultures to watch and wait. Their eyes were hard and hungry and filled with hate.

The time was not yet. The forces of Hapdjefi were still gathered, as numerous as locusts, on distant sands. But every day drew them near. The stink of war was getting to be more noticeable in the air. At its height there would be the looting, the raping, the paying of old scores. Long live Hapdjefi the Hurrian, who so avidly worshipped strange Indus—spawned gods.

CHAPTER NINE

The dying day glowered, a sullen black and scarlet in the sky. The sun was a baleful eye glaring down at the earth. The stretch of wilderness was bathed in shadows. But everywhere there glittered cooking fires serving a great legion of soldiers' tents.

The huge royal marquee of Hapdjefi stood in the centre of shelters erected for the use of the finest of hand-picked men. Great Hurrian warriors headed by their heir apparent, Hapu. All round and stretching out of view, were chariots, pack animals, noble horses, camp followers, servants and slaves.

They had come to make war. Men were geared up, excited, as taut as bow strings pulled.

Everyone was in readiness for combat to come. It would all begin when the King gave word. But first, it was rumoured, The Great One Most High, had to sort out an immensely private and important thing. It was whispered that it all had something to do with negotiations with the enemy. The loathsome Egyptians of all people! It was really very strange.

Oil lamps lit the luxurious interior of Hapdjefi's abode. There were tapestries hanging from the woven wool walls, and coloured carpeting covered the desert floor. There were colourful cushions and carved stands on which stood oil jars, lamps, dishes filled with sweet meats and dried fruits. Long wooden chests which contained treasures with which to pay the army lined one wall. Other chests held fine linen or else luxurious robes for the King to wear. There was a many breasted, many armed god leering in its gold shrine, incense burning before it. A large bed bearing a hard cushion for a pillow and a blue woollen rug was set back in the dimness of a recess. An upright, gilt covered throne on which sat the King, stood centre of all.

A ray of light like a blood red finger fell on Hapdjefi's face. He was a curious looking personage. He had very prominent cheekbones and his soulless black eyes were sunk deep into his face. They were almost hidden by strong over-jutting brows. One gained the impression from the statue-still figure, that he had known great evil, and that he was hiding dark secrets all the time.

The King's bony hands, heavy with rings, rested on the white robe that covered his knees. His over jacket, ankle length, was purple, thickly fringed with gold and bearing gold set jewels on the chest. He wore a wide gold banded crown over a purple head cloth that hid the spareness of his hair.

Sitting at Hapdjefi's feet, her face as awful and as ugly as the years of hate made her, sat Ese. She was rocking backwards and forwards, cackling quietly to herself. The silent guards and slaves in attendance round the walls were rigid with fear. The whites of the rolling eyes gleaming in their dark faces. Ese was lifting cubes of human bone in the air and dropping them again into the palm of her hand. Hapdjefi seemed unaware of her. Her impatience grew.

'Most High,' she babbled. 'You will have me read?'

'I will have you begin,' Hapdjefi's voice was a ghostly sigh. 'You tell me that the spirits insist that I will need this girl?'

'Ai! To rejuvenate you when you get to the other side, O King of Kings.'

'And there I will be young again and in good health?'

'In the next world, Most High, you will be as a god and you will reign supreme. Have I ever told you wrong?'

'You have never disappointed me,' came the eerie, whispering reply. 'But I am puzzled to know why I need an Egyptian female at my side in death. I have never lowered myself in such a way in life.'

'The spirits call to me from the mists of time, O King. They sob out the name of your long lost daughter. The child who had her indentity taken from her, who was renamed by the Egyptians and called Sitamun. So, obeying the spirits, I threw the bones. They fell in the shape of the name Nefer.'

'This puzzles me. Throw the bones again. Perhaps we will learn the reason for this riddle.'

At that Ese called aloud for her divining tray. A shivering slave crept forward carrying a sheet of polished bronze. Then Ese took the tray and set it on the ground with her own hands, so that it lay like a shining pool gleaming under the lamps. Her voice, at first guttural, gradually raised to a pitch so high and wild that it stung against listening ears. Ese began chanting mysterious words to bring forth the spirits who carried the messages of gods. The chanting grew higher, then reached up in a scream that seemed to last forever, then slowly, sobbingly the cry descended into a mournful wail, then stopped. In the moment of intense silence that followed, Ese threw the bones.

Beads of sweat had broken out on the faces of both guards and slaves. They knew that the witch woman had called up the Jins and they were here, in the black patches all round the marquee. Jins were gibbering, had pointed teeth and fiery red eyes. Ese's distended gaze was on the bones.

'What do you see?' the old King asked.

'Your daughter, Most High, the young beloved!'

'She has been gone too long,' the old man whispered. 'She is now only a far away memory.'

'Listen! She speaks!'

'I hear nothing, only the heavy breathing of the guards.'

His tone was vindictive and the guards tried not to breathe.

'Drink of the magic potion,' Ese commanded and handed the King a goblet of gold. 'Drink and you too will hear the voice that cries out from a million cubits away. I promise you, Oh Great One, she speaks!'

'What does she say?'

'That to live again you must follow ancient customs. That you must repeat the rites as carried out by a long ago governor of this region. He lived in the reign of the second Ammenemes and he was called Hapdjefi. Yes, O Great One, Your name! He was born in Asyut.'

'Old woman,' the King hissed. 'I have no interest in long dead Egyptian governors. Be careful that I do not call for hot pincers to tear out your vile, shrivelled tongue.'

Ese cackled and wagged her finger admonishingly.

'My Master, My God, you have always had ears for me. You know that there is no one more close to you than I. And who else, but me, can brew the magic potion that always gives you joy? I have something to tell you of great importance. May I go on?'

A slight inclination of the large bony head gave the assent.

'It is true that this man was an Egyptian,' Ese went on. 'A civilised man, so they say, though what that ineffectual term means I cannot tell. But the governor learned many truths when he came out here, to the edge of nowhere. He came to recognise the strength and the power of your own beloved god. He learned that there was a quicker and far more effective way of reaching the Second World.'

'Get on with it, you old blabber mouth.' The sibilant voice was growing impatient.

Ese looked over her shoulders, into the shadows and black patches the spluttering oil lamps made. She smiled and leered at unseen things and rubbed her hands together in a wickedly evil way. It was a terrifying scene.

'The quickest route,' Ese said, 'to the Land of Hereafter is through *sati*-burial. And when you are surrounded by all those you need, I will say the magic words that will ensure your safe transport. You will be there in a mere wink of an eye.'

'That sounds promising,' the old King whispered and lapsed into silence again. A gust of air shivered round the marquee, sending flames leaping and hissing in the oil. Shadows danced in a wild macabre way and made Ese's face look almost skull-like as she went on:

'Think of it, Most High. Imagine it, if you can. There will be no facing of Egypt's Black Jackal. No having your soul weighed against the Feather of Truth. There will not be a list of dangerous situations to side-step as listed in the Book of the Dead. No! It will be *sati*-burial, then the magic rites as called by me, and you will be there with your beloved Sitamun.'

'Why does my daughter cry out to me from beyond? Why does she wish to take such a great step?'

'She was brought up by Pharaoh and lived in his house. She knows that Egypt's subjects must bow to their laws, that your burial must be their way. But she also knows how much easier the old ways are. She remembers how long it took her to reach the glory of Elysian Fields. How many years it took her aboard the boat of Ra. She is afraid that she will have to wait too long to see you again. Listen! Listen hard and you will hear how wildly she laments.'

There was a deep silence and the darkness seemed to grow stronger, the glow fading from the lights. Then, faint and far away in their imaginings there came the sound of sobbing and a woman's voice whispering:

'Father, Great Lord, come to me—'

The King's strange face set in a simian expression, his small dark eyes seemed to go even deeper into his head. He appeared to shrink as he listened intently to Ese who now gave way to a new wild torrent of words. There was a bargain to be made, he knew it. There always was!

'Your daughter,' she was gabbling, 'knows how you can fold back years and

285

be young again! In return for this favour, and for making the Lords of Death open Immortality's doors, she asks the King, her noble father, to bring with him her own dear childhood friend.'

'Friend?' Hapdjefi's eyes glinted. 'Old woman, did you say that Sitamun wishes me to bring a friend?'

'Sitamun cries out through the aeons of time, Great One. She is lonely for her friend Nefer to travel at your side. Thus she can step through the portals of the After Life.'

'You are mad!' Hapdjefi's eyes glinted and his thin lips sneered. 'And not even your magic is strong enough to make me wish for an Egyptian bride.'

'Drink the magic potion,' Ese persuaded. 'O Divine One, drink, listen and see!'

And the King's claws went round the drugged potion that Ese handed to him again. He drank, his eyes almost fascinated by the wise woman's distended glare. Gradually he began to accept that the old way of holy *sati*-burial was necessary and right.

In a dream he saw the large tumulus where he would be. He would be surrounded by his servants, women folk and slaves. They would be given the sleeping potion and suffocated where they fell. All would have the great honour of accompanying their master to the Other World. But the success of the whole business lay with the wishes of his dead daughter. She wanted, no insisted on the presence of Nefer, who had once been her friend.

'It shall be as Sitamun wishes,' Hapdjefi said in his soft sepulchral voice. 'When we have stormed and taken the citadel, and the sky reels under the weight of our victory cries, I will have the Lady Nefer brought to me here.'

'But you will not ask for her first?' Ese enquired fiercely. 'You will bargain for her, Great Lord? You will visit the citadel and make your demands?'

'I do not see the necessity, Wise Woman. The deed will be accomplished. The Egyptian girl will be ours when we have won the fight.'

'But Divine One,' Ese said quickly. 'She could be maimed, or even perhaps kill herself when she witnesses defeat. She must be in perfect condition to bring about the delight of Sitamun. It will be wise to bring her here before the battle begins. In the name of Amun, it is—'

'Amun?' There was terrible venom in Hapdjefi's eyes. 'Do you call upon the vile god of Egyptians?'

'No!' Ese recanted quickly even though her gaze was as mad as before. 'I would go to hell for ever before I did such a thing. I was merely using the name of the girl's god in order to damn her the more. Drink from your goblet again, O Great One. Feel the joy and pleasure of your soul flying free. While you live, Nefer lives, and she will be like ripe fruit in your bed.'

The King sipped again, then:

'I will tell them that if they give me the girl, I will go in peace.'

'And will you keep your word, my lord?'

Hapdjefi's chuckle gusted out like the faint rattling of Ese's dried bones.

'Of course,' he said. 'But then, I speak only for myself. It will be another matter entirely for Prince Hapu and his men at arms! Now I am thinking and wondering about just what we will do if the Egyptians refuse to hand over this girl, since her presence is so necessary here and now.'

Ese laughed in a terrible way.

'There is someone within the walls of Citadel Amenemhet who would slit the throat of his mother for two rings of gold. I need only to offer a pitcher full of precious things and he will be less than a slave.'

'So be it,' Hapdjefi rustled the words, rather than spoke, and sipped at his drink again. Then he added slyly:

'But I am not anxious to make my

journey to the next world, Ese.' A significant pause. 'And if things do not go well, you will have your hands and feet cut off and you will be boiled in oil.'

'And then I will be eaten?' the crone laughed. 'Will you eat me as you have munched on others born with talents you admired? Eat up my flesh and spit out my bones if you will, but it is my head you must chew on if you wish to learn of the dark unearthly things. If you do not wish to continue to dream strange dreams, and hold a magic fire for ever burning and scorching at the base of your skull, kill me!'

Hapdjefi went into a stupor deep inside himself, wherein his own devils of torment played. All the while Ese rocked herself backwards and forwards again and laughed ...

Nefer walked in the garden that even now was only barely beginning to take shape. She had made a plan, one with many dangers, perhaps, but one that might work. Amosis had told her that he would be outside the citadel on the following day. He and a platoon of his most impressive men were going out to meet Hapdjefi.

'They will arrive, the Hurrians, with their king, his entourage and a mere token force of men,' Amosis had told her. 'But

I'm willing to wager that there's a whole army gathering somewhere out there. Still, the royal visit stands us in good stead. We'll listen to their terms while our spies go out foraging again.'

'They—they have discovered nothing, my lord?'

Amosis smiled grimly.

'We'll never know, my lady. You see, they have never returned. I feel that Hapdjefi's visit will be the signal for the Hurrians' advance. We will be beleaguered perhaps, but we are mighty in strength. You have no need to fear.'

'I am not afraid for myself,' she had said quietly. 'My greatest concern is for Nesmin and Pepy of course, also for my parents who are due to arrive. Who will step ashore and into a hornets' nest. Please Amosis, send men down there to fetch them up here to safety. Oh please!'

He shook his head.

'I am sorry. I am truly sorry, but I cannot spare my men.'

'Not even one—to at least warn them, Amosis?'

'Don't you understand even now?' he replied. 'There are spies abroad. We dare show neither unease nor fear. To go scuttling to Kerma on an errand of this kind would be a clear indication to the enemy that we are forewarned. That there'll be no surprise in their attack. We wish to have the element of surprise on our own side!'

'But it would look as if we are merely being courteous, Amosis! And what would be so unnatural about going to the wharf to greet parents? I simply don't—'

'But they are not your parents, are they, Nefer?' He was staring at her very haughtily now, irritated because she would insist on pressing her point home. 'They are merely visitors of no great account, a man and a woman! I thought secrecy was necessary. I understand that this visit was to be kept quiet. That the newcomers were coming here to shelter, incognito, away from Pharaoh's might.'

He had been right, of course he had. She had no courage left to plead more. Then she had learned that Amosis would be taking the red chariot and Ra and Sphinx to greet the Hurrian. Yes! The red and gold ceremonial chariot. It was not the time to don the war helmet of blue. Officially the Hurrians were subject to Pharaoh at Thebes. They lived by the laws he lay down. Their customs were those of Egypt. They made sacrifices to Egypt's gods.

Thutmose had surely forgotten that Prince Hapu was now set free and on his own ground. He would not even remember Sitamun, the only other royal Hurrian hostage he'd had. There would be no holding the Hurrians now, but on the surface at least, they were at peace. Because of this, the disruptive element in the fortified city at Kerma would wait. For the moment Egyptian travellers would be safe.

Nefer could hardly wait for Amosis to leave. But when the time came and Nefer stood among the crowds of cheering people, she could not take her eyes off her Lord Husband. He stood so strong and tall in his chariot. In one hand he held the reins of the two horses, in the other the standard of the Pharaoh, whose messenger he was. He wore body armour of beaten gold and he looked like a god. Women were crying out his name and Nefer heard herself calling him too. She wanted to run to him, kiss him, tell him to take care! Looking at his powerful arms reminded her of the feel of the man when his arms, like metal bands, held her close. He was Mighty Warrior. He was her Lord Husband! The thought made her go weak at the knees. He did not look her way.

He was in place, ahead of his separately organised chariot corps. Handsome, arrogant, he was grim faced. Toadying was not in his scheme of things. However, Governor Khonsu had insisted that expediency must be the order of the day. He raised his hand in command and the noble black stallions Ra and Sphinx adorned with red ostrich feathers and bells of gold, began to trot handsomely towards the gates of the citadel.

Suddenly, Nefer found herself wanting to run after him. She wanted to throw herself into his arms and lift her face up to accept his kiss. She wanted to look into his eyes, breathe his name. She wanted to tell him—what would she say?

Confused she turned to Oyahbe who was holding Nesmin in her arms. Next to her, Yati with little Pepy. Both young women were smiling and laughing. They were excited at the peace talk celebrations that were soon to begin. But it was all a cover-up, Nefer thought. Amosis's welcoming words would have a hollow ring. As hollow in fact as they were when he called her My Lady Wife. He did not love her, he had said as much. He had merely admitted to having become accustomed to her face! She watched the departing men again.

The last chariot had vanished through the citadel gates and Nefer said to the two women:

'It is over. There will be no more excitement for a while. Nothing will happen until My Lord Husband has escorted the

Hurrian safely back here. Come along do. I wish to return to the house.'

Once they reached House of Amosis, Nefer left Oyahbe in charge of Nesmin and hurried to the ovens outside where Uronarti was passing the time of day with Paihuti. Kanes was there too, watching Uronarti with big dreamy eyes. Nefer dismissed her, then turned anxiously to the men.

'I have come to beg of you to help me,' she told them. 'I have heard that my loved ones will be at Kerma. Their ship will have arrived, or at least be due to arrive at any moment now. I want you to go and meet them. They must be brought safely back here. I do not need to tell you that we live in dangerous times.'

Paihuti was watching her closely. Uronarti was plainly puzzled and looked away.

'My lady,' Paihuti said, 'we are your servants and your wish is our command, but there are difficulties ahead. All of the camels here belong to the army and they will not be let go. It is the same with the horses. We could hire litter bearers, but a man can only run so fast. To carry out what you have asked us surely calls for haste. I cannot see—'

'Paihuti, it must be accomplished,' she cried. 'I am holding my breath in fear!'

He frowned, then asked:

'Who are we to meet, my lady?'

'My mother and father,' she wept. 'Oh beloved Paihuti, help me, please!'

'But—how?'

'Take Duat and Horus! My mother is slight. She will ride with my father. You two must be one at each side. Guard them, defend them with your lives. I—what is the matter with you?' She broke off exasperated. 'Your mouths have dropped open. You look stupid like that!'

'My lady,' Paihuti's voice shook, 'we dare not!'

'Not ride to Kerma? You are afraid?'

'We will die! The Lord Amosis would kill us with his bare hands. Those great and glorious animals are the light of his life. He has given orders to the animals' servants and slaves. No one may get near enough even to breathe on Duat and Horus.'

'I can!'

'But, my lady—'

'And I will! Now this is what I plan—'

'My lady,' Uronarti breathed out, horrified. 'I know nothing of horses and—and I fear the Lord Master's rage.'

'Think of this,' she told him. 'The journey will be over and done with quite quickly if you ride like the wind. The celebrations here are set to last at least two nights and days. There will be much feasting and drinking. Many speeches will be expounded, many pleasures will be laid on. My Lord Amosis will have no time to visit the stables—and should he even think of doing such a thing I—I have ways of making him change his mind.'

'We will return to our deaths,' Paihuti said flatly. 'But for my beloved Lord Per Ibsen and sweet mistress Zarah, I will go.'

'I—I do not think I have your courage,' Uronarti stammered. 'I am only a peasant born. I am less than the dirt at your feet, my lady.'

'Nonsense,' she told him. 'You are a king in Kanes' eyes. You have seen the way she looks at you?'

'She is as above me as the stars,' Uronarti said. 'I worship at her feet.'

'Go with Paihuti, get my parents safely back here, and you shall have Kanes as your wife.'

It was sufficient only to smile at them both in her sweet pleading way after that. They both agreed that if she could get the stable minders to let the horses go, and if she could get them past the guards on duty at the citadel gates, they would attempt to do what she asked.

They went with Nefer to the stables. The men there knew her well, for she took Nesmin to see the horses every day.

'It is my wish,' she told the horses' Chief Caretaker, Sekhti and slaves, 'that you take this opportunity to relax from your duties. I have two men, Uronarti and Paihuti, who will guard these great beasts with their lives, and will exercise them. In the meantime, I give you these bands of gold and this bag of fine beads. Go in peace and enjoy fat goose, fruit and beer.'

'My lady,' the eldest and bravest man whispered, 'we have been ordered to stay here at all times.'

She fixed him with a tight determined smile.

'My dear Sekhti, am I not the Mistress of Lord Amosis's house?'

'Ai, my lady.'

'And when my lord is not here, is it not correct that you do as I say?'

'Ai,' he replied, then dared to add, 'but not where his prize horses are concerned.'

He knew the Lady Nefer had it in her power to have him cut down or stoned and remained waiting for the blow.

'Sekhti, I make you this promise,' Nefer said urgently, 'if we are found out, the Lord Amosis will know that it was I who gave you these orders. That the gold I insist on handing over to you all, belongs only to me. The Lord Amosis will have it made quite clear, by me, that you had no alternative other than

297

to obey me. Please take the gold and go. But first make the animals ready for me, please. They will have a hard ride and with luck on our sides they will be back before My Lord Husband returns.'

When the great animals were led out it was clear to Sekhti and the others that Paihuti and Uronarti had no understanding of horses. It was then that Nefer had to throw caution to the winds.

'Sekhti,' she said, 'I will need your help. We must get to Kerma and meet those that Paihuti will recognise. Bring them back safe. And if you do this thing, risk your lives for me in this way, I swear by all the gods, that you will be repaid a million times!'

'But the Lord Amosis—'

'Will return and hand Ra over to Bata, as he always does. Bata who loves Ra and Sphinx like sons, will act as usual and lead them back to the stables here. The Lord Amosis will himself go straight to the Governor's House—where I will be waiting for him.'

'And—and the guards by the gates, my lady?' Paihuti asked quietly.

'See? Here is the Mighty Warrior's scarab that bears his seal. Take it and show it to the guards.' She handed over the green stone beetle that had ruby eyes. 'It will be as good as a direct order. Do you believe that?'

Sekhti watched as Paihuti took the scarab, then he wordlessly began to ensure that the animals were correctly harnessed and prepared for the ride to Kerma. They were fine animals and could take the journey in their stride. All would be well providing Mighty Warrior never found out.

Feeling victorious, Nefer returned alone to the garden, sure in the knowledge that Paihuti would comb the length and breadth of the city until he found those so dear to her heart.

She would see Lady Zarah again and be held against Per Ibsen's heart. How they would adore Nesmin. How Mother would croon over him and how pleased Per Ibsen would look! They would stay here safe in the citadel, while she fussed and fretted over them both. She would herself wait on them hand and foot. Excited, happy, she began to sing the love song she had learned at old Natalia's knee.

'She stands upon the further side,
Between us flows the Nile.
And in those waters deep and wide
There lurks a crocodile.

Yet is my love so true and sweet,
A word of power, a charm—
The stream is land between my feet
And bears me without harm.

For I shall come to where she stands,
No more be held apart.
And I shall take my darling's hands
And draw her to my heart.'

As the words faded she bit her lip, because now she had got her own way, she realised the enormity of the thing she had done. She had *forced* helpless workers and slaves to do as she ordered. She had been more cruel than any slaver, because she had overridden their desire to carry out Amosis's instructions. They were probably now in mortal terror. Their lives were not their own. She had placed them in an impossible situation. She should have known better! She was suddenly enormously distressed and ashamed.

What if he finds out, she thought frantically. If he goes to the stables and finds his most prized possessions gone, I will throw myself before him. I'll grovel. I'll do anything! He can beat me, kill me, do what he will, but he must not blame the poor servants and slaves. I will not allow him to punish them for doing what I, and I alone, made them do. They cannot be blamed.

She began making frantic bargains with Amun, if only the gods would keep Amosis away from the stables until the horses' safe return.

I will go to My Lord Husband, she thought feverishly. I will make passionate love to him. I will let him see me as the very goddess of love. I will make him alive as he has never been before. He will not be able to take his eyes off me. He will not want me to leave his bed.

Try though she did, she failed even to convince herself. She went back into the house and played with Nesmin until it was time for him to sleep. Miserable, feeling sick with guilt, she accepted when Bebu came fussing in, saying that it was time to get ready. To make sure that she looked more beautiful than the loveliest flower!

'Please Amun,' she whispered over and over again, 'for just once in his life, let my Lord Husband forget his fine horses and think only of me.'

'What did you say, my lady?' Bebu asked. 'Are you ill? You should be as excited as us—' She smiled archly. 'And do not forget that you can look forward to Mighty Warrior's return.'

'How can I forget, Bebu?' Nefer whispered and went white to the lips.

CHAPTER TEN

There was a great deal of laughter and excitement around Nefer after that. She was washed and perfumed with the sweet-smelling oil of flowers. Her fingers and toe nails were painted with henna. Her sweet, pretty mouth was the colour of peach as was the rouge she wore. Her eyes were outlined with khol making them look larger than ever. Green malachite shadowed her lids and stretched like cool water up to the fine dark arches of her brows.

The material of her dress had been woven so loosely that it was like a fine pearl-pink mist about her. Over her shoulders, she wore a matching cape that was edged with little pink stones set in chains of gold. The deep collar she wore was a marvel. It had been a New Year present from Per Ibsen some time before. It was a wide latticed half-moon shape of gold set with lotus flowers fashioned from rose coloured gems. It was a collar of such delicacy and beauty that there was only one man who could have fashioned it. His name, Ananias. It was Nefer's pride and joy. She had cried out her pleasure when she had seen it among the things so carefully packed by Bebu.

Amosis had not seen it before, simply because she had believed him to prefer blue. She wore pink lilies in the dark beauty of her long hair. In contrast the earrings, bracelets, anklets and the belt were all of fine gold chains set with glittering red jewels.

Bebu, Kanes, Yati and the other women who had attended, surrounded Nefer, smiling and clapping their hands.

'You look like a little wisp of morning cloud,' Bebu told her. 'And, my lady, you are almost too beautiful to be true.'

'Thank you,' Nefer said quietly, and loved them with her eyes. 'You are all very kind and I don't honestly know what I would do without you.'

'The master will think he has a little morning princess for his Lady Wife,' the bubbling Yati crowed. 'Mighty Amosis will be the proudest and the most envied man in Residence this night!'

'I would like that, Yati,' Nefer whispered and her smile was tremulous and unsure. 'And now you must go about beautifying yourselves because you will enjoy celebrations of your own. The food and wine, fruit and beer that you like has been set aside for you—and honey cakes. Yes, I made quite certain that there would be masses of honey cakes, if only for the sake of Bebu!'

They all laughed at that and teased jolly Bebu who was the plumpest lady of all. When Nefer smiled her dismissal they all went away still laughing, their spirits high.

As yet there had been no call from the look-out wall, no high trumpet cry. The visiting party escorted by Amosis was still nowhere in sight. The later they were, Nefer thought desperately, the less chance there would be of Amosis finding out about the missing Duat, Horus and Sphinx. On arrival, he would be in attendance and on guard at all times. This because it would be too terrible if a nationalistic Egyptian attempted, in his fervour, to kill Hapdjefi! There was a great deal of hard feeling in the ranks. And, too, there was a deep and deadly suspicion over too many mysteriously missing scouts. Each and every one of them having been a fine and brave Egyptian man. Animosity among all of the Egyptian soldiers was running high.

Worried, concerned, Nefer went outside to her small, greatly treasured garden area and sat alone. The ache in her heart was so deep now, so sad, that tears came to her eyes. The perfume of the lilies she was wearing made her go back in time and see a magical, golden, sunlit scene.

There had been so many flowers. Masses and cascades of them, and their strong, intoxicating perfume had seemed to swirl all around her, like a fine veil flowing out on the breeze. Her senses had been so alive, yet she had been so shy. Her heart was singing when he had been at her side, flying high, floating like a bird up to fluffy white clouds. Her soul had been filled with longing, yearning, the uniformed, silver-splintered dreaming of a shy small child.

How she had looked up to that tall, raw boned young man! How she had quivered with delight at his slow, wide smile. And when his strong fingers had curled comfortingly round her own she had felt like a fledgling again, flying joyously to the highest peak in the land of the gods.

She had been so lost and alone before his arrival, so incredibly afraid when he had gone. And he? He had suffered, he had said so. Perhaps even far more than she.

When Ese had gone and she, Nefer, had been allowed back into Per Ibsen's house, her life had about faced again. She was held tight and warm within family bonds of love. Unlike the hurt young Amosis, facing a harsh and cruel world on his own.

Yet in spite of all Zarah's love and care, Ese had left her mark. Her bony pointing finger of fear still lay like a black bruise on Nefer's trembling immature mind. She regularly had bad dreams of the terrible woman. Also she could not forget darling Natalia's death for a very long time. And—and she had waited so wistfully to hear Amosis's name!

Gradually the gold glittering, lotus eating existence of being daughter of a favourite at court had re-woven her days. And as always there was dearest Twosre, quiet, diffident Sebni—and Khaleb.

She had come to adore the young Prince, who was so handsome, so merry and so good at getting his own way. It had been Khaleb who finally seemed to have been the magic to make her forget that other larger, tougher more dependable boy.

Now Nefer recognised that the closeness that far away, innocent little girl had felt for Amosis had never really been banished. Had in fact always been there. The gods had taken Amosis the boy away from her, had replaced him with Mighty Warrior—the eagle-like man. The gods had also given her a second chance and made her his wife!

Love Khaleb though most undoubtedly she still did, she knew that she wanted to stay as Amosis's wife. She needed to be his 'Woman of the House'. He was the rock she leaned on. She was a mere, helpless sliver of moonlight shimmering against the strength of a valiant of the sun. She was weak but found herself wanting to be the woman in her Lord Husband's bed.

Her hand flew to her mouth. She felt a choking sensation. If he ever found out what she had done, if he ever sent her away, she knew that she would want to shrivel and die. She loved Khaleb, had been his slave, but the Prince was in the past. Amosis stood for the here and now. All too vividly, she could remember his love-making.

Nefer closed her eyes and recaptured the feel of Amosis's strong body beside her in the darkness. Thought of how she had so often listened to the strong steady beating of his heart, the slow and regular rhythm of his breath. In the deep purple world of sleeping, she had felt as if she were floating gently in a sea of security and content. Of all the people in the world, with Amosis, she felt safe.

Now, because of having her own way, there was every likelihood that he would clap his mighty hands together and in a cold fury, have her sent forever out of his House. The thought made her blood run cold.

There came a step behind her and she swung round. It was Bebu.

'My lady,' Bebu said, frowning. 'There

is something wrong. Paihuti seems to have vanished from the face of the earth. Kanes has searched for Uronarti. He too has gone. I must confess that I am feeling almost as badly as the girl in my distress.'

'Oh Bebu,' Nefer whispered and gave way to tears. 'You won't forgive me, neither will my lord. It—it is too late now. They are gone and there is nothing that I can do.'

'My lady?' Bebu's usually jolly expression had been worried before, but now she showed fear.

In rapid sentences Nefer told her the truth. She was wringing her hands as she spoke, and unable to look Bebu in the eyes. She waited for the wail of horror. None came. Instead Bebu was business-like and quite matter of fact.

'Of course they had to leave,' she said. 'Just as Paihuti's grandfather had to risk his life on your behalf all those years ago. My Lady Zarah and the Lord Per Ibsen are our light and our love.'

'But—but I forced them to make the journey, Bebu, and they—they have taken Duat and Horus.'

'Which is all the better,' Bebu said stoutly, 'because with such magnificent beasts in charge the task will be achieved the sooner.'

'And—and if my husband finds out?'

'We are all in this together, my lady. We will therefore make quite sure that Mighty Warrior never knows. Come, cheer up! Wipe your eyes and allow me to call the girls. You need fresh paint again now. This night of all nights, you must look your best.'

Relieved that Bebu knew, happy to share her burden of fear and guilt, Nefer allowed them all to fuss and fret over her again. At the end of it all, Bebu stepped back and said softly:

'No wonder your mother calls you Nefer, Nefer, Nefer. You are indeed thrice beautiful!'

Just then, high and clear there came the clarion call of the trumpets on the watching towers.

'Amun, save me!' Nefer whispered, her face tragic. 'Guard and protect me. Unseen One. Don't let Amosis find out that his horses are not here.'

As Hapdjefi rode in splendour with the Egyptians making a guard of honour on either side, he was thinking:

Kerma is the one stronghold that Thutmose will not keep. By my own strength I will take this city. We will be the one enemy that Pharaoh will not beat. We will smash his proud boast that he rules all the world. I am old, but I am pig-headed. I will survive long enough to hand Kerma over to Hapu. But first, I must and will have Nefer, the Egyptian girl.

Ahead, now clear to view, the Walls of Amenemhet Citadel stood proudly on the highest elevation, like a guard overlooking all. The 'Tower of the Wilderness' was the safest place of refuge, far better than Kerma itself. Its walls were less massive than the walls surrounding the city, even so, as a stronghold, it was superior in might. Within, Hapdjefi well knew, were situated the Governor's residence and the homes of government ministers—and Amosis, Chief of Southern Armies.

The Hurrian's eyes gleamed. The citadel was the last stronghold of refuge and resistance. When his men breached the city walls they would have to fight through the streets to reach the tower. It was not going to be simple. Kerma had in the past hundred years or so, expanded in size. The walls of the older establishment had been left standing and new walls built to enclose them all. The citadel was therefore a city within a city. Both sections must be overcome before the attackers could get to the great tower itself. There could be another way. The gates on the far side of Kerma looked directly on to the river, where there was always so much going on. But Hapdjefi had no ships. His was a wilderness army, and within their own sphere, they were supreme.

'Victory will be ours!' Hapdjefi whispered. 'There is no doubt about that. But I have had to come here in peace to get the girl. The rest will follow all in good time. I must be ensured of the goodwill of my daughter, Sitamun. She has the ear of the Lord of Death!'

Amosis, catching sight of the old King's twitching face and moving mouth, thought: He is talking to himself. He is in his dotage and clearly mad. Where is his son, Hapu? Just what mischief is he at behind all this play-acting that Hapdjefi's putting on? Why did Khonsu fall for this nonsensical peace treaty talk? This wily old son of Set is up to something that will bear ill for us all.

They reached the approach to the gate. Massive, wooden, and with heavy beams of metal, it was open wide to allow inhabitants to go freely about the business of the day. Towers were situated on either side of the gate so that defence efforts could be concentrated there.

As Amosis, the King, soldiers and entourage entered the city, the people crowded to watch them and cheered. Palm fronds were thrown in their path and Hapdjefi smiled in a thin, hard way. There was a faint uplift to Amosis's firm lips too. He was thinking of a pair of wide anxious eyes, of a cloud of shining dark hair that every so often swirled under his chin. Thrice Beautiful, he thought, yes, the name suited her well. She had brought no great disruption to his life after all, and she had pretty feminine ways. Yes, he was quite looking forward to seeing her. In fact he could hardly wait.

A large vessel floated near the shore of the Nile. Two men left the vessel, one of them holding a young woman in his arms as he waded ashore. Paihuti, watching, was puzzled. But even so, his duty was clear.

He waited silently, his thoughts like bees buzzing in his head. The trio meant trouble, he thought, deep and terrible trouble for the beloved Nefer. Why had they come instead of the two she expected? What had gone wrong?

Lord Amosis may have welcomed Lady Zarah and Lord Per Ibsen with open arms, but would that apply to Twosre, and to Sebni, who he Paihuti personally disliked? And to make matters a million times worse, with the brother and sister, there was none other than Prince Khaleb.

Paihuti had the distinct impression then, that his own days were numbered. Mighty Amosis would be terrible in his wrath, because, no matter what had gone on before, the lovely Lady Nefer was the Woman of Amosis House. Prince Khaleb would be as welcome in the citadel as a heap of jackal's dung. The Prince would not care a curse about a small thing like that. In fact he'd probably quite enjoy his position of power and Amosis's helplessness in the game.

With a calmness that he did not feel he signalled Sekhti and the others forward. Trouble! he was thinking. Nothing but trouble. Amun, Greatest God of All, please watch over our little Nefer. None of this is her doing. Do not allow her to take the blame.

The Governor's residence was large and sumptuous. The grounds were divided in efficient, orderly fashion. Minya's formal garden was set off with a lotus pool, shrubs and small decorative palms. There were cow pens at the rear of the house. In the forefront, work rooms, kitchens, servants' quarters, stables and shelters for the slaves were all crowded together. The whole establishment was managed with precision by the Steward. He always courteously referred to Minya, but otherwise had a free hand.

All was light and laughter, music and golden goblets filled with sweet water, beer or wine. Professional harpists had been hired, flautists and drummers. Servants and slaves had been busy all day and a great feast had been prepared. There was pigeon to eat, duck, goose and roast oxen. There were at least forty varieties of cakes and bread. Fruits were piled pyramid-high.

The ladies were separate and their chairs were set against one of the walls. Nefer sat next to Minya. With them also were officials' wives, daughters and a bevy of harem favourites dressed in their best. They looked like a host of exotic flowers in their coloured dresses, wide collars, beads, bracelets and rings. Many wore waxy incense cones on their elegant coiffures. As the evening progressed the slowly melting oil of the cones would seep into their hair.

Specially chosen serving girls handed round dishes of dates, grapes and sweet meats to the élite, who smiled on the girls and were gracious indeed. Any one of the girls could be favoured that night and thus risen in importance by the next day. It was wise always to play safe.

Opposite, on a tall chair, looking regal and stern, there sat Governor Khonsu. He usually insisted that his beloved Minya stayed at his side, but since the guest of honour was Hapdjefi, this simply would not do. Hurrians thought of women as less than the beasts they rode, be they camel, oxen or horse.

Suddenly, warningly, there came the strident cry of trumpets. Khonsu stood up, not a tall man, oval-faced, rather plain, but dignified for all that. Everyone fell silent.

Nefer, watching as eagerly as the rest, was fully caught up in the magic of the moment. She gasped in awe as Hapdjefi appeared. The old man was a magnificent sight, dressed in purple and gold. He all but glittered under the weight of jewels and the heaviness of his gold crown.

Hapdjefi came forward slowly, as stick-brittle as a desert thorn. His strange small-eyed face did not seem of this world. Behind him came his Hurrian soldiers wearing leather helmets that were small enough to show the crisp black curls covering their ears. They were bearded and wore knee-length woollen tunics with leather belts at the waist. All had high-strapped leather sandals on their feet. Without exception their noses were strong and their faces fierce. Behind them, marching proudly between the Governor's own guards, there came Mighty Amosis and his men.

From that moment Nefer had eyes only for her husband. How large he was, how dominating and grand.

A signal was given and slaves in Hapdjefi's service hurried forward to present caskets and gifts. Khonsu graciously accepted jewels, incense and myrrh. In return, he gave the Hurrians soild gold in the shape of heaps of little glittering Egyptian gods. What Hapdjefi thought about this was hard to tell.

Speeches of welcome and acceptance were made. Hapdjefi took his seat next to Khonsu. The feasting began.

During the first course dancing girls wearing only the tiniest of loin-cloths began their high kicking routine. Their long hair was pigtailed, on the end of which there swung large weighted discs. Some were gold, others red, green or blue. And the dancers swung their heads and the discs glinted and flew high and wove amazing and intricate designs. Crouching singers clapped and chanted in merry rhythm, their faces wreathed in smiles.

Nefer shivered and felt as though someone was walking over her grave. She looked across the room and caught sight of the King's black lizard-like eyes. She turned away quickly and saw that her Lord Husband was watching her too. She felt herself blushing and looked down.

The evening progressed at pace. Great quantities of intoxicating liquor were consumed. Men and women grew more flushed. Nefer, almost hypnotised by the continuous turning towards her of those black soulless eyes, noted that Hapdjefi drank very little himself.

Hired dwarfs arrived and they juggled and tumbled, made fools of themselves and generally amused. Wild acrobatic stunts were achieved by a group of wiry-haired men, then new dancers came. Beautiful, sinuous, slow and erotic, they moved to the music of harps in suggestive, seductive ways. Revellers began leaving their seats, the men trying to catch and hold the dancers while the others clapped and cheered and urged them on. More wine, fast drumbeats, music of a fiercer, more compelling kind. Men and women danced together now, fell into each others' arms, wanting and needing and not ashamed to say. This much to the enjoyment and delight of those who remained in their seats. What Hapdjefi was thinking was hard to tell.

Nefer sat where she was. There were empty chairs on her right for the harem girls, on orders from Khonsu, were making themselves pleasant to Hapdjefi's men.

'The Hurrians are not tempted,' Minya whispered behind her hand. 'They are all on guard, Nefer. We are not entertaining friends.'

'I am afraid of that king,' Nefer replied.

'He has the face of a lizard one minute, and like a monkey the next. It must be the light, the shadows, those awful deep-set eyes because he—he reminds me of a Jin!'

Amosis, looking over to the other side of the room a little later, thought his wife was worried. She seemed small and very vulnerable sitting there, like a delicate blossom in pink. She was, he considered, the most beautiful person in the room. He caught her eye, but she blushed again and looked away. He wondered why, not realising she was now consumed with anguish and guilt over the horses and the fear of her husband finding out.

A servant approached, stretched his hands before him and bowed low, saying:

'My lord, the King of all Hurrians requests the pleasure of having your Chief Lady at his side.'

Amosis stood up, hiding his displeasure at the thought, but with quiet deliberation, made his way across the crowded room. He towered over Nefer, his eyes roving over her in a proud, proprietary way.

'Nefer, Nefer, Nefer,' he said, 'I am proud of you. You delight my eyes. You make all the others look plain.'

'My lord!' she breathed and felt immensely pleased. 'I would have been happy just to have you join me, but to hear you

318

say such nice things makes my heart dance.'

She was rewarded by his wide slow grin.

'And you're not so bad at pretty speeches yourself. Come, the Hurrian wishes to meet you. This is most unusual. A high honour in fact. Whatever you do, take care.'

She looked up, suddenly afraid again. His tone held such a strong warning. But she relaxed again because his eyes were smiling into her own. If it had not been Amosis, Mighty Warrior, she would have believed him to be teasing her in his rough and ready way.

'Why must I take great care?' she asked and dimpled up at him.

'Because, given half the chance, I am sure that he would spirit you away. He must have realised that you are high above any of the others here.'

She was serious now, and asked:

'Have I any reason to be afraid? My lord, throughout this evening, he has been watching me and—and I do not think it is because he likes my face. I—I feel almost that there is something evil reaching out from him.'

Amosis laughed and his steps were slower as they lingered together, pretending to be held up by the cavorting crowds.

'Don't tell me that you have heard and

believe all the stories spread about that old reprobate?'

'I have not!'

'They say that in his time he ate the hearts of the heroes he killed in battle. Now it occurs to me to wonder what happened to all the pretty girls that went through his hands.

It had started out as a joke, but now Amosis had a serious expression on his face and Nefer suddenly felt very unsure. She looked at the old King, the soulless, secretive look on his face made her shiver again.

'Amosis,' she said breathlessly, 'you would never let him, or any other enemy take me alive, would you? Promise me!'

His arm encircled her waist like a comforting metal band. 'Small Person,' he said quietly, 'no one will ever lay hands on you. To this I swear.'

For all the calmness of his tone, he was shocked. A great unease filled him. He was remembering battles that he had himself been in and won. There had been no mercy shown to the vanquished. Men had died, women and children taken as slaves. Some, the lucky ones, found good homes as servants in rich houses. Others had quickly succumbed, working in the choking horrors of the turquoise mines. What would happen to a delicate flower like Nefer? It would take less than a night, he thought grimly. Just one night of such cruelty and her little flame of life would be gusted away. He knew then that he would defy even god himself, Mighty Pharaoh, Horus over the world, to keep Nefer safe.

He could play for time no longer. The men at the head of the room were looking uneasy. There was irritability on the old King's face. Amosis led Nefer to Hapdjefi and found himself dismissed. He sat down, disturbed even more, for he had not liked nor understood the sudden flame that had leapt into the other man's eyes. This even though there had been no other expression on the Hurrian's face.

In the centre of the hall a wild Kushite dance was now in full swing. Dozens of savage native figures twirled round in a circle. As the music quickened so did their pace until they were moving round like spinning tops, going at an amazing speed. And all the time they were letting out flesh-creeping shrieks and screams. For the first time the Hurrian smiled. Looking at the grimace made Nefer feel sick. Although she had been seated next to the King he had taken no notice of her apart from the first quick scrutiny that had made her flesh crawl. Hapdjefi was intent on the dancers. Unaware of anything other than the mêlée before him. Lamplight gleamed on the excited faces of the watchers. Many of whom now sprawled on the ground, clapping their hands to drum music, encouraging the entertainers with loud cries.

By midnight the fun was running at its highest. Totally unnerved because although he had spoken no word, Hapdjefi had signified that she may not leave, Nefer sat very still. She was thankfully aware of Amosis's watchful eyes.

As the orgy continued Governor Khonsu and Hapdjefi began to talk. They spoke low and no one else heard what they had to say but clearly, bargaining of some kind was going on. At last Khonsu held up his hand in a firm, but negative way.

'I am sorry Great Hapdjefi,' he said, 'this is not up to me, but up to the lord who I am quite sure, will not accept your terms.'

Those nearest to the two great men froze. The frenzied excitement of the evening died away and it was then that Nefer realised that the Egyptians all around her were not so drink-sodden as they had seemed. There were still noisy revellers of course, and several drunken figures staggered round in a hazy whirl. But the people of note near Khonsu and the King were alert and sober, and very aware indeed.

'I will keep the peace,' Hapdjefi said firmly. 'Kerma will stand but I will have my price.'

'It is too high,' Khonsu replied.

'You mean,' the sepulchral whisper held surprise, 'you value Kerma less than one girl?'

'You are playing a trick, O King. I think that you are playing a very peculiar game.'

'I have stated my price. If I do not get it, it is only fair to warn you that I have hundreds of thousands of men in the wilderness just waiting for my word. There will be no peace if I do not have the girl.'

'O King,' Khonsu replied, 'you have been asking for trouble for a very long time.'

Before the conversation could go further three people came into the banqueting hall. Three people dressed up and clearly all ready and willing to have a good time.

'My Lord Khonsu!' Khaleb cried out and his face was lit by his wide handsome smile. 'My Majesty Hapdjefi! Peace and good will to you. May thy nights be happy.'

'And may thine be happy and blessed,' the Governor replied courteously. 'We did not expect the honour of receiving Egypt's great Prince.'

'Only the second greatest,' Khaleb laughed. 'My brother Amenhotep sends his greetings from Thebes. He says that perhaps he will be seeing you soon.'

A small muscle beating frantically in Hapdjefi's temple was the only indication of his sudden flare of unease. Amenhotep stood shoulder to shoulder with Mighty Amosis in strength and valour. If Amenhotep was heading this way he would not be travelling alone.

Nefer was unable to describe her emotions at that moment. She was utterly taken aback at seeing Khaleb, delighted almost to the point of tears at seeing Twosre's charming face and Sebni's expression of unease. Great functions like this one were, for Sebni at least, much too much. Then, over and above her shock at not seeing her parents, there came relief. Their arrival meant surely, that Paihuti had met *them*. If that were the case the horses were back safely.

Hapdjefi signalled that he wished to retire. The celebrations for this night at least, were at an end. The guests, those who were in the way, fell back respectfully, as he was led to the sumptuous room set aside for him. With this leave-taking, people were free either to stay or go home.

Still on official duty Amosis watched and

waited. He had seen Nefer's expression and did not recognise relief. He saw only the inordinate pleasure Khaleb's presence gave. He was surprised at the non-appearance of Per Ibsen and Zarah of Anshan, but rather more concerned with the rapid changes of emotion chasing across the face of his wife. He was suddenly coldly, killingly angry. His mood grew no better when, with pretty little speeches of gratitude for their hospitality, Nefer bade Minya and Khonsu farewell. Then she walked towards him, having merely smiled at Twosre.

'My lord?' she said softly. 'I may leave?'

He replied grimly. 'Since you have already spoken your farewells my permission is unnecessary I would say. But I am surprised, Nefer. I would have thought it too soon for your sister and the Prince to leave. Surely they've only just arrived?'

'They will stay, Amosis,' she replied, shocked at the cold look he gave her after the loving words he had given before. 'It is only—I am tired, that's all. And I did not enjoy having to sit next to that horrible old man.'

'He is a king, Nefer,' he replied crisply, his tone authoritative and seeking to put her in her place.

'I am sorry, my lord,' she replied and looked up with an expression in her eyes that spoke of over strain, and the sudden release from the fear of discovery. Then, openly defiant she added, 'King or not, he reminds me of the Devil of the Deserts, and he makes me afraid.'

'Really?' he snapped. 'Even though I have sworn to keep you safe. Not forgetting that now you also have Khaleb to hand?' It was a cruel barb.

She drew in her breath and gasped.

'I will take my leave, my lord. I wish you goodnight.'

He stood tall and straight, looking more noble than any king, and watched until she was out of the long columned hall and his sight. Then he grimly turned his attention on to Khaleb who was thoroughly and quite wickedly enjoying all the adulation he was receiving. Twosre went to Amosis.

'Mighty Warrior,' she said sweetly, 'I cannot thank you enough for receiving my husband and I into the bosom of your home.'

'Your husband, my lady?' he asked, taken back. 'The Prince has taken you to wife?'

'Khaleb, Amosis? Goodness no! I have married Sebni.' She looked over her shoulder and smiled so warmly at the silent sickle-eyed young man that Amosis's bewilderment grew. 'Sebni, my brother, is dear to my heart. He and I refuse to be parted and that is the real reason why we came here.'

'So the two people in trouble are you and—'

'Yes, Sebni and I. It is a long story and one that I must explain to both you and Nefer. Then—then, Amosis, if you wish us to leave—'

He brushed her words to one side.

'Twosre, my sister, why has Khaleb come here?'

Twosre eyed him tragically and in a voice barely above a whisper replied:

'My lord, I feel that you know!'

'No!' he said sharply. 'I will not permit it! I have Pharaoh's seal.'

'You also have his grandson, Amosis!'

'Nesmin is my own,' he replied harshly. 'He is my son.'

'Then I shall bear solemn witness to the fact,' Twosre said firmly and tossed her head so that her hair with its pretty gold ornaments swung wild and free. 'I will set a seal on my written oath. I will personally challenge his word. And now, with your gracious permission, may Sebni and I go to your home? This sort of affair quite literally gives my poor husband a pain in the head. We came because Khaleb insisted that we must. And you know as well as we do, that when royalty snaps their fingers, we mere mortals must obey.'

Suddenly Amosis smiled his great wide grin.

'My Lady Twosre and brother Sebni,' he said. 'I welcome you with all my heart. Nefer will be burning incense to the gods in her joy at seeing you. I will not myself return to the house for a while yet. When I do we will talk and eat and drink and get to know each other far better than we do now.'

'That will be our great pleasure,' Twosre replied, then turned to take her tired looking husband's hand.

Amosis called for slaves and front runners with lighted flares to show them the way. Before they had left he had forgotten them. He was watching Khaleb, and there was cold distaste in his eyes.

CHAPTER ELEVEN

When Twosre, followed by Sebni, walked in, Nefer, who had been waiting, ran to her with open arms.

'O Beloved,' she cried. 'What a pussycat you are and how pleased I am to see you. You also, Sebni, my brother.'

He looked bemused and sat on a chair in a slow, weary manner. But Twosre was bubbling in her happy, breathless way, taking little or no notice of him.

'You were so pleased to see us that you ran away the moment we came in sight, Nefer? You left that banquet looking like a wounded deer!'

'Forgive me, but I had to escape. Everyone's attention was on Khaleb at that moment and I took the chance to get away. Twosre, didn't you take a look at that old king? I was made to sit next to him, an honour they said! But he kept looking at me in a most disgusting way. All I could do was sit there and smile and pretend that I was aware of how honoured I was. The truth being of course, that I was feeling sick unto death. Once he put his claw-like hand on my knee and I found him obscene!'

'Well, all of that is over now, my beautiful, and you are free.'

'Not so, Twosre,' Nefer said and there was a hunted look on her face. 'I think there is more to it than that. I believe that something is about to happen. Something quite horrible and I am afraid.'

'You should not have such a refined and delicate air about you,' Twosre teased. 'You often look very unworldly, you know. Most men like the challenge of tearing down the defences of a sweet young goddess. I expect ancient old Hapdjefi would give his eye teeth to have you on his arm.'

'You don't understand—'

'I know only that you are afraid of shadows, Nefer, very unlike me! If that dried up old man had smiled on me, I would have tickled and teased him and so tired him out that he'd have no further heart for the game.'

'Twosre!'

'Don't look so shocked, Sister dear,' Twosre laughed in her merry lilting way. 'That is how I get out of difficult spots and you never do. Don't you see? By taking that old man's challenge up I would have made him aware of his own inadequacies. No man likes to feel a fool. So—I would be on the winning side for I would very pointedly make him see that he was the one unable to fulfil me! He would be the one at fault!'

'And then you would be killed for your pains! We are not playing little court games here, this is reality. But that is enough about me. Why are you and Sebni here? I was waiting to greet our father and our mother. When are they due to arrive?'

'They are not coming. They are very happy in Thebes. Indeed, our Lord Father sits on Pharaoh's right hand and bathes in his smiles. Mind you, the temple Father has built in Thutmose's name is so marvellous

330

that even a god can't fail to be pleased.'

Nefer was nonplussed.

'Then—then it is you and Sebni that are in trouble?'

Twosre made a wry little face and shrugged saying:

'By Set and all devils, we are in trouble and that is the truth.'

'And it is so awful,' Nefer asked wistfully, 'that you had to forget your loyalty and—and bring Khaleb here as well to discover me?'

Twosre was very repentant and sincere.

'Believe me, my sister, we had no choice. He found us even though we believed we were well hidden. He followed us to Pepi's, and after that he came after us in his own boat. We had no say in it, Nefer, and there was nothing that we could do.'

Nefer's heart was beating too quickly. She was trying to forget the warm ringing sound of Khaleb's laughter-filled voice. Trying not to see the charm of his smile. His eyes, as dark and shiny as southern grapes, had looked directly into hers. It had only been one quick look, but it had been enough.

She dared not admit to Twosre that she had run away, not because of that foul old king, but because Khaleb's one quizzical glance had been enough. He had come after her to find out about her baby for himself. He would take one look at Nesmin and he would know. Soon, very soon now, she would be given an ultimatum. Either she and Nesmin could go back to Thebes under the protection of Khaleb, or else she could stay and Nesmin, sweet baby Nesmin, would travel with the Prince alone.

'No!' her heart cried. 'No, no, no!'

Nefer tried to concentrate on matters other than her own.

'You must tell me all the news, Twosre, and explain to me why you and Sebni had to leave Thebes. There was secrecy in it? Fear?'

'I will tell you everything, beloved.' Twosre's tone held great urgency and the laughter in her eyes had gone. 'But first, please call your servants that they might help me to get my Lord Husband to bed. See? He sleeps. That is good, a release for him since he had another bad pain in his head.'

'You—you have married our brother?'

'Yes. Joyfully! His love for me is the most complete and utter madness that I have ever known. It is hard to live up to, believe me.'

'And do you love him, Twosre? Really and truly love him?'

And then Twosre looked at the sleeping figure who somehow managed to look so lost and forlorn, and there was infinite compassion in her eyes.

'Yes, I love him,' she said gently. 'And he loves and totally relies on me. Now, please call your servants. He really does need to be taken to a comfortable bed.'

Bebu came as did the other girls, but Nefer noted it was Twosre who held Sebni close and her lovely face was tender, her eyes full of concern. I never thought I would see the day when Twosre would actually care, Nefer thought, and went so far as to say as much when her sister returned. Twosre smiled in a faint, sad way and replied:

'Sebni needs me. He always will. He—he is not like other men, Nefer.'

'He has always been quiet and shy and liked to keep himself to himself, I know. But it's you I can't understand, Twosre, you of all people are in love with Sebni?'

'He is not like other men,' Twosre said again and then added starkly: 'In the head! He has pains, Nefer, and they are agony for him. And once—just once out of love for me, he did an enormously terrible thing.'

'Sebni,' Nefer smiled, 'is not capable of doing a terrible thing.'

'Listen to me, O Sister. Let me tell you how we came to be here. Once you know the truth you must act as you think is right.

Either let us stay here or else send us away for ever. Either way, just by coming here, we have put your life in jeopardy. I think that it would be best if you turned your back on us. But, I did have to see you again, just this once. You are dear to me, Nefer.'

'Twosre, no matter what has happened, I would never send you away from my house.'

Ignoring Nefer's protestations, Twosre carefully told Nefer what had happened. She left nothing out and ended by saying:

'Our brother is not aware of the thing he has done. He has a faint inkling of it now and again, but he believes it all happened in a dream. He clings to me now. And I? It has come to the point where I do not know what I would do without him. Whatever happens. Nefer, if they catch us, don't let them send him away.'

Nefer's compassion outweighed her shock.

'Beloved,' she said carefully, 'should Sebni not be taken to the temple to see the physician of the head? He has been known to work miracles in his time. Our father would pay for the top man, no less, and—'

'Do you honestly believe that the Law Officer would agree to this?' Twosre asked fiercely. 'I met him and found him an awesome, quite frightening man. How do you think Sebni would cope, standing before them all in the Temple of Law? His head would hurt him and without me he would go really mad. No! We must leave him in peace, Nefer, and pray that Imhotep, the great God of Medicine will hear my prayers. I fear that Sebni is beyond mortal aid.'

'My dear Twosre,' Nefer's voice held all of the love and sympathy in the world, 'don't look like that, so panic-stricken. You and Sebni are no longer alone. Sebni will get better all in good time and both of you will be left in peace here. But—Twosre, does Khaleb know?'

Twosre looked tired, her eyes were wide and sad. She held her hands out in a wide helpless gesture and nodded her head.

'We are all in his clutches and well he knows it,' she said bitterly. 'And to think that all the days of my life I have loved and adored him. That all the escapades I have had, every time I laughed and left a man in despair, I really was thinking only of him, and wishing it was our dear sweet Prince I was paying back. Oh Nefer, Nefer, Nefer, don't tell me that you did not know?'

Unbelieving, Nefer stared at her younger sister. Never by word or deed had Twosre given her secret away. No one had ever known, till now.

'Why did you not tell me?' she whispered

frantically. 'I can hardly believe that you are telling me the truth.'

'Can't you? Not really, Nefer?'

'And when he came to Ramose and he and I—'

'He was playing a game, using you to go against me. All my life I have fought and squabbled with Khaleb. All these years I have gone out of my way to beat him at his own game. Then, when he came and—and made things as they were with you, I knew I would never forgive him.' She laughed and it was a bitter sound. 'Yet, until that time, Nefer, there were actually times when I won! Now the games are over and it is Sebni that I must care about.'

Nefer was barely listening.

'I never knew,' she whispered. 'I was so passionately in love with him that I could see and think of no one else. Oh, my dear little kitten, forgive me! How you must have suffered and how wicked he—'

Twosre's face lit up and she was herself again.

'Don't look so tragic! I have survived and believe me, I always will. Now, I will let you into a secret. I have brought you a present, Nefer, no several in fact. But I will show you in the morning because, at this moment, I feel very, very tired.'

Nefer retired herself shortly after that, her thoughts in a whirl. She knew that she had taken too much on herself, saying that Twosre could stay here in her Lord Husband's house, but what else could she have done? I must throw myself on Amosis's mercy, she thought feverishly. If Sebni is to be helped at all, it is Amosis who will know what is best to do.

She fell asleep and dreamed wild dreams. Someone was taking her baby away. Little Nesmin was screaming, but her legs refused to move and there was nothing she could do. She was calling out for help, but the demon riding away with her child was getting further and further away. Then the demon turned round and the hood fell away from his face, he was laughing, laughing in a diabolical way.

'Khaleb!' she cried out and awoke with tears running down her face. It was morning, and Amosis was standing before the bed. He stood tall and angry, his arms folded, his legs astride.

'My Lord Husband,' she wept, 'I dreamt that Prince Khaleb had taken away our son.'

'No man takes what is mine, Nefer,' he said coldly. 'And no woman, come to that.'

'But when he sees Nesmin, he will know! He will claim him and there will be nothing that we can do for Khaleb will

337

be looking at his own likeness and we will be lost.'

'See his own likeness?' Amosis raised his brows in a tight, supercilious way. 'What foolishness is this? Nesmin is the double of you.'

She held her breath, hope springing, her eyes shining with wonder and joy.

'That is your honest opinion, my lord?'

'My honest opinion,' he replied stiffly, then added: 'I can only believe that seeing Khaleb's likeness in the boy is wistful thinking on your part.'

'No!'

'You woke with his name on your lips.'

'I told you, my lord,' she said frantically, 'I dreamt that he was running away with my—our son. I was trying to follow. I was unable to move. Please, please believe me.'

Instead of weakening, his anger grew more fierce.

'Why did you tell me untruths, Nefer?'

'I—I did not not, my lord?'

'Was there not something about having your parents met?' he asked silkily.

'I truly believed they were in trouble. I never dreamed that it was my sister and Sebni—'

'And Khaleb?'

'No!'

His eyes were narrowed and his face

338

looked as though it had been chiselled from stone.

'You knew who the visitors were to be, *knew!* And, my lady, you were so anxious to see Pharaoh's Divine Son again that you went out to the stables and browbeat my men. And in so doing, you have committed the sin that I cannot, nor will I ever forgive.'

'Oh! My lord husband, please—'

She could not speak further. The words died in her throat, her mouth had gone dry. How stupid she had been, how ridiculously naive. Had she honestly thought it possible to have her Lord Husband's beloved horses removed from the stable? Have them used as mere travel animals, without it becoming common knowledge to the whole of a shocked and disapproving world? The great and noble beasts who were Amosis's pride and joy—worse, to actually pick up the very man whose dishonourable actions had brought about their master's marriage to a woman who he must now despise. How despicable I must look in my husband's eyes, she thought and felt physically drained.

Where just moments before she had been lying on the bed like a crushed and wilting flower, she now sat up, entreaty in her eyes.

'I confess,' she said urgently, 'yes,

Mighty Warrior, I confess! I went to your stables and I was like a wild and terrifying person, so determined was I to have my way. I told them that I would have them cut up into little bits and pieces. I had my way—and Amosis, now I am glad that I did. Twosre and Sebni are in terrible trouble and I want above all else to help ...'

'I heard how it was!' Was there a faint lessening in the tightening of his face she thought wildly? He went on: 'And I cannot quite see you as a wild and terrifying person, for all you say. But you did bend my men to your will, and worse, you knew very well that you were doing wrong.'

'The punishment must be mine, Amosis,' she cried. 'Whip me, it is nothing less than I deserve. But I swear by the gods that Paihuti, Uronarti, Sekhti and the rest of them were placed in an intolerable position. They obeyed me simply because there was nothing else that they could do.

He made no reply and she lapsed into a miserable silence. He was gazing down at her in an insolent, arrogant way. When he spoke next, his voice was harsh and held only contempt.

'Unworthy creature you may be,' he told her, 'but you are mine. You belong to me. Do you hear? Only to me!'

'Yes, my lord,' she whispered. 'I know.'

'You were a plaything used by Khaleb and when he was through, he cast you aside. Then, just because it suited those who I must obey, I was ordered to take you to wife. You *are* my wife, Nefer, the Woman of my House. Should any of this make me feel proud?'

'No,' she choked and was quivering with shame. 'I am sorry, my lord. Please forgive me and please—please do not send me away.'

'Because while you stay, so might your sister and her man?'

'No, Amosis. I—I want to stay.'

'And so you shall, my lady. I intend to ensure that you do at least do your duty in one respect. You will give me children. I will fill you to overflowing with my seed. Mine! And since there is no time like the present, prepare to accept me now.'

He began coldly and deliberately to take off his clothes. She flinched as he got into bed and unfeelingly pushed her down. She lay there, tears running down her face. He was going to punish her the best way he knew how. Humiliate her and show her his utmost contempt.

There was no love in the savagery of his onslaught, no tenderness. Only fury and ruthlessness and the angry battering of brute strength. And even though she sobbed out his name, begged for forgiveness and told him she was sorry over and over again, he thrashed into her as grim and as uncaring as any man using a whore.

When he had left the bed, was dressed and staring ruthlessly down at the crumpled figure that lay there so desolate and forlorn, he asked cruelly:

'Tell me, what did Khaleb give you as payment after he had eaten at your table?'

She did not, could not reply.

He took a wide gold band from his wrist, a bracelet that had been decorated with holy scarabs, the ankh sign of life, and Amosis's own name. He threw it down cynically, looked her over in a hard and contemptuous way, then swung on his heels and left.

Crushed and more deeply hurt than she had ever been in her life, she stayed where she was for a very long time. She did not want to see anyone, felt too despairing even to call for the ministrations of the beloved Bebu. Never Bebu. She had such wise, all-seeing eyes!

It was Twosre's arrival that made her pull herself together and to hide her feelings as best she could. Twosre who could still smile, for all her trouble, could still laugh and tease and all but say 'to Set with the world!' Twosre who right then and there made Nefer try desperately to get things in their true perspective again.

'Nefer, you are not still here! Aren't you even a little bit interested in the presents I have brought for you?'

'Oh I am, I am! I had forgotten, that's all.' Nefer smiled obediently and jumped out of the bed. Twosre clapped her hands for Bebu who came bustling in.

'Hurry, Bebu,' Nefer said lightly. 'My sister has surprises in store for me. I cannot wait!'

Amidst much laughter and teasing Nefer was dressed and her face painted. Her hair combed till it shone and a deep collar of red, green and blue was fixed round her neck to brighten the plain white flax-linen straight dress she wore.

'Let her go now, Bebu,' Twosre pleaded, her face alight with love and laughter. 'Now Nefer, come with me. Try to guess what it is that I have brought you.'

'Gem stones? Beads? Flowers? Oh, a new collar?'

'All wrong! But you'll be very happy, I promise you.'

Twosre continued to act mysteriously until they reached the small side room next to the entrance hall. They entered and, in the middle of the room, Nefer saw a plaited rush basket.

'Open it up, then,' Twosre insisted. 'And mind how you go—it might hold vipers, had you thought of that?'

'Twosre! Now—let me see! Oh!'

She was gazing down at two pairs of sleepily blinking blue eyes. With a joyous little exclamation, Nefer sank to her knees beside the basket and kissed each little grey stripy face in turn.

'Kittens!' she said unsteadily. 'Oh Twosre, what a wonderful thought. And they are so beautiful and so sweet.' Gently she reached inside the basket and picked up the two diminutive furry little creatures and held them close.

'Oh, how I'll adore them and cherish them, Twosre. I shall never let them out of my sight. I will guard them and if anyone dares to frighten them or upset them or treat them wrong, I—' She stopped then and remembered that her Lord Husband had pets that he adored too. Great wondrous horses and she—in her blind selfishness had put them at risk. She made her immense pleasure over the kittens her excuse for her sudden upsurge of nervous tears.

'I can see that Priestess of Bast will have no cause to admonish you,' Twosre remarked, 'nor kill you, come to that.' She was referring to the death penalty received by anyone wicked enough or rash to kill a cat. The animals were sacred and had vast temples built where they lived in close proximity of the Cat Goddess Bast. And Nefer, rubbing her face against the little creatures who had begun to purr was remembering her other darling pets that Ese had had sent away.

'They were born aboard the boat,' Twosre explained. 'Pepi's son Tu brought us here, remember him? He won't be parted from his cat. He calls her Star of the Morning. Star had her kittens, all six of them and Tu wanted to keep them all. I plagued the life out of him until he agreed that I might have two. What will you call them?'

'Khephren and Khufu, after those two pharaohs Father told us about. The ones who built the pyramids over one thousand years ago.'

'You are not remembering long dead pharaohs though, are you?' Twosre asked. 'You were thinking of your own past and feeling rather odd about it. Your face went quite white just then.'

'It—it is Ese,' Nefer had to admit. 'I suppose I will remember that dreadful woman all the days of my life. She always appears in my mind when I'm worried or sad.'

'If you're worried about Sebni and me being here,' Twosre said quickly, 'we will go now at once. I swear I would kill myself if I thought I was making you feel bad.'

'My house is your house for ever,' Nefer said firmly. 'The grief I have, I brought upon myself. I—I have greatly annoyed my Lord Husband. He—he flung this bracelet at me in his disgust and contempt. See?' She held up her arm to show the over-large wrist band that Amosis had thrown down. 'And Twosre, this I swear, one day I will give Amosis this monstrosity back. I—I shall pay him in kind.'

'And I shall clap my hands when you do,' Twosre said stoutly. 'And cry out with joy. How dare Mighty Warrior descend so low as to upset you!'

They smiled at each other in a dewy way and went back to the general room. Nefer was lovingly cradling the kittens in her arms. Kanes, Yati and other serving girls were there, all laughing and joking and busily replacing the lamps that had been cleaned and newly filled with rich castor oil. Then they saw the kittens and were clustering round them at once. Oyahbe and Bebu, holding the eager-eyed baby boys drew near. Khephren and Khufu were kept safe out of their way for everyone's sake. The whole world knew how holy cats could scratch, even in play.

Sebni sat alone. He was smiling, but withdrawn in a happy world of his own.

But every so often he looked across—just to make sure that Twosre was near.

Khonsu and all the officials were uneasy. Hapdjefi had still not deigned to appear. Grim-faced, Khaleb sat with the others, waiting for the forthcoming talks to begin. He was unsettled, and he had been for a long time. Ever since he had faced Twosre's look of loathing and scorn in the garden of Ramose House when he had so blatantly seduced Nefer. He had followed Twosre and Sebni on an impulse. He had heard rumours of Nefer's condition, but he had found that no great concern. It might not have happened if he had not been so outrageously bored. He cast his mind back to how it had been at home.

He had been in his palace at Thebes, outraged and revolted. Hunting had been bad, fishing a failure. Not surprising, since he was not allowed to go too far away. Polite court society and its meaningless talk made him feel bilious. But at Pharaoh's command he'd stayed near to home. He had felt that almost all of what his First Wife's friends said or did was completely incidental to real living. It was a round of superficial pretence, and all of the time, underlying everything, they were after the main chance. They would grovel and bow and scrape, do anything to take a step nearer to any favours handed down from the Throne.

He had looked up still scowling, as the woman he had married on Pharaoh's command came into the room. She was tall with a beauty that was refined rather than ostentatious. Her features were good, her cheekbones high. Her dark eyes were heavily outlined with khol and her red painted mouth belonged to a woman of determination. Her name was Neith.

'My lord,' her voice was well modulated and yet there was curiously little softness in her diction, 'why did you let her go?'

'I do not know, My Lady Neith,' he had said honestly. 'She is young, very lovely. She loves me. No, I do not honestly know.'

'You could go after her. She would be made very welcome in the women's house. Our only delight is the pleasure of our lord. We realise that our little dancing and gossiping sessions are of no interest to you. Not even the talk of the killing. But since the daughter of Per Ibsen was involved—'

'Killing?' She had his interest at last. 'What is this?'

'It was committed by Per Ibsen's adopted son, Sebni, who is quite mad, of course. The Priests of Law had quite a time trying to make up their minds whether Per Ibsen's daughter Twosre was involved. They have now decided that she was not. Since the natural uncle of Sebni was old and not favoured by the gods, the Priests of the Law have decided also that Sebni was driven by the spirits to take his uncle's life. In this way allowing the old man's properties to revert to the crown. Is that not all very strange, my lord?'

'Explain this to me more fully,' he had said. Pleased that she had broken his bad mood at last, Neith told him all she knew.

After that it was a case of sifting the facts from a wealth of half-trusts and innuendo. Khaleb caught and acknowledged two things. One, that Twosre was married to someone else and two, that the idea of Twosre belonging to someone else filled him with an unreasonable hatred for that other and ineffably fortunate man. He came back to the present because the Governor was speaking.

'My Lord Prince,' Khonsu said quietly. 'I fear that Hapdjefi's demands will remain the same. I do not understand his wishes, but there is one thing I am certain of. Give him the young woman or not, it will be all the same. He means to declare war.'

'Do you intend to order Amosis to give up his wife? Does he know the terms?'

'Not yet. I thought it expedient to

wait to hear if there is anything new that Hapdjefi has to say. The old man could have indulged in too much wine, of course.'

'But you do not think so?'

'On the contrary. The King ate and drank very little. I am afraid—'

'That he has come after Nefer for some vile purpose of his own?'

'I heard a whisper, Lord Prince, that there is an old crone who is as mad as all the Hurrians seem to be. She, they say, is edging the King towards *sati*-burial. If that is the case—'

'But that, you believe, will not bring about peace?'

'No, Lord Prince.'

'So!' Khaleb was stroking his chin with his hand. 'We must consider whether we can play for time by letting Nefer go, or else flatly refuse and have the old man finally commit himself to all-out war.'

'Exactly, my Lord Prince!'

'I see.' Khaleb's expression was very direct. 'Tell me, Khonsu, had I not been here, what would you have done?'

'I would have called upon Amosis and let him decide.'

'Because he knows about war?'

'Because as well as being Chief of Pharaoh's Southern Might, he is a loyal and honest man. If, by giving up his wife, it will allow us the advantage of more time, he will see it as his duty to let her go.'

Khaleb found himself picturing the young sensitive girl he had come to love as a sister. She had been like moonlight in his embrace, unlike Twosre who was like a raging fire in his arms.

'I feel a great pity for Amosis,' he said and there was genuine concern on his face. 'I would not be in his place for all of Egypt's grain.'

'Hapdjefi may not continue with this nonsense,' Khonsu remarked. No man present could quite believe that. Nefer was as beautiful as she was good. She was as pure as a lotus flower on the living Ra's arm. The old King was sick, but he was not blind!

'By Set,' Khaleb grunted. 'What is the old dog doing, keeping us waiting like this? I swear I'd like to slit his throat. I would give a great deal to have this murky business over and done.'

Then came a great rush of feet as serving girls ran forwards throwing sweet smelling palm fronds and flower petals before the threshold. Trumpeters blew high, thin salutary notes. Khaleb, Khonsu and all the councillors stood up. The hard bargaining was about to begin.

Unaware of the weight of events, Twosre, the women and children had gathered on the gorgeous flat roof of House of Amosis. A large striped awning gave shade and made a play area for the boys. The kittens were playing with goose feathers and were a delight to behold. There was much laughter and clapping of hands.

Sebni sat alone in the courtyard. He was happy. Twosre had given him thin strips of red and gold linen. Had showed pride in him.

'O Beloved,' she had said, 'you are so meticulous in your work, so clever. Our Father has always said how brilliant you are in design. Do you think you could fashion two tiny, very light collars for the kittens? Nefer so adores them, and you are the only man I know capable of making collars for kittens more lovely and delicate than the rest.'

Filled with great pleasure, anxious to please Twosre, he had concentrated on plaiting the collars. They were miniature works of art and when completed, Sebni felt satisfaction. His pleasure grew beyond all proportion to the task. But collars were the things his lady desired above everything else. Collars of red and gold linen, collars of blue. Collars of Star-Stones that glistened and gleamed and blinded a man's eyes. Collars were omnipotent! The faint noises that he always had in his head began to grow. Sebni gave himself up to them and to the voices that were whispering that he had sublime power. That he was master of all he surveyed. He saw the world as if it were a million cubits away.

He thought he saw Twosre and was surprised that she had decided not to go on the roof after all. She was sitting alone, unaware of him, and seemed to be very sad. Someone had given her a bracelet of gold. It was much too heavy and far too large. He would get her a better one. Yes, he must shower her with delights. She was wonderful and she belonged to him! Joy burst over him like a shower of glittering sparks and his feeling of power grew more strong. He would creep towards her, give her the kitten collars, and she would kiss him in her delight and allow him to kiss her. But wait! There was something wrong. Two bestial looking men were creeping up behind his beloved!

Quietly, panther-swift, Sebni began to move. The knife he had used to make the collars held in readiness in his hand.

He reached the first opponent who turned at his approach. Sebni saw a face. And a vision was hovering and dancing in Sebni's head. He saw the uncle who had sneered at him and accused him of being less than a man. And Sebni struck his uncle, direct to his heart, and killed him stone dead. A light came blazing into Sebni's head and he knew he was the conqueror. He leapt at the second figure who was seeking to do his wife harm, and beat at him, pounded at him, and Sebni was no longer the despised son of a wandering man.

He felt a sudden searing agony as a dagger blade cut into his chest. He looked down at his own blood. He had the sensation of falling rapidly through space. And in one infinitesimal fraction of time Sebni knew! He knew that what was happening now was utterly and absolutely right. This was for Twosre.

'I love you, my dearest dear. I love you!'

The words hung in his mind like jewels. Then he fell face down over the corpse of the would be abductor not of Twosre, but of Nefer.

The snivelling traitor who had killled Sebni was trying painfully to crawl away. Shocked, and showing no mercy for the enemy of the house, servants and slaves rushed forward. They began beating and kicking the screaming victim of Sebni's second, but unsuccessful, fanatical attack.

'Stop!' Paihuti commanded. 'Let him stay as he is, whimpering and grovelling in the dust. Send for our Lord Master. He will want to know a great deal more about this.'

Twosre, looking down from the roof, felt her eyes open wide with horror. 'No!' she breathed. 'Oh no!'

Then she was running like the wind down the wide, stone steps that led from the roof down into the main hall. She flew along the vast columned place, panting, her breasts heavy with fear and dreadful premonition, then out to the garden that was Nefer's delight. And Twosre's hand crept to her mouth to still the low anguished moan that trembled deep in the base of her throat. She sank to her knees beside Sebni and took hold of his slim pale hand.

'He is a hero, a valiant warrior,' Paihuti said. 'With no thought of himself he leapt at both men and in so doing, he saved Nefer's life.'

Then the moan in Twosre's throat escaped at last because she felt as if she had lost her loving and trusting child. Nefer knew how it was for her as, white-faced, she went to her sister and knelt at her side. The tears they wept together glistened as brightly in the sunlight as had Ananias's collar of Star-Stones all those far full moons ago.

There came great cries from the gates, then the sound of Amosis's hurrying feet. He reached them all and took in the scene at a glance. He held up his hand for silence.

'I cannot hear with all of you speaking at once,' he stated flatly. 'Paihuti, you be the one to explain.'

He listened, his face cruel and thin lipped as he looked across at the wounded man. When Paihuti finished speaking Amosis said flatly:

'You need an explanation, all of you. Well, the situation is this. The Hurrian desires the Lady Nefer as his wife, in this life and in death. For this reason he came here offering peace. King Hapdjefi is at this moment preparing to leave this place—alone. We are now at war.'

'And this murderer, my lord?' Paihuti said, vengeance in his eyes.

'He will be taken to those who best know how to get the truth out of him. There are many things we need to know.'

He turned away, but Nefer, horrified to the core at what she had heard, heartbroken for the brother she had known and loved all her life, cried out:

'Amosis, my lord, please do not leave me.'

He looked at her, his brows raised in a sardonic way. His tone held contempt as he asked:

'Are you not flattered enough, my lady? Old kings hold up a war—for you. Brothers

356

die—for you. Princes leave the wonders of Thebes—for you. A Lord Husband rejects overtures that I am ready and willing to hold up my troops—for you?'

As he turned away, weeping servants came to lift the honourable dead. Sebni would be placed in the small private Temple of Peace Everlasting. Then, they believed, just as soon as it could be arranged he would be carried down the streets of Kerma and would finally be lifted on to a waiting boat. This vessel would sail down stream of the City of the Dead on the west bank beyond Thebes. There, Sebni would be embalmed and placed in the Per Ibsen family tomb.

Before he left Amosis decreed:

'A statue will be built in the likeness of Sebni of Per Ibsen House. The statue will bear words at the base—that all the world may know of the brave deed that this young man achieved. Who, by this action, saved the life of Amosis, Mighty Warrior's Lady Wife.'

Twosre lifted her tear stained face to enquire in a choked and bitter way:

'Why did these men come here? Why did they want to kill my sister?'

'Nefer was not going to be killed,' Amosis said crisply. 'They meant to abduct her. She was going to go to Hapdjefi, and on his death she would be buried alive.

In that way he would please his gods. He offered us peace, but the terms were unacceptable.'

He impatiently turned away, closing his ears to Nefer's frantic, heartbroken sobs. Then, when a little slave crept forward and handed her the two lovely kitten collars her brother had made, she and Twosre began weeping all over again.

Their loss was so all consuming, so personal, that it quite blotted out the fact that now they were all under threat of war. All that Nefer knew and realised was that she could not bear Amosis's contempt. Could not stand the idea that he thought so little of her that he had paid for his pleasure. Had settled the debt by throwing down the bracelet she herself now so determinedly wore. This man, this great, proud man now meant so much to her.

It came to her in that moment. That, had it been Amosis killed in place of Sebni, she would want to lie down and die herself. She loved her husband! Loved him with all her heart and soul and every fibre of her being. And the awful, most tragic thing was that he did not love her. He would keep her, he had said so, but only to mother his children. She was his Lady of the House by Pharaoh's will. In all probability, he would be relieved and delighted if Khaleb put in a petition and Pharaoh revoked his decree and allowed Khaleb to take her and Nesmin away.

I must prove my love, she thought desperately. I must make him love me! I will do everything I can to let him see that he is my earth, my sun and my moon.

'Oh please God, let him learn to love and adore me. Show me how to prove to him that I am worthy to be his wife. Amun, let me carry his seed. Let me give him a son!'

She walked to the great planning room, hoping to find him alone. But there were many men present. Captain Rama, Nehi the Lord of the Kush, Khaleb and Khonsu, as well as other high men in Pharaoh's Southern Might. As she hesitated, Amosis looked across and saw her. His chiselled features grew more remote, his eyes distant.

She was in the way and quite out of her element here. Nefer, crushed, turned and walked back to the women's quarters of the house.

Twosre had changed already, she had become like a pale shadow. She kept whispering over and over again:

'Beloved husband, sweetest brother, oh my dearest dear, it was all my fault. You will never know how greatly I came to care for you. Sebni, the guilt is mine! Sebni, what can I do?'

'Twosre!' Nefer sat next to her on the ground in the room that her brother and sister had shared. 'Beloved, try not to do that! No blame lies with you.'

But Twosre was not listening. She crossed her arms and began rocking forwards and backwards in a paroxysm of grief. And in spite of her own determination to remain strong, Nefer found herself remembering that boy who had always been there, like a quiet, effacing, sickle-eyed shadow in the background of their lives. He had been so shy to them, so anxious to please. They had taken him for granted, had used him. Now he was dead. They would never see him in this life again.

Surprisingly Khaleb came then, his face solemn for once.

'Twosre,' he said, 'I am sorry.'

Twosre looked up at him and at that moment seemed to be like a heartbroken child. She stared tearfully into his eyes.

'Thank you, Khaleb. For once I—I believe you to be sincere.'

'You will always be a part of my life,' he told her gravely. 'You always have been, every since you plagued the life out of me when you were a little girl. You belong to me, Twosre. To me!'

She shook her head.

'No!'

He went away then and Nefer thanked Amun. The Prince had not asked to see Nesmin. Was not, at this moment of time, concerned with the fact that he might have a son.

Twosre was rocking backwards and forwards again and desperate to break the wall of sorrow that was cutting her little sister off from the world, Nefer said gently:

'Did you hear what Khaleb said? He must have been as serious in his affection for you as you for him! Can't you think a little more about him at this present time?'

'Could you, Nefer?' came the fierce reply, and the curtain of numbness had been broken because now Twosre had anger in her eyes.

'I—I was only thinking of you, my sister,' Nefer tried to explain.

'Don't do that!' Twosre rejoined bitterly. 'I have spent very many selfish, self-centred years avidly thinking of just myself!'

Accepting that at this stage nothing she could do or say would help, Nefer went in search of Bebu and Oyahbe who would be caring for the boys. Both women looked up at her approach, sad-eyed, worried and frightened. It was not satisfactory! It made everyone insecure, realising how very easy murderers had found it, to enter their home. They said as much and Nefer gasped and shivered. Her frightened gaze flew to Nesmin. He was asleep, a plump little fist bunched up against his mouth. Pepy slept also. Two dear, charming, friendly little boys—and so vulnerable!

'We must have more guards, Bebu! Yes, that's it. I will see to it that the babies are watched over at all times.'

She hurried to find Paihuti, and asked him to go to the Lord Master with her request.

'It will do no good, my lady,' Paihuti replied. 'The Master will be able to spare no armed men. We prepare for war!'

'Paihuti!' She wrung her hands in despair. 'What shall we do?'

'Slaves, my lady. They are watchful and, because you are kind to them, they adore you. I will put it to them. They will guard the little ones by night and day, that I promise you.'

'Tell them that they will be greatly rewarded, Paihuti. They will eat the same food that is set at my table. They shall have gold bands, and they shall have bright beads to wear.'

'They would prefer a jar of oil each,' Paihuti observed. 'And they would be greatly delighted with a small box in which to keep their things.'

'If they keep the boys safe and secure,'

Nefer promised, 'they shall each have a jar filled with oil, a wooden chest to hold their possessions, gold bands to use for barter and beads to adorn themselves with. To this I swear!'

Paihuti stretched his hands, palms downwards before him and bowed.

'I honour you, Mistress. There is no lady in the world so gracious as you. Never have slaves been treated so well. You are like a goddess in your kindness and loyalty to those in your sweet service.'

'Oh, Paihuti,' she said and her voice trembled even though she smiled. 'I do wish that everyone thought as you do. I am afraid that the Lord Master ... Has he given out punishments to those of you who ...'

'Mighty Amosis turned the other cheek,' Paihuti said. 'He accepted that under the circumstances, there was nothing that we could do.'

'Oh, thank Amun!' She was smiling and relieved at that. 'Paihuti, I am afraid that I will never be as just and fair as my Lord Husband.'

'You have a woman's heart and a woman's mind,' Paihuti replied. 'And a woman's generosity. The Master would never have accepted that a belongings chest was necessary to such lesser beings as slaves.'

363

'Which reminds me,' she told him, 'I will go personally and order them now. So shall it be written, so shall it be done. I will go to the scribe and have the agreement we have made set down on papyrus. Tell the slaves, though, that for this I will expect them to lay down their own lives for my son.'

Once she had made the necessary arrangements and had it all signed and sealed, Nefer found that she did not want to sit with Twosre, did not want to stay still. She wanted, no had to do something. Anything would be better than just thinking of Sebni—of what Amosis had said about the requirements of the terrible old King—and even worse, witnessing Amosis's open contempt for her own miserable self.

In order to be able to speak to Amosis in a knowledgeable way, she decided to learn all she could about the predicament they were in.

She knew that the character of the citadel was as much a matter for observation as defence. That the height of their position was because not only was the river route involved but also the overland trails used by the camel caravans. The Walls of Amenemhet overlooked all.

Kerma was a six-day land journey south of the last fortresses of the Second

Cataract at Semna. Kerma being a town of quite considerable size. Here an almost completely self-sufficient group of Egyptian officials, scribes, soldiers and many others lived peaceably among the local dark-skinned Kushites—who, until overthrown by Egypt, had been even more powerful than the Hurrians.

And so, Nefer thought, there must be Kushites as well as Hurrians ready to fight us down there. No wonder Amosis was so strict. He was being sensible, not merely overbearing as I thought. By Amun! What a stupid person he must think me to be.

She pushed this miserable thought away and tried to concentrate, as she knew her husband must be, on the actual position they were in. It was important to remember that Kerma was situated at the head of the Dongola Reach of the Nile, which was the terminus for numerous caravans, the routes coming from the west. It was all getting very clear to her now, and seriously concerned, she went back to the garden where she found Bebu speaking to Paihuti. Oyahbe had taken the little ones back to the house.

'Oyahbe and the little ones are all but surrounded by slaves, my lady,' Bebu's fat chins wobbled merrily as she laughed. 'Whoever heard of such a thing? Fine wooden chests for slaves?

They'll be wanting grand belongings to put in them next!'

'And why not, Bebu?' Nefer asked, while a small part of her mind was registering how quickly people were able to put grief away. It was almost as though beloved Sebni had never been on this earth by the merry sparkle in Bebu's eyes! Because of this, her tone was not warm when she spoke briskly to Paihuti.

'I want to know why the Hurrian King is so set on smashing us. Why must he begin his battle here?'

'Because we are in a key position, my lady. Between us and the Fourth Cataract there lies Dongola, Debba, Korti and Kereima. From all those points caravans go overland. These stretch as far, even in some instances, as the vast sandy waste known as Khartoum.'

'And this means—'

'If Kerma falls, my lady, it is almost certain that so also will Dongola, Debba, Korti and Kereima. Our position is vital. We must withstand the enemy at all costs.'

'How do you know so much?' Nefer asked wonderingly. 'How very wise and learned you are Paihuti.'

'Not so, my lady,' Paihuti laughed. 'It is just that I have big ears. I overheard the Governor instructing a scribe. A message has been written on papyrus and is already travelling down river to Thebes. Let us hope that Pharaoh sends us more soldiers, and that in plenty of time.'

'I see,' Nefer said thoughtfully and knew that with the arrival of the message, everyone would know of their trouble in Thebes. She bit her lip, thinking of her beloved parents' fear and grief—and the immeasurable sadness that would well up inside them when they learned of Sebni's death. But the message would have been written in full, she was sure. Mother Zarah and Per Ibsen would learn how courageous Sebni had been, how loyal and sincere. They would be proud and, outwardly at least, hold their heads high. But deep down a loss was a loss, that and nothing else would count.

A servant came hurrying out.

'The Lord Master requests your presence in his business room, my lady,' he said. 'And if it pleases you, hurry! Mighty Warrior has stressed that he has little or no time to spare.'

Obediently, Nefer hastened to do her lord's bidding, only to find a white-faced, defiant Twosre was already there.

'This cannot be, Amosis,' Twosre was saying. 'My husband is to be bound in fine linen. His organs placed in canopic jars. He will wait till the ship comes that will take him in all honour, back to his beloved Thebes. This must and shall be done!'

'Not so,' Amosis replied. 'I cannot spare men to take him on this final journey. It will not be safe for him to go unaccompanied, attended by mourners alone. So—I insist that my brother is laid to rest outside the walls here, and in the desert sands. In time a monument of much distinction will be raised in his name.'

'My husband is the son of a great lord, Per Ibsen,' Twosre cried, beside herself with anger and grief. 'He is not a peasant to be cast on the sand as food for scavengers. With no burial at all!'

'He is not going to be cast on the sand, dear Sister,' Amosis replied patiently. 'He will be buried, deep down, where he will be safe.'

'He is not a poor person to be just cast aside. He will have many needs in the After Life and—he is my husband, my sweet lord! He is—'

'Going to have a deep place in which to rest until his turn comes to live again. There will be all that he needs beside him as well as a wooden boat and oars with which he can get himself back to Thebes. He shall have food and drink, and oil for his skin. There shall be lamps to light his way, and beads and gems and rings of gold for him to wear. It has all been arranged.

'No! No! No!' Twosre cried out.

'I will see to it that your husband's name will continue forever because there are fine words written down already, and many signs that bear the means of Sebni, Brave Warrior. A carved likeness of him shall be made and it will stand with other great statues of heroes in Pharaoh's Victory Hall. In this way, Sebni, your Lord Master, will live in honour, for ever.'

'I beg of you,' Twosre whispered, 'let him be prepared correctly and well. Let Sebni be returned to Thebes to rest sweetly by the side of the Nile. Let him, in his final slumbers, hear the river's gentle lullaby.'

'I am sorry,' Amosis refused bleakly again. 'I have done what I must. Already there are men digging a great pit in the sands outside the wall. At the right and proper time you may accompany him. But, I warn you, the whole business must be over and done with very quickly. We do not know where or when the enemy will attack. I do not want any of you at risk outside the citadel walls.' He turned to Nefer. 'Take your sister away and comfort her if you can. I am not unfeeling. There is no other way.'

'I know and I understand.' Nefer was herself, openly weeping now. 'And I realise how kind and considerate you are being, my lord. Particularly since we are living in

369

such dangerous times.'

His eyes were empty as he looked at her.

'I do my best, Nefer,' he told her. 'And that is all that any man can do. Now I must leave you, for I am due at the Governor's residence.'

Unable to look longer into his wife's large tragic eyes, Amosis turned and left with no further ado.

Amosis joined Khonsu, Khaleb and other high officials. They began holding a council of war, but their hands were tied. No one knew exactly where the Hurrians were and so it was impossible to carry out any particular strategy plans. Hapdjefi, so it was rumoured, had returned to his great desert city beyond the oasis of Hurrians. But spies had been busy. They had reported no sign of the enemy army on or near their home ground.

Clearly it was going to be a cat and mouse game.

CHAPTER TWELVE

Twosre left the small stone-built Temple of Peace Everlasting where Sebni lay in his fine wooden coffin. There were carvings on the side, of the gods of heaven, of the

Jackal Anubis and the ibis-headed Thoth. Twosre walked slowly and mindlessly, her guilt having grown, rather than the reverse. She wished that she could run away from the heartlessness of this frontier place. Run back for ever to the beauty and richness that was Thebes. She wanted her mother. Her dear, gentle understanding little mother. But the next best in the world, she thought, was her sister Nefer.

She hurried then, back to the garden where Nefer sat. The kittens were playing with the boys' pretty linen balls which was making the children gurgle with delight. Nefer looked up and smiled wistfully.

'How quickly all young things grow.'

'And how rapidly we older things shrivel and die,' Twosre replied starkly.

'You will never grow old, Twosre. Even if you lived to be a hundred years, you would never be old. You have such young and pretty ways.'

'Don't be kind to me,' Twosre said fiercely. 'I do not deserve any kindness. I am too selfish to warrant even a second thought.'

'Yes, you are selfish,' Nefer agreed serenely. 'Because you are insisting on thinking of all the things you should or should not have done. Why not forget your own point of view and allow our brother his heroism for a change? You are so busy blaming yourself that you have forgotten all about how brave and splendid Sebni was. He was like a warrior, Twosre! Can't you think about that?'

'A warrior? One who is to be laid to rest in the sand?'

'Is he any the less for that? And hasn't my Lord Husband chosen a most tall and impressive stone to mark where Sebni lies? There are words to be chiselled on it, marvellous words that will last forever.'

'Oh Nefer!' Twosre choked. 'How sweet and wise you are!'

Nefer held Twosre in her arms and stroked her tangle of hair and soothed her until her storm of weeping had passed.

Twosre seemed more able to come to terms with her loss after that, but her eyes remained large and desolate.

All around, men were busy inside and out of the citadel, preparing to march. But where? As yet the Hurrians' position had not been found. Amosis and Khaleb were concerned with men's work. Affairs of the heart had to be put aside. They were speaking about the situation they were in, when a thin, wiry scout was shown into Amosis's council room. Hot, dusty, near to exhaustion, the man stretched his arms before him and bowed low.

'Life, Health, Mighty Warrior,' he gasped. 'I have found them at last. I have learned the destination of the Hurrian army and lived to tell the tale.'

'Life, Health,' Amosis replied. 'Give me your news.'

'They are heading towards the city of Setesh. They are mighty in number, O Lord, and their chariots are as numerous as locusts spreading over the sands. The infantry, too, are many. I was near enough to see that they had been joined by many members of the Bega tribes. One can tell their wild fuzzy hair anywhere.'

'Setesh?' Amosis's eyes had narrowed. 'The city who kneels before the Scorpion God? This is indeed treachery on a grand scale!'

The scout remained where he was. His chest was heaving. His bare feet were bloodied and raw. His arms looked as though he had been hiding in, or forcing his way through thorns.

'Come forward,' Amosis commanded.

The man took one further pace towards Amosis, then fell deferentially at his leader's feet. Amosis slipped a wide gold arm band over the wrist that had once worn the bracelet that weighed so heavily on Nefer's arm. He handed the band to the scout.

'You have done well,' he said. 'Take this as my written seal of approval. Your name shall be written down on papyrus and this our Divine Pharaoh will see!'

'I, too, would like to show my admiration,' Khaleb said, and took a gold ring set with a green gem stone from his middle finger and handed it to the man.

The scout accepted the gift and remained still, waiting for permission to leave. Amosis called for a servant.

'Take this man and treat him with all honour. Give him food and drink and find him a fine bed in a good house. It is my wish that he be known as the Eyes of Amosis from now on.'

When he had gone Khaleb smiled.

'I have just seen a scout who would willingly lay down his life for you, Amosis. It is the same with all of your men. They give you loyalty without question and will obey your every word.'

'Then I thank Amun for my army,' Amosis replied, stonily. 'I only wish the Woman of my House would feel the same.'

'Your wife is as beautiful and as pale and perfect as the moon,' Khaleb smiled. 'She is a goddess, pure and marvellous, and high above my head. Nefer, Nefer, Nefer loves you. I know it.'

'And you, Lord Prince?' Amosis asked, a closed expression on his face.

'I will always adore her. She is to me, perfection. She is the gentle warmth of the sunrise. She is the sweet sister that I will always love.'

Amosis was frowning, angry, unwilling to hear more. But Khaleb continued even so.

'It is Nefer's young sister that plagues me. Twosre is like an irritation under my skin. Twosre makes me happy, angry and sad all at the same time. I have taken her, and I would willingly keep her in my house all the days of my life. But she will never give in!'

'You mean,' Amosis said, 'that you have not come here to claim Nefer?'

'How can I? Divine Father gave her to you!'

'And her son?'

'Ah!' There was a sudden stillness in Khaleb's eyes.

'He is my son,' Amosis said firmly. 'While there is breath left in my body, Khaleb, I will keep him. I say again. The boy is mine!'

'So be it,' Khaleb said crisply. 'But there is one favour I will ask in return. I will ride with you, fight alongside you, but I want the reins of Duat and Horus in my hand. From now on, they are to be mine!'

'And Nesmin?'

'Is that his name?' Khaleb asked, then catching the cold fury in Amosis's eyes, shrugged, saying, 'Thotmes? Khaleb?

375

Nesmin? It is all the same. The boy is yours. He can never be mine. Pharaoh my father is not stupid and he knows how long it all takes. He must never guess that perhaps the baby is mine. As it is, Pharaoh often looks at me with anger and impatience in his eyes. Amenhotep has always been his favourite son. To be honest, Amenhotep is a great favourite with me! But for once, I would like to show my father that I am a great warrior. I wish to do well in this war.'

'You are above me in rank, Khaleb. You are Prince of the Realm. Our victory will be your victory. You will—'

'No! I wish to learn from you, Mighty Warrior. I wish only to be a good officer under your command. You know this terrain. You will guess the kind of fight the Hurrians will put up.'

'We will be brothers in arms,' Amosis replied. 'We will beat the Hurrians, swat them as effortlessly as we kill flies. I have annihilated resistance before and I will do so again.'

'Amun!' Khaleb agreed. 'Amun! Tell me, Amosis, what are your plans?'

'To attack Setesh. We will leave a token force here, but for Setesh we will need all the men we can get. I propose to take four sections, Amun, Ra, Ptah and Setekh. You will head the Army of Ptah, Khaleb? They are all fine and upstanding men.'

'Ai! Ptah will carry my standard as well as its own. And you?'

'My bodyguard troupe and the Army of Amun will form the van. We'll have the Army of Ra about a mile and a half behind us. The Army Setekh will take the south easterly route. We will march on Setesh and keep the Hurrians prisoners in that deceitful city's walls. We will starve them and when they come out to fight we will beat them into the ground. We will quickly put an end to Hapdjefi's little game.'

Bright eyed and alert now there was something to be done, the two men found to their mutual surprise that they were getting on.

'In Pharaoh's name!' Khaleb said and drank from his cup of wine.

'In Pharaoh's name!' Amosis toasted his reply, his chiselled features softening as he looked at his Prince.

It was late when Amosis went to Nefer. He found her in the sleeping room. She was standing by the window and looking up at the stars. She turned when her husband came in and she smiled, like a child, sure by the look on his face, that she would not be rebuffed. A wide, lazy grin spread across his face. Somehow, she thought, the smile and the grin had reached out across the room and met—had seemed to capture their relationship in space.

'Well, well, Small Person,' he said quietly, 'you look beautiful standing there.'

'Thank—thank you, my lord.'

'I bring you good news, Nefer. I know how afraid you have been and so I have spoken to Khaleb. He will make no claim on our son.'

His words released her terror and his tone was such that it washed some of her hurt away. The way he was looking at her made her very aware of the immediacy and purity of the present. In spite of herself, her love for Amosis stayed there, balanced on a shining shaft of air between them. And such had been her faith in him, she replied now, that deep down she had never really believed that he would allow Prince Khaleb to take their son. Then her heart sank.

He was staring at her in the way he had done so before when he needed her. But he does not love me, she thought sadly. He cares that I am in some ways content, but he does not love me as I adore him! She knew before he spoke, just how stark and to the point he would be as he made his request. He stepped closer.

'You will come to my bed?'

Her voice was so quiet when she replied that he had to bend his head to hear.

'Thank you—for Nesmin, my lord.'

'Then I am forgiven my rough and ready ways?'

'I will forgive you, Amosis,' she said gravely, 'but I will not forget. One day I will return your gold band, but for now I am content to keep it on my arm. To remind me always.'

'Nefer,' he began stiffly, 'our relationship—'

'Was arranged! Even so, in the beginning, it was pure and beautiful, Amosis, unlike now. Lately it seems to be weighed down with irrelevance.'

'You should not have taken the horses.'

'I know that now, and I am sorry that I did what I did. However, I am glad that—that Twosre arrived and is safe. If—if Sebni died as he did here, in your house, my sister might never have survived down there in the city.'

'Even so—'

Nefer was uncaring now. She should never have dared to break into her lord's conversation, not only once, but twice. She said quietly:

'I am very sad that the first part, the pure part of our relationship has gone. In—in the beginning,' she continued wistfully, 'everything was so simple and unencumbered, Amosis. Our feelings for each other were unformed I know, like a flower held tight in a hand, but we had friendship, and we had sympathy.'

He was frowning, his eyes searching her face.

'You speak as if you are saying goodbye,' he said sharply. 'How can this be?'

'You have left me in a way, my lord, or at least the wife part of me. Now you need only what you can get from any woman. I am sorry, Amosis, but it will not do.'

'So what do you propose?' he asked her angrily. 'May I know my lady's plans?'

'My lord, once Sebni has been laid to rest in the sands of the desert, Twosre will have no reason to stay here. She needs our mother quite desperately and—now all of the warm happiness you and I shared is gone, so do I.' Tears slipped down her cheeks then as she thought of the beloved Zarah of Anshan. 'Oh, my lord, so do I!'

'You cannot leave!'

'Not now, because of the situation, I know. But, at the first moment—'

'So be it,' he snorted furiously. 'Have it your way.'

He stormed out of the sleeping room and left Nefer sobbing. Not once had he disagreed with her. He had gone along with it all, even remaining silent when she had spoken about the prostitutes who were so openly available near the barrack walls. She felt the weight of the gold bracelet, her payment! All her hurt and humiliation rose once more and she repeated her vow.

'One day he will take his band back,' she whispered. 'I have said it once and I repeat it again, one day I will make him take this monstrosity back ...!'

The whole population came to cry out and cheer and make much of the army. At the head of the men was Mighty Amosis and he looked very austere and grand. The chariot of war he was standing in was a wonder to behold. Its framework of light wood was bent to make a curved front. The canvas walls had been covered with gesso and modelled with scenes of bound captives kneeling before Pharaoh. The whole front was covered with sheet gold with a border inlaid with glass and coloured stones. The harness of Ra and Sphinx was of leather and all the metal used was gold. The horses were adorned with blue ostrich feathers fixed in the gold bands across their heads. The same blue of the matching war helmet that Amosis wore.

Watching the scene, Nefer could hardly accept that Khaleb was there in a chariot drawn by Horus and Duat. She mentioned this to Paihuti who smiled and looked very wise.

'Tell me!' Nefer commanded.

'The Lord Amosis gave them to the

Prince,' Paihuti said behind his hand, so that no one else could hear. 'And only my sweet lady can know why!'

She stood there, holding Nesmin close to her heart. Her Lord Husband had actually parted with two of the animals he revered above all else? For Nesmin? In that moment, Nefer's love for Amosis was so great that she wanted to run to him, and in front of the whole world, thank him for what he had done. But she must do no such thing. Her Lord Husband's mind was on war, not on emotional things.

Amosis raised his hand high in signal to shout. The horses snorted and moved forwards. Nefer cried out his name, but with the mêlée of movement and noise, the sound of her voice was gusted away.

Chariots led the way, the charioteers being the élite of the men. There were other organised divisions, complete with units of bowmen, axemen, and spearmen. Camels were there, fast runners and also the more slow moving package carrying kind.

Following Amosis the army marched in columns. The chariots bumped along behind horses that held their heads as high as the warriors holding the bearing reins. As the men from the citadel marched out, the waiting forces fell behind them. Camels made wide splodgy footprints in the sand.

Camels that only a short time before had been snarling protests, and making menacing backward sweeps of the head at every attempt at loading and having saddles put on. Ox-carts were laden with food, wine, water and all manner of things that were important and necessary to the army. There were treasure chests with which to pay the army, wide gold bands to reward valour; clothes and weapons, oil and grain, and as always the masses of toil-weary slaves. There too, were the prostitutes who served the army and who followed the army or starved.

All was heat and dust and organised confusion as the army moved on. Bright in colour, steady in resolve, and secure in the love of Amun. The men of Egypt were on the move and spirits were high. Lean, tanned, keen-eyed men bristling with arms were on the way—and heaven help the Scorpion lovers, the traitors of Setesh ...

The thin sad line of mourners followed the two oxen that pulled Sebni's coffin into the wilderness. Twosre and Nefer walked behind it. They were silent in their grief, numbed by the finality of the event. The only comfort being that the two sisters were together and holding hands.

They reached the pit that had been dug to receive their beloved brother, husband

and friend. Slaves came forward once the shaven-headed priest had intoned a few ritual words, and with little or no feeling, began filling the pit in. At the head of Sebni's resting place there had been erected a tall column of stone. Already Sebni's name had been chiselled on it. A message bearing witness to his bravery had begun.

It was wearying, Nefer thought, just to watch how quickly the slaves worked at the filling in task. Wearying and sad, because the very matter-of-factness of the disposal of Sebni, made the whole point of living seem worthless somehow.

She stood there, beside Twosre, trying to think of words of comfort, but none came. Bebu and Yati were weeping obligatory tears. Kanes had eyes only for Uronarti, the quiet loyal man to whom she now belonged. Bebu and Paihuti stood side by side, their faces unreadable.

It is as though my brother never lived, Nefer thought and now also, it is as though my Lord Husband had never lived. He might never come back! Amun, my god, I beg of you, watch over my Lord Husband. Keep him from harm. If he dies, I will die too!

As they turned away from Sebni's grave there was a movement over the sands. A strange figure dressed in a long black robe, was riding on the back of a camel and heading directly towards them. Such was the shock and horror raging through Nefer now, that her throat went dry and the blood turned to ice in her veins. The scream rising in her throat was choked at birth, but in her heart and soul and every fibre of her being, she was crying out the name of Amosis. Praying and entreating all the gods in the universe to send Amosis. To recognise her desperate need to have her beloved lord come to her rescue here and now.

Frozen, hypnotised, she watched as the awful crow-like creature drew near. Ese—O yes! In spite of the passing years, it was Ese who was perched like a carrion bird on the camel's back.

The woman had come for her, just as deep down Nefer had always known that she would. Ese who was the dark side of god, the avenger, the bringer of death.

Sensing her horror, Uronarti and the servants and slaves jumped into position before Twosre and Nefer. In this way blocking the old woman's path. Ese halted the camel and Paihuti stepped forward in a belligerent manner and held up a warning hand. Ese ignored him, her black eyes glittering over his head.

'Life, Health, Lady Nefer,' she screeched. 'Do you know why I'm here?'

'Say what you have to, Ese,' Nefer replied, 'then leave us. Can't you see that we have completed a very sad business this day?'

'Not half so sad as new dawns will bring,' Ese sniggered. 'There is another Lord Husband who will be buried beneath the sand very soon. That I promise you.'

'Kill her,' Twosre said tonelessly. 'Get that evil old witch out of my way.'

Uronarti made to move forward, his attitude as aggressive as the rest of the men—apart from the priest, who seemed to have melted away.

'Wait, Uronarti!' Nefer said sharply. 'We shall hear what Lady Ese has to say.'

They stood there while the old woman let out a high pitched tirade that was making little or no sense.

'She is mad,' Twosre intoned. 'And she is unclean. Her hair is matted and her face has sores and how you recognised her I simply do not know. Why you refuse to have her struck down is a puzzle. She is offensive to me.'

'She is Ese,' Nefer replied quietly. 'I can never forget her eyes. In spite of the ravages of time I recognise her as the woman who once terrified me.'

'That Ese?' All of Twosre's heartbreak blazed out in hate brought about by the intensity of her grief. 'That crone who all but destroyed you? Why should such vileness continue to live when all the gods stepped aside and allowed my sweet Sebni to die?'

Ese cackled.

'As Mighty Amosis is about to succumb unless my king has his way. Think about that!'

'Stop it!' Nefer's voice cracked with fear. 'Ese, get out of my way!'

'Removing me will make no difference to the fall of the bones,' she screeched again. 'Enemies surround Pharaoh's might and every man of Egypt will soon be biting the dust. The Hurrians have been watching and they know every move. Amosis will be cut down and Egypt crushed.'

'No!' Nefer gasped. 'No!'

'It will take one word to save Amosis,' Ese continued. 'Just one word, Nefer. Mine!'

'Lady Nefer,' Uronarti said urgently, 'let me put this old woman down. Let me trample her into the dirt. Let me stuff up her evil, lying mouth.'

'No.' Nefer's voice was quiet now, strained. 'I know why she wants me. She is after revenge because I was the reason she was banished from Thebes many years ago.'

'And my king wants you,' Ese said sibilantly. 'The great Hapdjefi believes that you are his passport to the After Life. He promises peace if you go to him, prepared to lay at his side in death.'

'It is a trick,' Twosre cried, her fear for her sister momentarily outweighing her grief. 'With or without you the Hurrians mean to have a war. Who on earth would want to listen to the vile babblings of a crazy old king?'

'His own people,' Nefer replied.

Nefer found herself looking up into Ese's distended eyes and the years fell away. She was a child again, as helpless now as she had been then. Ese had the whiphand. She knew that Nefer would go, had to, must try! If she did not and Amosis was cut down as the old woman predicted, she would never be sure if the blame lay with her. She would know guilt all the days of her life.

White to the lips, Nefer whispered: 'You must give me time to say farewell to my son.'

'No!' Twosre shrieked, high and wild. 'Nefer, this cannot be!'

Nefer turned to her and held her in her arms.

'Sister, beloved,' she murmured against Twosre's cheek. 'Would you not have done the same thing for Sebni? Tried anything that might have given him even one half of a chance?'

They were all sobbing as they made their way back to the citadel. And while Nefer cradled Nesmin and tried to comfort her shocked and distressed servants and friends, Twosre ran like a wild thing to the Governor's residence.

Khonsu listened in silence and then held up his hand for the full attention of all those present.

'Hear this,' he said, 'Nefer, wife of Mighty Warrior, has taken the decision that I had hoped her husband would on the night the Hurrian was here. By her action she shows patriotism beyond all call. Her name shall live to Everlasting. By her action, even if peace is not the outcome, the Lady Nefer will perhaps have gained us some respite.'

Defeated, hardly able to take in such callousness, Twosre crept away. She went back to Nefer who had a small basket at her feet that held a few necessities she had asked the servants to pack. Bebu and Oyahbe, holding the babies in their arms, stood with tears running down their cheeks. Yati and Kanes had run away weeping. Paihuti was grim-faced but calm for he knew that his lady was doing her duty as she saw fit. Uronarti was sadly looking down at the ground and shuffling his toes.

Nefer took Amosis's bracelet from her

arm and handed it to Twosre.

'Beloved,' she said shakily, 'please give this to my Lord Amosis. Tell him that now he owes me nothing. That I too, have paid a debt. That we stand equal at last.'

'I—I cannot do this thing, Nefer.'

'You can and you must! I leave my little boy in your care, Sister. Adore him always and see to it that Pepy and his mother are always cared for too. And Twosre, beloved sister, one final thing. Be kind to Khaleb because for all the arrogant façade he puts on, you are dear to his heart.'

Twosre was unable to reply, and Nefer left her, and all of those of whom she was fond. She went, quietly, dazedly, like a sleepwalker, out of the house. There, waiting, looking like an evil grinning Jin, was Ese.

There came shock after shock after that. Once Nefer had gone through the gates, on foot, Ese rode the camel, she went down towards Kerma. Hot, tired and dusty, they at last reached the streets. And now it was clear that the Hurrians did have many on their side, for many recognised and gave honour to Ese. And Ese rode proudly for she had come into her own.

'Revenge is sweet,' she cackled, once she had ordered her camel to kneel, and eased herself off its back. 'What price pride now, my lady? What price deceit? Amun has caught up with you at last. Now you will die for him as you should have lived for him all those years ago.'

'I am not to die in the name of Amun,' Nefer said stonily. 'But in the name of a vile Hurrian god. You are not making sense, Ese. No more than you were all those years ago.'

Ese pushed her inside a dilapidated mud brick house and carried on: 'When you die, my lady, your soul will belong to Amun, so it is of no great significance as to how and where your demise is accomplished.'

It was useless to argue. Ese was insane. Worse, the men that Nefer saw now, all huddled in the shadows, looked on the old woman as a great and powerful force. They were clearly afraid of her wicked spells, and of her proximity to Hapdjefi their king.

Low and cunning, they gathered together in a stifling dark and evil smelling room. They were able to tell Ese the route the Egyptian army had taken. The old woman nodded and sniggered and claimed that the Scorpion was on the Hurrians' side. That fortune was going their way.

'Your victory will be the greatest, your recompense more sweet,' Ese told the listening men, 'if I get to Seshet by the quickest route—and go by the opposite way.'

'You will need fast camels, Wise Woman,'

the head man growled. 'And someone to take Hapdjefi's deathbride off your hands.'

'And your price?'

'A bag of gold pieces and five sacks of grain.'

'So shall it be,' Ese laughed. 'And for this shall you take this woman before you. Hold her so that she is as helpless as a trussed goose! And remember, she is important to god.'

Nefer turned very slowly and stared at Ese with utmost contempt.

'Oh, what a loathsome, suspicious old woman you are! I came back here of my own accord. I will not try to go back on my word. There is no need to truss me up like a goose. As Amun-Ra lives, I will keep to the bargain I made. The only uncertainty is that your despicable old king will keep to his!'

This was too much for the man. He felled her with a blow. She felt herself being tied hand and foot and there was nothing that she could do. And all the while, high and wild, she was calling in her mind, Amosis, my dearest dear. Amosis, my love, think kindly of me ...

The Egyptians made good time. Morale was high. There was a sense of victory in the air. Amosis was looked up to, a man among men, ready at all times to side with those he held dear. At ease in masculine company, he roared out the victory song of the Nile as loud as the best of them. Alert, lean, his eyes missing nothing, his lips always ready to turn up in the grin that his soldiers knew so well, he seemed like a god.

And if, when the camp fires sent up showers of sparks from burning thorns, he remembered other nights with Nefer, he kept it to himself. If the purple shadows of night were reflected with visions of her wistful little face, he refused to look and see. But the mystical desert night was alive with memories of Nefer, with longing for her, with love! When a man loves on Pharaoh's command, Amosis thought, he loves mostly as horse loves mare. But with Nefer it was not like that, even though I've refused to accept this fact for so long. The trouble is that I let devils roost in my mind and forgot that other black devils ride the black steed of tomorrow. My devils looked like Khaleb and now I know I was wrong. But I have left it too late.

He cursed silently and faced up to remembering the teaching of the priestess of Isis, 'The one flower that should always be plucked when it is in bloom and desired is the flower of love. For no flower, not

393

even the white star lily of the field withers so rapidly.'

She loved me once, Amosis thought, I know it. She cried out my name and there was yearning in the sound. Why did I not recognise it till now?

Softly like a whisper in the pulsing murmur of the night, he heard her name 'Nefer, Nefer, Nefer.'

The following morning the army was on the move again. The basic formation they travelled was of hard red sand, in immense undulations, like a troubled sea many times magnified. Occasional superimposed sand hills of a paler colour were sometimes solid, sometimes horse-shoe shaped. In their depressions lay patches of white gypsum and not quite so frequently, water-holes.

As the going grew more rough, the camels came into their own. But the camp followers steps grew slower. Horses neighed and protested, oxen plodded on, the expression unchanged in their large doleful eyes. The heat grew more intense, the nights more cold, but Amosis rode ahead, suffering the same as his men. All was going as planned.

At last the forerunners saw the walls of Setesh. With grim faces and a hardening of attitudes, Amosis and his men proceeded to pitch the main camp, to the north west of the city.

Within Setesh, Nefer heard the talk. She sat very still and quiet, in the women's section of the Great House that had been set aside for the Hurrian King. She was feeling dazed and was quite often unaware of what was going on. She was not treated unkindly but in the name of purification she was not given food. Clothed in a robe made of material she had never known before, she was dressed like a queen. There was a diadem of rubies in her hair and they shone as brightly as did her ankle-length skirt of red silk. There was gold at her waist, wrists and ankles. Ruby pendants hung on gold wire swung from the lobes of her ears. Her face paint was always perfect as were her nails on her hands and toes. She was growing more fragile by the day.

Hapdjefi had summoned her just once. His lizard-like gaze roved over her and made her feel sick as the liquid Ese insisted on pouring down her throat. Nefer hated the drink, knew it was a drug that made her helpless, so that her mind flew away on wings up to the clouds. She fought it and at times won—but the nights seemed to be days—and the world swivelled round in an aimless, timeless way.

Even so, in her rare lucid moments she

was able to grasp that things were not going well for her love. Amosis did not know that the Hurrians were not within the walls of Setesh, but were in fact hidden behind it. So while Amosis pitched his very rich and comfortable camp to the north west, the Hurrians moved to the south east and fell on the army of Ra as it was crossing a ravine. The route of Ra was complete. Men lay screaming in agony or else died. The rest fled in disorder and burst upon the unsuspecting Amun division pursued by Hurrian chariotry.

'Please God of the Sun, Horus, Isis and Ra, help them!' Nefer whispered and cried out in agony as women pulling back her head, poured more of Ese's filthy potion down her throat.

Amosis was faced with chaos. His infantry men were panic-stricken and they fled leaving him only with his bodyguard and chariots to face the exultant enemy. The Hurrian chiefs flung the whole of their chariotry in an encircling movement at the small, remaining Egyptian band.

The situation was desperate, and with the courage of despair, Amosis put himself at the head of his force and charged his enemy as they came up from the south. And such was the surprise of attack, where Hurrians had believed that all that was necessary was the killing chase, that

Amosis halted them.

Mighty Warrior re-grouped his men. There were many dead, the dying littered the plain. He again took action, attacking when the enemy expected him to hold. After that all was heat and dust, blood and sand, shrieks and moans, the high clashing and rasping of shields withstanding arms, the awesome cacophony of men at war.

And just when it seemed that even Mighty Amosis's strength was done there came the far away stridency of blaring horns. Khaleb had arrived with the Ptah division, heading the others who had reformed. He attacked the Hurrians in the rear.

The fighting raged. After four hours, the savage response to revolt broke the back of resistance. Both sides were exhausted, but it was Hapu, son of Hapdjefi who withdrew his troops. This time they entered Setesh and stayed.

Amosis and Khaleb returned triumphant to their camp. They met and looked into each other's eyes, then Khaleb asked humbly:

'We are brothers, Mighty Warrior?'

'We are brothers,' Amosis replied.

They prepared to make siege of the city.

High above the orange plain, clouds of black feathers wove in the sky. Vultures, the rag-pickers of the desert, watched and waited with beady, greedy eyes.

Much later the gates of Setesh opened again and a deputation came out. They were bearing the flag of peace.

Nefer, very pale and ill sat on a throne-like chair barely able to understand what was going on. She was in a large room which was harsh with light and thick with incense, but she could only see the awesome looking priest. He who wore a Scorpion mask over his face and head. And this terrible monstrosity's attention was on the shrivelled figure sitting on the throne next to Nefer. In a dream-like way she understood that it was not the King in power, but the priest. And the cold animosity of the Scorpion was searing to the soul.

'Your continued existence is a menace to the fortress of this city,' the Scorpion said, its voice hollow, unearthly, echoing as it did through the mask. 'We had a treaty of kinship and went along with your treachery, but now we are lost for our pains.'

A terrible cackling came from the background and Ese's voice, harsh with defiance cried out:

'You run like hares, Scorpios! You deserve to be boiled and eaten for the

398

scared desert pests you are.'

The priest continued to look in Hap-djefi's direction, but his order was clear.

'The woman is not magic and she has told many lies. Our army is shattered, her predictions were wrong. The gods are not on her side. Take her out. Fill her mouth with sand till she chokes and dies.'

'I go to Amun at last,' Ese laughed in her wild way. 'I go to my god at last!'

She was silenced in an abrupt and terrible way.

'She called upon Egypt's god?' Hapdjefi's sibilant voice held disbelief. 'Oh Amun?'

'You heard her,' the Scorpion replied. 'Where is your wisdom, your authority now? You have led your people and mine to defeat. You are not a fit king.'

'I have a fine and noble son!'

'One who was brought up in Egypt's court. Who spoke out against the war from the start. Who fought simply out of loyalty to his father the King, who is from this moment deposed!'

Hapdjefi's hoarse protests were un-availing. The Scorpion had made his decree. Hapdjefi had brought dishonour and disgrace upon them and he had to go. Since he had himself decided on the macabre fashion of his own funeral, so would it be written. So should it be done.

Hapdjefi began to cry in terror, but he had to go.

Drugged, helpless, Nefer felt her chair lifted. She was carried outside behind Hapdjefi. All his servants and slaves followed with fatalism in their eyes. They were watched by huge crowds of silent Scorpios.

They were taken to a deep well that stretched wide. The gibbering Hapdjefi was lowered into it, on his throne. Nefer, mourning, followed, and so, wordlessly, did the servants and slaves. A priest climbed down on a rope and placed a piece of dry hide over the King's head, and men began to gently pour in sand, so as not to hurt him. And now the Hurrian's fear and honour made him scream out for mercy and for the help of his son.

It was then that Hapu appeared. He was a middle-sized man of dark complexion with small black eyes and a hawklike Armenoid face. He was thickly bearded and had a curiously soft voice that held determination for all that. He held up his hand. The inhumation ceased.

'You called me, Father?' he cried out.

Hapdjefi was too terrified to make a sensible reply. All he was capable of was crying for mercy and calling out his son's name.

Hapu folded his arms, and stood with

his legs astride, and stared down at the quivering wreck he had once revered.

'If you can go so far as to forget all the instincts of a civilised Egyptian, and accept this local barbaric custom,' he said flatly, 'you have gone entirely native and you are no father of mine.'

'Hapu—my son. I beg of you ...'

'It is no longer my concern, Father.'

The pit fillers made as if to begin their work again, when a voice rang out in fierce command:

'Wait!'

Hapu held up his hand, then turned and looked with expressionless eyes at Amosis. Mighty Warrior had come in person to see that full justice was carried out. It was he who had been the one to insist that the traitor King should receive the punishment he so richly deserved. But the conqueror was looking not at the vanquished enemy. He was staring with unbelieving eyes at the slight figure that was held captive on a grotesquely carved sacrificial chair.

Nothing moved in that oppressive moment of heat and suspense. Not a human whisper cut the silence. But there was the harsh, grating cry of black ill-omened carrion birds who watched and waited with spiteful, predatory eyes. The huge circle of human spectators waited. Many still bore

401

hate for the Egyptian and all they needed was a chance.

Amosis felt an agony in his heart, and a terrible fear. He wanted to yell and kill Hapu for the barbarian he was, but he knew he had to take care. He had to tread softly when every instinct in him was crying out to leap down and rescue the girl who was staring before her and into eternity with such dreamy, wistful eyes. He had come to this spot with only a handful of men, who as victors, were off guard. They would all be cut down in an instant should the watchers let caution fly away. He stepped towards the edge of the pit and forced himself to stare coldly down at the dribbling old man, who cowered and began weeping in a helpless, senile way. Then Amosis turned back to Hapu, saying:

'You are a credit to Egypt, O Son of Hapdjefi. Pharaoh will hear of how loyally and exactly you intended to carry out the law. I can see now how faithful and how valuable you are to Egypt. It is our will that you take over your father's throne.'

'Then the inhumation shall continue?' Hapu's near black eyes held no expression in them. 'Shall we progress with the ritual you think so necessary to prove that the battle between us has been well and truly won?'

402

'Hapu,' Amosis replied evenly. 'I came along here personally to witness how far you were prepared to carry out your oath of obedience. Also to see that your father received the fright of his life. I am satisfied this has been done. You may now continue this farce in such a way that your father may know just where he stands. Let your people accept that we are fair to our vanquished, and just. And not the devils they believe we are.'

'Hapu!' Hapdjefi called. 'Mercy, My Son!'

'O Father, do you now accept that you are under my thumb?'

'I bow to you, Hapu. I am under your thumb!'

'You kowtow before Pharaoh and accept his might?'

'I am subject to Egypt, if that is your will. Hapu bring me up!'

Hapu turned contemptuously away and signalled to those who waited. They ran forwards and began pulling all of those in the pit to safety.

'The young woman is an Egyptian,' Amosis said and his voice held cold fury. 'By Amun, they had better be careful of her.' He faced Hapu with such an air of suppressed savagery that the vanquished Hurrian stepped back a pace.

Watching and waiting was the hardest

thing Amosis had ever done. He wanted to cry out, yell to the gods, fight all these evil devils and take his beloved in his arms and carry her in safety to the citadel. He could do none of these things. One word, one look from him and they'd kill her. In the name of their obscene Scorpion god, they'd cut her down before his eyes, and joyously bear the consequences later on. They would be fanatic if their new king allowed them off the leash. He, Amosis, had to stand there, act the man high above them all, seem unmoved! Should Hapu suspect the trump card he held in this game, should he even have a glimmer of how precious Nefer was, he would about face and the bargaining would begin—for Nefer's life.

Cold-faced he watched and waited and did not relax until Nefer had been carried away, back to the shelter of the King's house.

'Let her be looked after and given great care,' Amosis told Hapu. 'She will leave with me when the ceremonies are at an end.'

The city of Setesh was *en fête*. Was not the Mighty Warrior of Egypt being entertained by their new king? Was it not a blessing to be at peace again, safe in the fold?

From all the streets of the city came

the sound of drums, music and people singing merry songs. Inside the palace the feasting and merriment continued. Hapu, now wearing the crown, watched the proceedings with satisfaction. Yet he felt uneasy every time he looked at his guest of honour. There was something tigerish about Amosis, an anger only barely held in control. Hapu found it in his heart to pray to the gods that the Egyptian girl had come to no lasting harm. Should she not survive, he felt that he could be put in the pit alongside his father and the whole of the court. And also by the look in Amosis's eyes, sackfuls of vipers would be thrown down on their luckless persons as well. He felt relief when Amosis said crisply:

'At first light I will return to my camp. It will be expected that the Egyptian female will be in readiness then.'

Dawn came, and the night cold began to fade before the rosy, waking sun. Amosis, waiting at the head of his men, seemed not to notice the litter that held within it the crumpled form of Nefer, but his hands clenched in an agony of feeling over the reins. He raised his arm in signal. They began to move forward until the walls of Setesh lay behind them and at last they reached the camp. Then and only then did Mighty Warrior's iron will give way. With great haste he dismounted and strode to the litter and groaned in agony when he saw the desperate condition of the captive inside. Amosis took the limp figure into his own strong arms, his expression held fear. He whispered to her of love and held his face against hers. And far away though she was, unreal as the world seemed to be, her faint moans died away. Two tortured eyes opened, and she breathed his name like a sigh. Then long lashes fluttered and heavy lids closed again.

That night Mighty Warrior, Chief of Pharaoh's Might, knelt by his Small Person, who was so weak, almost unable to move, barely conscious, but just alive. And as he knelt there it seemed that he had loved this young creature for many lifetimes. That she was, and always would be, part of his own heart and soul.

'She will live, my brother,' Khaleb said as he came in. 'By Amun, she will live!'

The sharpness of his voice roused Nefer. She opened her eyes with a start, gazed at Khaleb in alarm, and her small hand crept out to Amosis and clasped his fingers in a weak nervous grasp. Amosis looked down tenderly.

'You must get well very quickly,' he told her. 'Because, O Woman of the House, I cannot wait to take you home.'

For nearly a full turn of the moon Nefer

flickered on the verge. She cried in her dreams, calling for the beloved brother who was now sleeping in Eternity and oh, so very, very far away. And Amosis felt fear, a fear that he had never experienced in his life before. He could fight the might of an army, but he knew that he was afraid of living out his life without this precious Small Person. Then, her faint weeping and whispering would start all over again as she called to Sebni, so far away in his narrow sand bed. Only Amosis's arms around her could soothe her and allow her some semblance of peace.

Then the day dawned when, at last, Amosis and the few men who had stayed with him in the now thoroughly subdued Setesh, set out joyfully for the citadel.

They arrived amidst tumultuous welcome. Crowds gathered to cry out their hero's name and throw palm fronds and flower petals in his path. But Amosis hardly noticed the crowds. His eyes were fixed on the litter that was carrying Nefer. He did not relax until she was safe in his house and resting like a small bird in the width of the great golden-pawed bed.

He left her sleeping and joined Twosre who was looking at Khaleb and saying coolly:

'So, O Prince, you have returned a hero! Did you know that Khonsu—how

I hate that man—has received a message from Thutmose the Great? You are to go to Thebes, for your Royal Father waits impatiently to honour you there.'

'Will you come with me,' Khaleb asked, daring her with his eyes. She looked him up and down. Then seeing the faint beginning of his smile, she glared. He hastily looked serious and waited. She shrugged and replied in an casual way:

'I might.'

'Sister,' Amosis said diffidently, 'Nefer has not spoken much and she seems to have become very remote. She has not told me about how and why she came to be in Setesh.'

'Then I will explain,' Twosre's voice was tomb cold. 'And while I am at it, I will return this.' She took his gold bracelet off her own arm and handed it to him. 'And when I am finished I will have you know that lord or no lord, you will do as I say. You will not go near my beloved Nefer. You will leave her in peace. I intend to nurse her night and day.'

'No,' Khaleb said quickly. 'You have half promised to come back to Thebes with me.'

'Let Mighty Amosis travel alongside you,' she flung down her challenge. 'For Pharaoh wishes to honour him too.'

'Twosre—' Amosis began, but she stopped

him and coldly told him how Nefer had come to be at Setesh and under Hapdjefi's sway. When she had finished speaking he said evenly:

'I commend you for your love and loyalty, Twosre. But now I must make my own position quite clear. No one, not even you whom I have come to love, will give orders to me. I rule my own house!'

A thin sickle of moon was slicing the black and silver sky high above when Amosis came to Nefer's room. For a moment he stood there, watching her slight figure, trying to still the hunger of his stomach, the pulse beating in his brain.

'Amosis?' her voice came softly, whisperingly, from the warmly scented blackness of the room.

'Yes, Small Person? I thought that you would be asleep.'

'No. I—I have been waiting for you.'

He moved closer.

'You knew that I would come?' he asked gently.

'I hoped that you would, my lord. I wanted you to come.'

He could see more clearly now. There was a filtered greyness that seeped through the wide window and he could see the ethereal silver of her body, half turned towards him, almost luminous. For a long time he stared at her, and in the waiting silence of the night there was only their breathing, soft and tremulous.

Nefer felt the faint beginnings of wonder, a dawning joy. She saw that his eyes were deep black shadows. He bent down and put his arms around her in a caring, uncertain way.

'There is nothing of you,' he said roughly. 'You feel as if you might easily break in two.' He groaned softly then and rested his cheek against hers. 'I wanted to kill him, Nefer. I wanted to put my hands round his skinny throat and—If he had—'

'He could not help being old and afraid of Ese,' she whispered. 'It was Ese, my lord, her hate, that had its beginning in the garden of Ramose all those years ago.'

'I loved you then,' he told her raggedly. 'And I love you now. Oh, my beloved Thrice Beautiful, I will always love you!'

'Oh!' She was weeping now. 'It has taken you so long to say that, Amosis. So very, very long.'

'Do you—can you love me?' he asked and his voice was harsh with uncertainty, taut with fear against her reply. 'I am not smooth, nor a prince like Khaleb. I am a soldier, down-to-earth, and I do not have courtly ways. Nefer, beloved, I am afraid that I am a very ordinary man.'

'You are a god,' she whispered shyly. 'My god! And as to loving you, Amosis, the truth is that I always have.'

He groaned and held her close. Her body felt cool and firm and fragrant. Her fingers touched lightly, flutteringly against him, and then as he put his mouth to hers, her arms closed tightly about him. He could feel beneath him her ripe, warm firmness, the tenderness of her breasts, the curve of her thighs. As he bent to kiss her again, she brought her arms up swiftly, to cup his face in her trembling hands. He could see her eyes, wide and imploring, as she breathed, 'Don't let us be parted, Amosis, not ever again.'

'Never,' he promised hoarsely. 'By Amun, I swear never, my love!'

Then he could feel the imperceptible yielding of her body to his.

'Amosis,' she whispered. 'Make love to me.'

And he made exquisite and gentle advances. He kissed her and was patient and kind, and finally passionate in the extreme. And Nefer gloried in his embrace and responded to him. The purity and golden splendour of their mutual adoration washed all the horror of the past away.

Thebes was rejoicing. The great temples and pylons and avenues of rams glittered

411

with colour and washes of pure gold. The streets were thronging with people, families gathered on the top of the roofs of their homes. There were flower garlands everywhere, and banners waving. Everyone had made sure of a place where they could witness the heroes' return.

On the top step by the river, Thutmose the Third waited. He was King of Egypt, God of Two Lands, the Omnipotent Ruler of all the Known World. In pride of place next to him there stood the noble Per Ibsen, on the other hand Amenhotep, Pharaoh's favourite son.

A little further away there stood the small lovely personage of Zarah of Anshan. Her eyes were greedy with longing as she watched. Then she gasped and cried out with delight. The ships were approaching, the vessels that held the adored ones of her life.

All was noise and confusion after that. Of music and drumbeats, of cheering, and high in the towers, the singing of hymns.

Zarah's eyes glistened and shone like stars because of her tears. Then she saw them at last, her dearest of dears. Two infinitely lovely young women—and Nefer was smiling and holding a quite enchanting small boy in her arms. Then there was Twosre, roguish, impish Twosre who was actually daring to tweak Prince Khaleb's ear. But it was to Nefer that Zarah's eyes went again, and her warm motherly heart was filled to overflowing with joy. Nefer had turned and looked up to the massive man who stood so squarely behind her, so solid, so firm. And the look that Amosis and Nefer exchanged told Zarah all that she needed to know.

Then they saw her, her two daughters, and they were laughing and crying and waving their hands, quite ignoring Pharaoh and all the pomp and circumstance waiting for them on the high royal steps.

A sob caught in Zarah's throat and she knew that her far distant dreams for her children had come true. She watched as they stepped ashore, each tenderly held by the men in their lives. Then, as the people raised their voices to sing the joyous theme of the Song of the Nile, Zarah's eyes returned greedily to the rosy-cheeked, happy, little boy.

EPILOGUE

Thutmose the Third was not only a great general in his own right but a statesman with high ideals. His treatment of conquered countries was always humane. Even the chiefs who fought against him were not executed, they were merely deposed. He reigned supreme and ended all wars between small kingdoms. Under his benign rule they reached prosperity such as they had never known before.

On the thirtieth of the month Phamenoth, Thutmose the Third ascended to heaven and his beloved son Amenhotep became Pharaoh of the Two Lands.

The publishers hope that this book has given you enjoyable reading. Large Print Books are especially designed to be as easy to see and hold as possible. If you wish a complete list of our books, please ask at your local library or write directly to: Dales Large Print Books, Long Preston, North Yorkshire, BD23 4ND, England.

This Large Print Book for the Partially sighted, who cannot read normal print, is published under the auspices of